THE
JEWEL

NEIL
HEGARTY

HEAD
ZEUS

An Apollo Book

First published in the UK in 2019 by Head of Zeus Ltd
This Apollo paperback edition first published in the UK in 2020 by
Head of Zeus Ltd

9 7 5 3 1 2 4 6 8

A catalogue record for this book is available from
the British Library.

ISBN (PB): 9781789541823
ISBN (E): 9781789541793

Typeset by Silicon Chips

Printed and bound in Great Britain by
CPI Group (UK) Ltd, Croydon CRO 4YY

Head of Zeus Ltd
5–8 Hardwick Street
London EC1R 4RG

WWW.HEADOFZEUS.COM

For John

'I see how shadow in the painting brims
With a real shadow...'

—THOM GUNN, *'In Santa Maria del Popolo'*

Prologue: The Jewel

London, 1839

The cloth was of linen. That choice had always been clear. And not white, but rather the colour of cream, of buttermilk, of good Scotch porridge.

Not white.

She flinched from the very thought of the harshness, the dishonesty of white. White was bridal, virginal, clean and unsullied, and she was none of those things. White would not do for the task she had in mind.

The linen, set out for inspection, was 'tabby-woven'. So they told her, there at the counter of dark mahogany and shining glass that ran impressively the length of the shop. Bolts of cloth lined the walls, in every colour, fabric and texture. It was not a term she had previously heard of or understood. 'Tabby-woven, madam,' the assistant said, and his companion – his superior, evidently – nodded approvingly to the right. 'As strong as linen can be, madam.'

'Irish linen,' the other interjected. 'The best, madam. Look at the quality,' he said, and ran a clean, proud hand over the cloth that was both rough and smooth at the same time.

Tabby-woven, and she thought of a cat purring and stretching in luxury. It was a pleasant term, although of course the words hardly mattered. The fabric was the thing: and it would serve admirably.

This was a day for adventure, beginning with the railway journey down from Watford: what an adventure, with the din and the steam of the train, and then Euston, with its vast roofs and its great arch. Best to consider the adventure and the glamour of it all, and to ignore the smoke and the coal dust, the coal smuts filling the air, the dirt clinging to the nostrils, and showing up horrifyingly on her handkerchief. Quite enough for one day, without London then to negotiate. The carriages raising a din of hooves and an explosion of dust with every passing; an odour of dirt and smoke and tobacco, and horse ordure to be avoided on Kingsway as she pressed through the crowds, lifting her skirts just a polite little.

Feeling the sickness, but holding it at bay.

A pressing London heat. Preserve me from this dirt and this place. But she had a task: so she had understood, waking in bed, feeling her illness anew, examining her skin for fresh sores and redness. Then in the train, then pushing through the crowds on the hot pavement. A something to accomplish, and much to hold at bay, and then directly home.

'It will serve,' she said now. 'It will serve, yes, very nicely indeed,' and both of their faces lifted at this effort of sprightliness on her part. She saw with a pang that they too were tired, for all of their pride in this porridge-coloured piece of linen, these bolts of cloth from across the Empire and across the world, the shining glass and glossy dark wood, and their handsome shop.

'Excellent, madam. It will last you a lifetime. A table-cloth?' he added, and raised an interested eyebrow.

'No indeed.' And then, to fend off further questions, 'I need eighty inches by sixty inches. Unhemmed,' she added, and then relented and essayed some humour. 'Not quite a tablecloth, gentlemen. An unhemmed tablecloth would be a very awkward tablecloth,' she said, and now she took a step back in her mind, and watched them rethink and recalibrate.

Still well dressed, of course, still a lady – but an eccentric, probably. One of the swarm of eccentric ladies that people today's London: one reads about them in *Blackwell's*. Perhaps this young lady's plan is to fashion an eccentric something by her own hand, a shawl or a wrap, and parade the item, as eccentric females like to do.

And, ought eccentric females be permitted to roam London, all alone? Where is her husband? Does he know she is on the loose?

Well, so be it. It was still good Irish linen, a pretty penny. They could still be pleased with the sale.

'Indeed,' the first man said.

'No, I am going to paint on it,' she heard herself say.

A polite pause, and then, 'Indeed, madam?'

She nodded: and now, for the first time today – the deed virtually done, the purchase virtually complete, the journey worth it after all – she felt a small pulse of pleasure and anticipation.

'Yes,' she said. 'I am going to paint on it. It will be my best piece.'

The men smiled, nodded. They had nothing else to say.

It will be my best piece.

The linen was stretched on a frame, now. And it was sized, the glue heated and applied rapidly. It was ready.

The water and the pigments were ready also, and set out in their neat little dishes. Cinnabar and lead white, azurite, ultramarine, verdigris and smalt; and beautiful, profound malachite.

She would prepare the distemper, batch by batch. The colours would blaze, if she had anything to do with it, and leap from the cloth, and live and breathe.

They would never be seen: but this was the very least of her worries.

This was the very intention.

Later, much later, days later – for the plan to begin and conclude this painting in less than no time, to execute it in a flash, with one eye on the sands of her life running rapidly, this plan came to nothing, it had to be done correctly, it had to be done with love and pride, how foolish she had been even to think of dashing this piece off in a trice – she could step back, and see this blazing and leaping for herself. The tiny sparks of brilliant white; and the cinnabar and the verdigris: yes, they were intense, they blazed, as though alive. The malachite, at the centre of all, breathed and inhaled and exhaled with life. The distemper, colour by colour, had soaked through the linen, as she had intended it should; the fabric now was heavy and sodden. But it would dry, and it would be rolled away, and she would leave her instructions, to the letter, and they would be carried out when the time came.

When the time came.

There was little time left.

She looked again. Yes: the smooth, dark horse haunch; the jewel embedded in the gleaming pauldron, blazing out, as she had wanted it to; the malachite shining as though lit from within. There it was, placed at the very centre of the piece: and the light welled from it. It was a living thing.

It would live for ever, it would live when she was dead. It would shine and swell in the darkness.

She thought again about the men – the kindly, confused men – who had sold her the linen. What would they have said? – and she reframed the conversation in her head.

Not a tablecloth. On no account.

I mean to paint on it, in distemper.

A thin brush, gentlemen, is best with this medium. Many, many layers, quickly applied. The distemper will soak and saturate, and then it will dry, and be complete.

I mean the colours to sing. Malachite and cinnabar and indigo and azurite: the most beautiful words, the most beautiful colours my means – reasonably ample, gentlemen, I assure you, as ample as I need them to be – can command.

Distemper, gentlemen: it fades, very rapidly indeed. We have few such pieces alive in the world. But I mean this piece to live for ever, as I will not.

No, I will not.

No, you see: I mean to have this piece placed upon me, as a coverlet, when I am in my coffin. Placed carefully, and carefully tucked, and smoothed.

A shroud? – by no means, gentlemen. I would not care to be wrapped, in such a Biblical way. How primitive that would be. And how confining!

No: I mean a rug, a covering, a coverlet, to keep me warm and keep me cool for all Eternity. A coverlet, and a painting that will live for ever, through the ages, in the darkness.

Yes indeed, it has a name. A good name. You will approve, gentlemen, I am certain. Would you like to hear it?

Very well, then: I shall tell you.

The name. I shall call it The Jewel.

Tidewrack

1

His was a seedy life.

Sometimes he told himself so, speaking to the mirror as he shaved in the morning. 'John, what a seedy life.' As bald as that, though at least he had the courage to square up to himself.

Of course, it wasn't merely seedy, it was thoroughly criminal – and yet it was the seediness that stayed with him, as a slick of oil on his hands, and a grubbiness on his skin.

The progression had been so straightforward: a career progression, if you cared to use such words. And it paid very nicely. A painter, a counterfeiter, a thief: one grade passing to another grade, up and up or down and down. In a world of relativity, a world without morality, you could go either way. It didn't really matter.

A painter.

'Look at them,' Stella had said, her loved voice filling

his memory, passing without effort down the years – low, a touch of huskiness, a golden-tawny velvet voice. 'Look at those colours. How did you do them?' She reached out, brushed a fingertip so gently against the linen cloth that hung from its makeshift frame. The linen moved with her touch, airily in the slight breeze from the open window. Its colours glowed: a murky day outside, but they still glowed. He had seen them glow – lit from within, or so it seemed – even more brightly, in yesterday's weather. The early sunlight, glancing on his memory, glancing for a few minutes on the sill of this north-facing room before moving away again: this cool early sun had lit his colours.

Now Stella could see and admire for herself.

'I don't know.'

'Don't you?'

'No. I don't know.'

And then a counterfeiter.

So he named himself, silently. Because what was it, in the end, but counterfeiting? Copying, again and again, a model that worked and that had once been true: eschewing colour for the grime, for the grey and the black that sold. The colour was leached out of his work, now.

'Everything you have,' said Etienne, looking over his shoulder at the canvases stacked against the studio wall, seeing them – John watched his expression change – converted into tidy bundles of banknotes. 'Everything, everything.'

And later. 'Will you meet with him?' And 'him', and 'him': these collectors, always men, who had no idea what they were collecting, who were collecting cash and not art, who wouldn't know a work of art if it was brought down hard on their skull.

'Sure.'

How Etienne would smile! He was a boy at heart: a boy who drank to excess, who was in all ways profligate, and who had much more money than sense – but a boy just the same, who liked to run with the glittering crowd.

'He'll be so pleased,' Etienne said. It was always 'he' and 'he' and 'he'. Women seemed to have more sense.

John smiled briefly, nodded. He sold and he sold. The collectors swarmed. His fellow artists envied him; and all was well.

And later: a thief.

'A small job.' It was nothing much, a small job, a small piece that a collector wanted. 'A special job, and I've been thinking that you might be the man.' Knowing the ropes, the lie of the land; the clichés flowed like water in a ditch. He knew the galleries, and how they worked; and in his greyness, he blended in. At first, a 'consultant', so they named it, to the actual thieves: a regional gallery, threadbare security, the shortcuts advised and made – and the job soon done, for a tidy fee.

And then another, and another. Soon he could do the job himself.

In West Berlin, and the halls of the Neue Nationalgalerie packed with students, the air rank and the attendants flurried: how easy, in such a context, to slip the piece of copper off the wall and into his pocket. The rush of adrenalin – like the strongest coffee in the world – and a stroll to the exit, and away into the city.

The newspapers breathless with the scandal of it all.

The authorities, screaming blue bloody murder. That had been the best of all: the point being that they couldn't have it their own way, always – not every single time. And he liked the cash.

And he was owed.

'You clever man,' cooed Etienne. 'You clever, clever man.'

And it didn't matter who owned these pieces. This was a corrupt world, and idealism was for mugs. So he told himself – though his seediness would not be gainsaid.

And now. Next on the list was an Emily Sandborne, in Dublin. 'You can do that, John, we thought. Man for the job.'

He held himself very still.

'The Dublin piece. That would be *The Jewel*.' It wasn't a question.

'That's the one.' A cheery smile. 'On linen. Famous, these days. Having a moment. Don't really see what all the fuss is about. Reminds me of the Shroud of Turin, you know what I mean? But there's an order on it. No accounting for taste. Are we agreed then, John?'

A little hesitation, before the colours rose in his mind: he had seen them, in reproductions and in catalogues, and had been staggered. How it would be, to hold this shimmering piece in his hands, for a little while. No: no hesitation. Only the pretence of one.

'That'd be a big job,' he said. 'Too big for me.' But Etienne scoffed at that: the gallery was completing a refurb, their systems would be weak, now was the moment.

'Come on, John.'

And in the end, the lure of the Emily Sandborne was too much. 'Agreed.'

Later, he felt a wash of shame at the eagerness and nothingness of it all. This would be the last of them: the world had surely paid off its debt to him by now. And besides, somewhere, far away, Stella was still sailing through life – or had been, last he'd heard. What would Stella say, if she could see him now? – an ageing, grey man, with an eye on the cash and a chip on his shoulder, who should have been someone else.

Yet he felt the excitement, just the same. In his mind's eye, a pauldron gleamed, black against luminous colour, leaping from the fabric. A horse's flank gleamed glossy black. A green stone gleamed, an iridescence like a dragonfly's wings, a lavish beauty of colour: *The Jewel*. This would be one to touch.

'You'll do it?'

He shrugged, nodded.

'Why not.'

'Great stuff. It'll be worth your while.'

'Yes. Why not.'

2

The charcoal dug deep into the paper. The paper was brown, and cheap, wrapping paper but not what his gran called *heavy-duty* wrapping paper; it had a cheap sheen, and that meant that he would have to work harder. So that was his heavy duty, you might say: to make it stick and stay.

Dig, dig deep into the paper.

Dig for victory, his gran would say, telling her stories of the war. Dig to make it last.

And the charcoal was everywhere. The Nazis were long gone now, but this was something to thank them for. Free charcoal, on nearly every corner. The charcoal scored and burned pictures that were nothing like the city around him, or like the Thames, or like anything at all. He would sit back on his heels, every time, and look at what he had drawn. Dark shapes, and whirls, and swirls. Open mouths, these shapes and gaps might be: were they? Or caves, or coal mines? He didn't know. And he couldn't show these drawings to anyone, they would laugh, and so there was no point, after all, in digging for victory, digging to make it last: forget Gran, and he would crumple the cheap brown paper into a ball, and throw it into the road, to join the rest of the rubbish, the sodden newspapers, and brown banana skins, and the paper bags that the traders in the market used for carrots and onions, the ripped rough hessian from the stalls. Up and down the High Street, the rubbish grew and grew, to be cleared away once a week, to come back, growing and growing.

This was how it would be, every time. Scrunch the brown paper into a ball, throw the ball away into the street. Feel in his pocket: there would always be more paper there, folded up into a neat square. And charcoal, rescued from the bomb sites off the High Street or down by the river. And seeds of willowherb, brought with it, tiny seeds that slipped into the seams of his pockets. Maybe they'd grow there, great thickets in his pocket, to match the willowherb that grew with the butterfly bushes in the bomb sites. Given half a chance. Or in his fingernails, if a seed found itself stuck in there: a butterfly bush growing out of his hand. Well, and why not? – if they can grow out of a wall, they can grow out of a fingernail.

Although, his mum would have a fit, if she saw willowherb growing out of the seams of his pockets and butterfly bushes growing out of his fingers.

His pockets filled with paper, and seeds, and charcoal. The crumple of paper, left there in the road. He had plenty of charcoal left, plenty of paper left, he would be drawing again, later, after his dinner. And the next day, and the next, and the next.

And always, tears in his eyes, big boy and all though he was, as he hurried along the High Street, through the crowds. At the thought of the drawing there in the road, thrown down as if he never cared about it at all.

North along the High Street, away from the river, towards Regina Road, and home. Nobody noticed such a little boy, not a big boy at all, as he ran and ran.

'Lovely,' Stella said, years later. 'Dig for victory. Lovely.'

It was easy to talk about his gran.

He never mentioned the tears.

Brown, they called the Thames. And stinking in summer, and filled with dead dogs, and wood, and every kind of rubbish in the world. Women, too: young women 'caught short', as his mum and gran said, with no cash to take them into the back streets to be scraped out and sent on their way again, and so nothing to be done about it but go into the river. *Scraped out*, they said to one another, low, in the kitchen. Such and such a girl. When they thought he wasn't listening. Over his head. They would be talking over the top of his head, and going on and on, a bit like a river themselves.

John knew to listen and not to interrupt – but sometimes his curiosity was like a live thing: it opened his mouth even though he tried to keep it locked tight, it opened up his clamped teeth, and out would come the words. Without so much as a *by your leave*; and that was another of his gran's favourites.

'Caught short? What does that mean?'

'Never you mind.'

They looked at each other, then, and moved away. Or moved him away: sent him up to the High Street on an errand, for this or for that, for a spool of thread or a needle, maybe, for his gran was forever running short of thread, and was forever losing her needles, who knew where? And off he would go. But he knew they were brushing him out of the way, out of sight and out of earshot. He didn't mind, but he wasn't stupid.

Nobody was stupid, in Deptford. You couldn't be stupid, not in a place like Deptford, and expect to get by.

(That was another of his gran's.)

His dad told him, in the end. A man-to-man, they had, one day in the house when the place was quiet. 'This is a chat to be had when the womenfolk are out of the way,' his dad said, 'and you're asking too many questions, and driving yourself up a tree.'

Up a tree.

Then his dad told him about the girls got in the family way, he said, by a man: by her young man, sometimes, and that was nobody's fault, these things happened; and people just got on with it, and the baby would be born, and that was fine.

But sometimes the girl fell in with the wrong kind of man, and that was not so good, and not her fault, and such a man would up and leave her. Get back on a boat and off down the Thames, and that would be an end to that.

And that would be an end to her, sometimes, too. To the girl: she would get the baby scraped out of her, if she was lucky, and if she had a few bob; or, sometimes, not all that often, but too often, she would go into the river, and never be seen again, or she would be fished out, right here at Deptford, or further east, or, sometimes, all the way down in Essex.

'You're too young for this, son, and too young to worry about it at the moment: but when you get a bit older, you need to treat a girl in the right way. In the right way, will you remember that?'

John nodded: he would. He didn't want anyone he knew to go into the river. He'd seen the dogs and cats in there, and they were bad enough.

'Gently, and you want her to treat you gently too, and that's the way to be happy,' his dad said, and he laid a large brown hand on top of John's head. 'Nothing rough, and nothing cruel, and you'll be fine.'

Another nod. That sounded good. Why would you be cruel, when you didn't have to be cruel?

He felt grown up, after that. 'Don't tell your mum,' his dad said. 'She doesn't like that sort of talk, and you're a bit young.' His mum went to church on Sundays – *she goes religiously*, his dad said – and sometimes at other times too, and his gran went too, hats and all, the pair of them. Togged out. Fancy. They liked it when John, not togged along but tagged along, but they didn't make him, and the truth was – 'the truth is, Dorothy, love,' his dad said – that John didn't really like it.

He was like his dad, that way.

Or, that he didn't like it enough. Sometimes, the sounds of the service lulled him, and time passed by, again a bit like a river running, and the service was over almost before he knew it, and the words made beautiful shapes and colours in his head: *The Lord is my shepherd: therefore can I lack nothing*. But then, his gran would press her ring finger into the side of his head, and the cold metal of the ring would feel cold against his scalp, through his hair, and he would open his eyes, out of a daydream.

That happened a lot, until the womenfolk became less strict, and he was allowed to stay at home instead. Only sometimes, but sometimes was enough: sometimes meant he was growing up.

And the times they made him go – at Easter, at Advent – *high days and holy days*, his gran said – weren't too bad. So long as they weren't each and every Sunday. *He shall feed me in a green pasture: and lead me forth beside the waters of comfort*. Bright green, the green of Greenwich Park in springtime, or like the fields out in Kent: as green as green could be, as green as emeralds in storybooks.

The colours glowed in his brain.

But then out of his daydream, they would make him scratch his head and wonder. There were green pastures only in some places, after all; they weren't everywhere. There were no green pastures in Deptford, or none that he had ever seen. And the waters in the Thames: these waters weren't waters of comfort, were they? It didn't seem likely: not when his dad was telling him the next minute that women in trouble ended up there. Bobbing there, floating out to sea, maybe. And the dogs and the cats (and the rats, only people didn't like you mentioning the rats). Where was the comfort there?

'Pipe down, son,' his dad said, when John asked him this. 'Your mother will have a canary if she hears that sort of thing coming from you.'

A canary?

But then – but *then*, Dad turned quickly and looked out the window, not that there was anything there, just the grey yard and the privy, and his shoulders moved up and down, and his ears turned a bright apple-red, and then – just like that – he burst into howls of laughter. He laughed, and wiped his eyes, and laughed again. 'You got me there, son,' he said. 'The Thames is no waters of comfort, I'm not going to argue with you about that.' And he laughed again, and went on laughing as he stood over the basin, peeling potatoes for Sunday dinner. 'It certainly is not.'

No waters of comfort. Not the brown, muddy Thames.

But – but there was a *something* that John saw there, sometimes. He saw – gold, sometimes, and yellow and orange, like the bright spices the women, the black women nowadays, sold on the High Street. A slice of red, late in the afternoon, the colour of cinnamon, that his mother sometimes bought in little twists of paper, to sprinkle on stewed apple. Glittering like gold under a blue sky; or a dark, hard grey like the charcoal he fished out of the old bomb sites. So, brown, yes, sometimes, but not often, and never the way they meant. And even the brown, the muddy old ordinary brown, when the sky was grey, even that was worth looking at.

And yes, he would draw, sometimes, with this rescued charcoal. It had begun – just like that: one day his dad fished a piece of *bone-dry* charcoal from the old gas works, pulverised, he said, during the war. Summertime, and hot weather, and the charcoal bone-dry, and 'Who needs pencils when we have this, just lying around?' Just like that: he handed it over; and later, in his room, John began drawing on a bit of paper. A house, with a narrow door, and a window downstairs, and two windows upstairs, a doorstep, and a door knocker shaped like a fish, a leaping salmon. He drew a house just like their own house.

And, just like that. It was easy.

That's how the drawing began. On old newspapers that his mum was about to throw out. On brown wrapping paper that his mum, his gran, folded and stored in a drawer, with string and odds and ends, in the kitchen. 'What's that?' Harry would say, and John would shrug. 'Nothing much.' Patterns in the way he saw the sky, or the river, or the northern shore of the river. The lines of the tide, the way the sun shone on the tidelines, the clumps of wrack at the high-water mark. 'Is that the river?' Harry would ask. 'Is that supposed to be that dog? It doesn't look like a dog to me.' Or, 'It doesn't look like the river to me.' Soon, John began to draw at home, only, upstairs in his little box room, never outdoors, never in front of Harry.

Never in front of anyone.

Once, he went into Jack's shop on the High Street, and stole some paper. Good paper, like velvet, a new line Jack was trying out – 'you never know what people might like' – and he stole it while Jack was dealing with a customer. Just stole it. Just like that. Jack knew him and liked him – 'There's the young man, himself: how are you, young John?' – and so he never stole from him again. Once was enough. He felt sticky with shame; the shame stuck to his hands like sugar. Once was enough.

But the paper that he had whisked away, that he had *stolen*: it was heavy, like cloth. The marks of the charcoal were different too. It was – how could this be? but the marks were – well, they were more black than on the old folded bits of wrapping paper, they were blacker than black, and the charcoal swept across the surface of the paper as though it ran on wheels. Slash, and turn, and mark, and he forgot himself, upstairs in his little room, and they had to call him and call him for tea: and when he came downstairs, his hands were black, his face and his forehead were black where he'd forgot himself and pushed the hair away from his eyes. 'The shape of you,' laughed his gran and went at him with a soapy flannel, and his mum laughed too and said, 'Never you mind, you do what you like to do,' and his dad touched the top of his head with a large brown hand. 'A bit of drawing never did anyone any harm.'

'What were you doing, to get into a state like that?' his gran said, when he began to take himself off to draw. The room upstairs, his little room, seemed too small sometimes: the river was large and the sky was large, and there was any amount of charcoal just lying there and waiting to be used. So he would slip off now, and draw outside, under the big sky, and now the drawings were changing too, and these were the pieces of paper that would end up in the gutter, in tightly wadded balls on the High Street.

'I was just drawing, Gran.' There was no need to say what he was doing, exactly, or why he was drawing.

Or, how it made him feel.

These were his sharpest memories, the ones he thought he would always carry with him through life, in an inside pocket: the acrid scent of charcoal biting paper; the feel of a powder of charcoal on his hands; the gorgeousness of wet, warm, soapy flannel on face, and forehead, and neck.

'Gran, stop!'

Never, never stop.

As for the colour, though: as for the brown staining the Thames – well, there was no point getting into anything like that. He would lose his dad, his mum, his gran, there – and that was a thing he didn't want. Once, he tried to say to his dad about the gold in the brown, the yellow lights and threads in the dank, smelly old brown, but it didn't seem to get him anywhere. 'I suppose you're right, John,' was the reply. And a little shrug and a frown. 'I suppose so. There's nothing wrong with brown, that's true enough.' Which wasn't exactly what John meant, but it would have to do.

Keep them close, keep them tight. Keep them in an inside pocket, and show them to nobody.

Never, never stop.

3

John liked to wander, and there was plenty of wandering to be had: at weekends, and in the summer, and in the other school holidays. You could wander to your heart's content, and he often did.

'Tell me now,' they would say, his mum or his gran, to the top of his head, 'where are you off to now, Mister John?' Or his gran would be in the privy – 'excuse me now, just a moment, while I step across the path' – and Mum with her hands red and scalded-looking from the washing. Just the three of them, for Dad was off and away to the docks with the lark.

'To the Quaggy,' he would say, 'with Harry.' It wasn't a lie, because that was where he would usually end up, for all of his wandering. 'Just down to the Quaggy.'

'Well,' Mum would tell him, 'and you be careful.'

She didn't need to be worried. John was a waterbaby:

that was what his mum liked to say, and he would look up proudly at his dad when she said it. 'A waterbaby: and we know where he gets that one from.' No need to worry, and they all knew it: the little lines around his dad's eyes would run out like a spider's web as he smiled. A waterbaby knew about the water, about the Thames and the Quaggy.

Regina Road was scrubbed today, as clean as a pin. Water on the doorsteps, and suds in the gutter, and the mums taking the air. He bashed on Harry's brass door knocker – shaped like a dolphin, but John's own brass door knocker was shaped like a fish, like a Thames salmon from the olden days, said the book out of the library – and Harry was there in a flash, and they were at the end of Regina Road in another flash; and Harry's mum was at the door, and shouting after them.

'And back at one! I need you to help me this afternoon!'

'With the blacking,' Harry said, and he held out his black hands. 'The kitchen stove yesterday,' he said, 'and the upstairs stove today.'

An upstairs stove. Two stoves in Harry's family, and Harry blacked them both.

John's house had one stove: but one was enough, his mum said. No house needed more than a single stove. Who did Harry's mum and dad think they were? And didn't their legs kill them, running up and down the stairs all day with their buckets filled with coal? John thought that another stove, a stove upstairs, would be grand, especially in the winter: then the air upstairs would be warm, and he wouldn't see his breath hanging like a Thames fog when he jumped out of his clothes and into his pyjamas and into bed, and his nose wouldn't be as red as red could be from the cold.

But no, his mum was right. No house needed more than a single stove.

They turned right. The High Street was filling up. Mums, and stalls, and some black men and black women among the people; and the shops open wide. Onions, and carrots, rope and string, spools of thread that shone like jewels, along with needles for his gran, potatoes and boxes of soap flakes. Fishes on white marble slabs, red and pink and white and grey, fat and flat, their glassy eyes watching as they scurried past; the smell of fish, and the smell of coffee, roasting. They followed the High Street under the railway bridge and along to its end, then the wiggles of streets, and then – a wide open sky, and there was the Thames. And it was brown today, and the sky white, and the further shore distant; and now the corner where the Quaggy flowed quietly out into the Thames, the sunny corner, no wind, where they settled themselves.

'What will we look for today?'

The Thames shore was brown and white, rough sand and shingle. The *foreshore*, his dad called it. Tidewrack, and wood white as a ghost and smooth, washed up from the sea. Metal drums from the ships, from the docks, and gulls in circles overhead, crying like the sheep crying in Kent when they went hopping, and little birds with black-and-white feathers and long beaks walking quick on the edge of the water.

'Dogs,' said John.

It was dogs, today.

Because all sorts washed up at Deptford. A sheepdog, once, heavy and bloated like a hairy black-and-white football, and smaller dogs, and sometimes cats. Sometimes they didn't look dead at all; sometimes, though, they did look dead, with pink tongues sticking out. 'You don't want to touch them, John,' Mum said – not that he would have, when they were all swelled up. 'They might burst,' said Mum, 'all over you, all that gas, and then where would you be?'

Still by the Thames, was where. What, did she think the gas would send them up into the air?

There were no dogs, today. No dogs, and no cats. No girls in trouble. Had Harry ever heard of the girls in trouble, floating out there on the water? – he was afraid to ask, because Harry was a bit of a blab; he might tell his mum, and something told John that he didn't want that to happen, because Harry's mum was a bit strange – 'a funny onion,' his dad said, once, and his mum said, 'she's funnier than any onion, that one' – and you wouldn't want her saying anything, or causing trouble. Girls in trouble, and Harry's mum: somehow John knew that she wouldn't be made a bit happy by that kind of talk.

So no, not a word to Harry.

But it was alright, wasn't it, to *secretly* wish to see a girl in trouble? Some time? It wasn't a sin.

And something else too: if the Lord made floods – and He did, because there had been a reading about it, in church – then he must have wanted things to be in the floods: wood, and cats and dogs, and even dead girls, even if Harry's mum wouldn't agree. And something else, that glinted in his memory: the brightest shine of yellow, a golden yellow like the sun, from the stained glass above the altar, above the vicar talking about the flood.

But there was no flood today.

Just the Isle of Dogs, and the early sun, and the river now all of a sudden not brown but yellow. That was really why he remembered the stained glass, was it? Yellow like twinkling gold. A few boats in the river, but no ships; the ships going, and the grey wharves emptier, now; and Dad had to leave the house earlier, and go further, and still no work, Mum said, when they get to where they're going, maybe; and coming back hang-dog.

Harry's dad had a different kind of job, an office job: Harry's family was lucky, so everyone said.

Two stoves.

'Nothing today?' – so his mum would say.

'The building sites tomorrow,' his dad would say. 'Good money there,' he would say. Said yesterday. In the past, in the summer, they would be off to Kent, hopping: but the hops brought in too little money now, when there was no money to be had elsewhere. Someone else would have to do the hops, from now on. So even less green, now, and no more sheep to hear bleating in the fields, the green pastures, before the sun rose. They'd sounded like little babies, tiny little things out there in the darkness, calling for their mums. 'I hear a baby, Mum,' he said, one time in Kent, 'is there a baby out there?' A baby was lost, somewhere in the fields. 'Hush, Johnny,' his mum said. 'It's a sheep, it only sounds like a baby, it isn't lost at all,' and he would listen and shiver a little under his blanket; but he would always go back to sleep.

All that was over, now.

The building sites: and his mum nodded.

'My dad's a river man,' John liked to say. 'And my grandad before him.'

'His heart's breaking,' his mum said. She meant his dad. She never said it when his dad was in the house. They needed the money.

The river, though, it was always here. He sat on the warm foreshore with Harry, digging into the shingle with a long white branch. And the sky was there, it was everywhere, it was bigger than everything else.

Harry went home first, to help with the blacking of their two stoves.

Later, John walked back slowly, alone. What had they done, all morning? Nothing very much: they skimmed stones into the water, and they fished branches from the Quaggy. Netting on the foreshore, and bottles with the glass worn smooth, and scraped into a misty silver; and rusted cans. And oily tidewrack with bubbles that you could burst with a pop. This, and that. *Flotsam and jetsam*, his dad said it was all called, once, and, *well, you could do worse with a morning*.

When Harry left, John fished out the paper, the charcoal, and drew what he saw. Black slashes on brown paper. But nobody would see. It was a secret.

'No dogs today?' Gran asked at dinnertime.

'No dogs,' he told her. 'But the river was nice,' and she nodded.

4

'That was when it started,' he told Stella years later, in the close darkness of Mildred's. The place was as black as Satan's waistcoat: so his mother would have put it, and he liked it that way. Smoke from a thousand cigarettes, hanging like a river fog. Sometimes he liked a place out of which the colour and light had been leached. It set his mind at rest.

'What?' Stella said. This was early on, before she accustomed herself to the ways in which his thoughts and speech moved: jumping here and there, like a hare in the grass. It took some getting used to, she said mildly.

'The river, the sky, the whole – ensemble.'

'Ensemble,' Stella murmured, and the plush banquette bounced and quivered a little as she snuggled into him. She was no twig, she was a composite of beautiful layers, she was an ensemble herself, she was delighted with herself and her shape. A little gleam from somewhere, from God knows where, caught and refracted on bevels – for Mildred was fond of her mirrors, if not of light to shine on them, and a whole series of them hung on the walls of this smoky room – and this splinter of light caught in her eye too, and gleamed out. 'Tell me about the ensemble,' Stella said. 'What was it like?'

What was it like? John remembered the sky reaching up, a vast vertical that dwarfed and diminished London, and the river, and the creek, and the empty wharves. Blue, in his mind's eye: a quivering blue in the gathering heat of a summer morning in London – and the river golden in the light.

'It was everything I wanted,' he told her in the darkness. 'If I could capture the light,' he said, 'I knew I would be happy.' Stella was silent: she understood; surely she would always understand. He drank. 'That was my mind made up.'

It was made up, over many days, mornings, evenings. Later, he would cruise the galleries: London in fog, London as Venice, *Nocturnes*: and then on and on, deeper into the adventure. He was not the only one: far from it. They were all on the same quest, maybe, to capture the light. But hardly any of them would make it. He would make it.

'And I will,' he told Stella, and felt her nod beside him. The banquette shivered. 'I bloody well will, too.'

'Black as Satan's waistcoat,' Stella repeated. He must have said it aloud, had he? 'That was one of your mum's sayings, wasn't it?'

'It was. Her own mum was from the North. My gran.

She made the best of it, but I think she was lost, you know, adrift, on the flood. London, Deptford, the whole bloody place, and all she wanted was to go home.'

'Which was impossible,' Stella said.

'Which was bloody impossible. So she had to make the best of it.' His gran hadn't been much of a talker, nor his own mum: but both of them had something about them. A way with language. Some intangible thing they had passed on, he felt: a way of looking at the world that made him feel rich.

Along with a freight of grief and rootlessness, a dreadful heart-stopping homesickness that never could be eased. He knew all this now – though God Almighty, it had taken him long enough.

And Stella. What a great woman to have in his life, the ballast when all the other ballast was gone.

Although, Stella thought she had him, that she could see into his heart. But she was wrong, there. He set a limit on such things.

'So you started off with black,' Stella said, and her voice was musing in the darkness, 'and you worked towards the light. Is that it?'

He nodded, although perhaps she wouldn't see this in Mildred's darkness. 'That's about it.'

They'd slipped out of the house onto darkness on Regina Road. John had shaved for the first time that morning: a straight razor, his dad watching, guiding, laughing a little, not unkindly. 'You can puff your cheek out a bit, that helps,' he'd said, and 'now, a nice tight stretch on your neck, go easy, you don't want to cut your throat,' and 'slow around your lips,' and 'your nose,' and 'your ears, that's the boy, good lad,' proud as anything, John could tell, and then they'd stepped in and he'd showed himself off, and his mum had looked and nodded, a shining of tears in her eyes, and his dad had clapped an arm around his shoulders. Two men in the house, now.

And now black night, and John had strapped lengths of rough hessian sack onto his boots – for the treads were worn to nothing, and he needed something for purchase, Mum said, on the snow – and his dad had his big boots that would take him anywhere and then home again. And now they walked, gingerly enough, past the house where Harry had lived, with the door knocker shaped like a dolphin, the house that was empty now, and turned right onto the High Street and through the wiggle of dark roads and lanes to the Thames.

Father and son. His dad hadn't wanted to miss this. 'You don't mind if I tag along, son, do you?' – and John had shaken his head. No, he didn't mind.

This was something to share with Stella: his dad, his mum, the house, the ice. The light in the sky, in the city, welling up and shining blue on the ice: this was something he was able to share.

No moon, but the snow and the ice. No light from the dark tangle of lanes and alleys behind him – but the light would be no trouble. He knew that London itself would lend him the light.

'Stay close to the shore, the two of you,' said his mum, and she went to the window as she spoke, and looked across the road to the black, lightless house opposite, the black lightless houses to its left and right. They had withdrawn even the street lamps, now, and the blackness must have hurt her eyes as she stood there, for she soon enough let the net and the curtains fall, and retreated to the fire. 'You know what the ice is like.' She herself kept far away from the ice: too many stories from Gran of dead boys and dead young men, plunging through the ice on this lake and that lake, peat-brown, in Northumberland long ago. Gran was gone, but the stories lingered. But John was stretched now, he was growing out of his clothes month by month, he was past telling what to do – and the paper said, besides, that the river was safe.

As for Alfred, his mum said, talking aloud: that was a case of like son, like father. She wasn't going to waste her breath trying to stop him.

'Safe as houses,' his dad said. And, 'Stop worrying, woman.'

The ice was piled up against the foreshore. That was the thing: the wind and the currents and the rest of it: they drove the ice and raised it high, and it was no good for skating. It was for clambering over, close to shore; and – in spite of what the paper said – John was none too keen to venture further out; for he had listened to his gran too, and picked up on her horror. And his dad was canny: he understood the river, he understood the water, he even understood the ice – even the ice, although nobody had seen such ice, nobody had seen the Thames like this. So they stood by the mounds of ice, and looked out across the expanse of ice. Out there it was smoother: they watched the skaters – but again, no temptation to join them, to clamber over the masses of ice and into the middle of the river. A deep horror kept John back. And now, the light was different again: plucked from the darkness, just a gleam here and there on the rutted and piled ice; and over it all a fitful blue London glow.

The skaters whisked and turned. A toboggan too, a rough sled – made of a piece of wood and a couple of lengths of metal, but fit enough for purpose – shared around. Young men, and girls; and younger boys: voices called and squealed across the ice, their breath smoked, the ice seemed to him to shift a very little, as though it were a vast raft, and to sigh, and squeak, and settle again. He watched. He was aware of his dad, watching; aware of his smoking breath, of the light. He would not join in; it was better to watch. The voices were joyous, giddy – even the men had lost the run of themselves, out in this strange glimmering once-in-a-lifetime world of ice and blue light and darkness.

'Would you look at that,' his dad said.

And suddenly, a change in the voices: from joy to fear in a moment. He was gripped by a sense of horror – but also of exhilaration. His gran would have snuffed the air and understood at once: a skater had slipped through a gap and vanished into the black water. He stood amid the piled ice, his breath white in the air, London sending its eerie blue light into the high sky, listening to the calling voices. To be in on a death: this was not new, but it had never happened in such surroundings, in such an otherworldly setting. Would they die at once? – or would the cold take them quite slowly? From feet to legs, from hands to arms, from thighs slowly up into the abdomen, the ice closing in on the heart and at last on the brain? This would be the way. They would be aware of death closing in on them. They would see the blue-black sky, maybe, last of all as they vanished below the water, and then it would be all black, and then – nothing.

'False alarm,' his dad said, and exhaled suddenly.

John blinked, and looked. It was – nothing, false alarm. The voices turned again to laughter. He gazed out across the ice, and saw the rough slab of sled thrown up into the air, crashing on the ice. A metal bar had come loose from the sled; it was fit for nothing.

His heart sank a little, though. The prospect of a thrill of death, now whisked away.

'So, all part of the ensemble,' Stella murmured in the darkness. 'Well, I can understand that.'

They had talked about it, many times. Colour, and the absence of it. It was the kind of conversation that John could never have with the others – the students now looking around at London, and wondering how they might manage. Winklepickers and tight cords and jeans, a de rigueur uniform of black, black, black: at least he could discuss with such people the texture and assets and virtues of the colour black, could he not?

So Stella had said once, laughing, knowing that there was but one answer to her question.

'Well,' John said, 'yes. I mean: yes, it was a—'

'Thrill,' Stella said. 'Death, right there and then.'

'Yes.'

'Under the lights,' Stella murmured. The banquette juddered a little as she sat up, animated now. 'The way you talk about black, you have them in the palm of your hand. And you work with your blacks and your greys so well. But when you talk to me, it's like your world is floodlit. Even at night, the world is blue: and in the daytime, it's all gold and silver and green. So, why not work with colour?'

With colour. Yes: exactly.

'I couldn't do that.'

'You could.'

'Not yet. I couldn't do it yet.'

'You could do it right now.'

Back home, on Regina Road, the light had leaked from the downstairs window; the fish door knocker was dull and filmed. Difficult not to feel chilled as he walked along – even here, on this familiar road that was being stripped around him, lined by houses being picked off one by one – and he jumped in the door.

'Murder a cup of tea,' his dad said.

Inside, the place was warm: but she had been crying again, and now she was sunk into her chair by the fire.

'We'll be damned if we're moving anywhere,' she had said in the summer – but they would be moving, now; something had shifted. The pressing darkness was too much for them.

'What about the river, then?' she said now, with an effort. His father's long legs were stretched out to the flames; his stockinged feet wiggled in the heat. She said, 'Many people out there?'

There were lots, John told her: lots and lots, a great crowd. 'But too cold to stay long.'

'What about the ice?'

'Thick enough. It was thick enough.'

'Just thick enough?' – and now John shook his head, and laughed, and described the hills of ice, a sight to behold. His dad nodded; his stockinged feet wiggled and wiggled. Who knew, he said, when they would ever see such a thing again?

'But safe, everyone felt safe. The ice must be as thick as anything. You could tell that they all felt safe.'

'That's right,' his dad said.

Safe as houses, John nearly said, but closed his mouth just in time. They felt as safe as houses, out there on the blue-shining ice. Death was far away.

His mum said nothing.

5

The first letters had arrived in the spring of that year. The season was stamped into his memory: there had been floods upriver, and April arrived with a tumble of dead farm animals and dogs on the Deptford foreshore. 'Tory animals,' his dad said, 'come down from Oxfordshire. All we need is a few of their MPs to join them, and we'll be in clover.' With the dead animals came blue spring skies, and bluebells in Greenwich Park, when they went walking one sunny Sunday, and then the letters.

These came as no surprise: even before the war, the County Council had been minded to demolish half of Deptford. That had been the plot; the Germans had put it all on hold, but even the Germans couldn't cancel it for ever. The place was 'too much,' said his mother, 'for all those chaps up there at the council,' and she waved a hand in an indeterminate direction, 'sitting in their offices and cooking up schemes to spend money and keep themselves busy.'

The shops on the High Street stayed open until eleven o'clock on Friday nights, and ten o'clock on Saturday and Sunday nights, and until eight every other night of the week; the stalls stayed open even longer; and the pubs – and there were dozens, throngs, masses of pubs – longest of all; and the street was alive day and night. The war years were far away, the place was thriving again. Costermongers and fishmongers, butchers and button shops and beaderies, hosieries and confectioners and brothels, Methodist churches and Congregationalist churches that opened their doors wide and welcomed all comers: they were all to be found on the High Street. And their own church, with its radiant yellow stained glass, that John liked to slip in to look at, now and again.

And now the postman, delivering letters that nobody wanted to see. 'The Lord give me strength,' his mum liked to say, and she said it more and more frequently, though the Lord's ears seemed to be pinned tightly closed just at the moment.

'Too much,' Mum said. The floods waned, leaving even more jetsam on the foreshore, and then the summer passed, and with the beginning of autumn came an opportunity to put on her camel coat on Saturday nights and link her husband and swank with the best of them: along Regina Road and onto the High Street to join the crowds. Sunset earlier every Saturday, the lights brighter, the smells and voices sharper in the cooling air. This was the life.

It was too much life for some.

'Where did you go?'

Mum and Dad had their various haunts – but it was the Prince Regent, this time, for their beers and their sherries.

'Did you see anyone?'

They saw everyone: where to start? John was growing out of his clothes and into his razor blades, but he was still too young to hang around the Prince Regent. Another year would make the difference: but until then, he had to taste this life through stories, from far away. He liked to hear about the captured moments, the glimpses of lives, and Mum was adept at capturing them for him.

'Mrs Saunders, poor love, though she's looking less sad nowadays. Isn't she, Alfred?' – and his dad paused in his filling of the kettle to look over his shoulder, and nod.

'She is.'

Mr Saunders had fallen down the stairs while drunk, and broken his neck. He had signed and signed and signed the Pledge, but it never came to anything; and nobody was surprised to hear about the broken neck. It was a shame, but that's the way it goes. The broken neck ('snapped cleanly,' they said, 'snapped in two, like a twig') was in May: now, in October, there was a touch of the merry widow about Mrs Saunders, so they said. She had never looked sad, though, not even for a minute in May.

'And poor Mr Riegler,' who had survived two wars, in spite of his German ancestry, by dint of being the greatest royalist in Deptford. They had smashed every single one of his windows, a score of times: he kept the glazier in business; he opened up again, a score of times, and an outsize Union Jack hung over his shop counter.

'Where was he?'

'Propping up the bar. Not too drunk, this time. I've seen him flat on his back, poor man. We saw the whole of Deptford tonight,' she declared, 'and every last one of them drunk.' She paused. 'The letters are flying around.' The kettle sang in a cloud of steam, and Dad took it off the hob. 'Flying through the air. Oh well, at least they put us first. We're first on a list, somewhere, isn't that nice.'

'Sweetheart,' said his dad.

'We're not moving.'

Cities in the sky, they were promised.

The brochures had arrived on the doormat a few weeks after the letters. They were promised cities in the sky: balconies and views, air and light, panoramas of the Thames and London and the whole wide world. The Eiffel Tower, if the air was clear enough. Hot water, central heating, fitted kitchens and the Formica that everybody talked about: it was all waiting for them. It was time to meet the future. All they had to do was say yes – and they wouldn't have to lift a finger. Except to pick up the pen and sign on the dotted line. Just sign, and the County Council would do the rest.

No more outside toilets, was the lure. No more front doors that opened up onto the street. Who could say no to that?

Mum looked around her own kitchen, and her lip curled with distaste at the thought of what they were promising. An inside toilet was a disgusting thing. They had spent money on their outside toilet, converting it from a privy to something much better – and something more hygienic too, for who could live with a toilet in the next room, just standing there, under the same roof? That was the point. No, it was disgusting, she said, however you looked at it.

Someone had said, on the High Street, that if the Queen had an inside toilet, it perhaps couldn't be too disgusting. Surely, this lady had said, surely if the Queen could settle herself comfortably and do her business on *her* inside toilet, maybe her gold toilet, up there at the Palace, surely that meant that they all could live with one?

'The Queen will do as she pleases,' was all his mum said in reply. She thought that this was disgusting too, that there were now two disgusting things going on. She didn't like the idea of a toilet, sitting there in the middle of her house; and she didn't want to have to think or talk about the Queen's toilet habits. Did they have to talk about where and in what manner the Queen used her gold toilet?

'It's hardly gold, the Queen's toilet,' said his dad.

'Lord's sake,' she said. 'Can we please stop talking about toilets, for five minutes?'

And she didn't want to live in the sky, either.

The letter gave them no choice, or hardly any choice – it was the sky, or nothing, that was the choice – but Mum told anyone who'd listen that this was England, they couldn't just knock down your house while you were living in it, they hadn't survived Hitler and the flying bombs only to see their front doors caved in with a wrecking ball. She had been just around the corner from the Woolworth's at New Cross when the flying bomb hit it and did for, what was it, one hundred and fifty, two hundred people? – and that included some people she knew, some girls from primary school. And now, what, the English themselves were threatening to bulldoze her own house while she was sitting in it, having her cup of tea? The Nazis would be pleased to hear that, if there were any Nazis still about.

'I don't think they plan to bulldoze the house with us still in it, sweetheart,' Dad said. 'I don't think that's the plan, exactly.'

'And what would I do, living up there in the sky? No,' she said, 'we're stopping, and that's flat.'

They had, in fact, been to view one such city in the sky, in the Pepys Estate. Nobody could point a finger and say that they weren't open to ideas, to suggestions. They went. The shadow of the estate fell across the High Street these days. Slender, with balconies and windows – but too tall, and it loomed there, in the corners of all their eyes. It gave his mum, she said, trouble sleeping. 'Just knowing it's there.' For John too it seemed to cast a shadow: across the neighbourhood, yes, but also across his mind. He could see this long shadow, slanting across his thoughts, by day, by night. There was a horror to the thing, it tied his mind and his imagination into a knot.

The lift moved up through the grey building: the colour reminded John of the shingle on the Thames beaches, when the tide was low. But lifeless: no strutting birds, no tidewrack, no white shells to lift the greyness; nothing up here. The lift stopped at last, on the sixteenth floor: it opened onto a narrow landing, with coloured doors spaced evenly beyond.

The man from the County Council, who had maintained his silence through all sixteen floors, stepped out, stepped across, turned the key in a coloured door, pushed the door open. A small hall, and stairs – steep, narrow – and a big room, big windows, a balcony. A maisonette, with bedrooms upstairs. The view was wide, and bright. They all, mother and father and son, stepped back automatically from the windows.

The room looked east, across flatness, to a distant emptiness. London stretched below them: Greenwich and its park, the grey line of the widening Thames with its wharves and its sheds, and in the distance, grey fields, an expanse of sky, a hem of sea-brightened horizon.

To John, the view and the immensity vibrated with desolation. How was she expected to deal with this? He turned to her, composing his face; beside him, the little lines around his father's eyes had vanished as his eyes widened. His mother's face was set – in shock, perhaps, or anger, or (he thought, later) a premonition of loss and loneliness. Before any of them could speak, however, the man from the council spoke.

'Of course, we wouldn't house you here. Not in Pepys. It's full up, already. No, you'd be housed in Charlton or somesuch,' he went on, 'where there's capacity.' He truly was oblivious to the expression on her face, on all their faces. 'Far away from here,' he said, and John watched as she gazed out at the wide view of river and city and sky.

The wind hissed, up here.

'Would we all be housed in Charlton?' she asked him.

'All?'

'The rest of us, the rest of us who live in Deptford now.'

'Not all of you, no. It would depend upon resources.' He paused, and then added smoothly, 'The ones who returned the letters, they've been allocated places here, of course. First come, first served, is the way it works, really.'

John turned on a tap, and hot water and steam came out.

'Turn that off,' she told him, above the hissing sound. He turned it off; the taps clanked and groaned and fell silent.

'Better than the little places you live in now,' the man from the council said. 'Dark, and no view, and outside toilet. Much better in a place like this. Look at that view.'

Toilets again, and his mum closed her eyes.

Later, at home, they talked about the letters doing the rounds. There had been other letters, was the talk, letters written by people on Giffin Street, complaining about the damp and the rats and the sewage, the black beetles and the dirt. Their children were sick, the letter-writers complained, and rats scuttled across the counterpanes as people slept in their beds. You have to help us, the letter-writers complained, you have to help our sick children.

But that was Giffin Street. Giffin Street was a black hole: you couldn't say that one street stood for the whole of Deptford. Which was what the council was doing.

It was criminal. They were cooking up a conspiracy.

'They want to plan the future,' his dad said, and his mum said, looking across her neat house: clean carpet, tidy room shining with brass and tinkling with china, three-piece suite with its starched antimacassars, warm stove with tongs and shovel and poker, 'But there's nothing wrong with the future right here.'

The house had foundations in the actual ground. In the earth.

John thought about the city in the sky. They were going there, he knew.

6

Soon afterwards, at the end of autumn, Harry and his family left. Not for a city in the sky, but for somewhere else again: for a *semi-dee* in Beckenham. 'Leafy Beckenham,' Harry's mum said, gaily. His father had a promotion, they were moving on, they were moving up, they were glad to leave. Soon afterwards again, the word went up and down the High Street that the first houses would be coming down. In Giffin Street, and in Adelaide Street, which was a little bit further away – but soon, the demolitions began and crept nearer. In Regina Road, another family left; then another, and then another. The windows of the empty houses and their front doors were fitted with corrugated sheeting; soon, half the street was boarded up. The street lights went out, and the services stopped.

'They're starving us out,' said his mum.

The ice provided some relief, for a few weeks. Nothing

happened in ice-frozen London for a little while: no pressure, no building, no more families packing their boxes and departing. John slipped and slid along Regina Road, and along to the river, and watched the skaters and the sleds, and the piled ice. The Quaggy was solid too, and the grey, coarse sand and shingle were slicked with ice. This was the last winter, he knew. He stood and watched the skaters in the blue-lit air, and watched his breath smoke, and then he went home to darkening Regina Road. This was it.

John sat on the stairs, his long legs bent, and listened. His father saw a way to make money from this city in the sky. They were building over Lewisham way, he said, and they needed hands and men. And he needed to make some money.

Mum threw a china cup against the wall. Her Royal Albert, with the pattern of red roses.

When his father started over at Lewisham, he and Mum didn't speak for a week. A few more families moved out in the course of that same week; and a little pool of something shit-smelling gathered in a dip in the road; the sewers on Regina Road, they said, were no longer being maintained. They liked their outside privies, they were perhaps saying up at the council: so, let them live with privy smells right on the street. That would show them. They might not like these smells so much after a couple of days.

After a week of this, the silence was broken – by Mum, who baked a special pie, apple, with a dusting of cinnamon from the market, and crisp, buttery pastry; and

Dad came home, and kissed her hand; and that was that. After another week, they went over to Lewisham on the bus, John and his mum, and walked over to where the city was rising into the sky. Hammering and scaffolding, ploughed, bare earth, yellow lorries and dust in the air; and the beginnings of another shadow – still fitful for now, but John could see the shape it would presently assume, a skeleton growing its flesh slowly, inexorably, and the lean and stretch of it, and the coarsening shadow growing across Lewisham's hills.

'Up there,' the foreman said, 'but you can't go any closer.'

They stood and watched. His mum pulled at her headscarf, and buttoned and unbuttoned her spring coat.

'What's the first thing you can remember?' Stella asked. Mildred's was filling now – the usual crowd, and the dark air filling too with smoke, and voices, and the music would be beginning soon – but the crowd seemed to sense the need to give him some space, to keep away for a while.

She liked such opening gambits, such starters: who knew where they might lead? He didn't know, he said, but she pushed him. Well, he said, what about you? – and she told him about a garden, and a picnic, all wicker and red gingham, and a race, and horses.

'You're making that up. Gingham, for God's sake, you're having me on.'

She turned to face him, on the quivering, jelly-surfaced banquette. 'A picnic. Wicker,' she said, '*and* gingham, *and* the races later. And probably I was wearing some sort of straw *hat* and making a daisy chain, though that I can't remember for certain. But all the rest of it is true. A certain kind of English person does actually live like that, you know.'

'With a nanny? Were you making a daisy chain with Nanny?'

'No,' Stella said, 'not with Nanny. Nanny had kicked the bucket by then. Mummy had her sent to the knacker's yard. Poor Mummy, she had to make the sandwiches herself at that stage. Imagine, shelling the eggs herself. The slumming of it. Mincing the cress, imagine,' she added.

That was how they began talking about memory, about memories, in the smoky darkness at Mildred's. About this memory, and that one. Gingham and picnics and daisy chains; and the Pepys Estate, and the flat on the sixteenth floor. And their first memories.

'Your turn,' said Stella, and he told her about the Thames foreshore at Deptford, and the branches bleached white, and the shingle and tidewrack and smell of salt, and the glossy brass knockers in the shape of salmon and dolphins, on the glossy doors of Regina Road.

'All gone now,' he said. In the darkness, she took his hand.

'In thee, O Lord,' he said, 'have I put my trust,' and Stella squeezed his hand a very little. For she had been brought up in the same way: the rhythms and the words, the liturgy and the stained glass gleaming on a Sunday morning. Little enough he had to explain to Stella – or so he sometimes felt. She seemed to know it all already. She seemed able to look through him, as through glass, the clear sort, and to bring the light shining through.

She was his last hope, as he later realised, and his best hope.

And yet.

They could quote the liturgy to one another all they liked, and feel pleased with this thought of their childhood selves bathed in the very same stained-glass glow of yellow and red, of the ties that were binding them together from afar—

And yet: there were certain thoughts that must remain unspoken, certain memories that must remain unarticulated. Stella had access to his heart, but only to a little bit of it.

Was she beginning to see this? Perhaps she was. She had given him access – to her heart, to her name. Was she beginning to see that there was an imbalance? Perhaps she was. But how could he talk about protruding bones, how could he talk about the dreams he still had, that he would always have, of white bones on a grey ground?

He would have to pour it into his work.

Surely she would understand.

The tower was clad in the same grey material as Pepys, something that was neither stone nor concrete. A sort of composite, he understood later, once he had learned the word. A sort of forcing together, a mixing of material to produce a greyness. There were winking glints embedded within: what looked like minute pieces of broken glass, and crushed specks of something white – seashells, perhaps. But the greyness dominated, overcoming the glinting glass and the hells. A grey shading to a light brown – and ugly, however you might look at it.

He stood, and forced himself to imagine the place in a different light, under a frosty winter sky, under a perfect sunrise. Surely he could capture such a scene, give it a new life on a piece of paper. But – no, there was no way to change this place. The glint in the composite faded away. The grey, fading to brown, was not the sort of shade to change itself.

They had travelled over from Deptford on the top deck of an unaccustomed bus. His mother was wearing a light spring coat – the air was fresh, there was blue in the sky, but a shower might make an appearance, later – and she had on her street face. Which was what he called it, taking a cue from his dad, who laughed at his mum's street face and her house face. 'Stop it, Alfred,' she would say, as she practised her face in the glass at the foot of the stairs, before stepping up to the Prince Regent on a Saturday night. She would smile a practice smile, and then glance over her own shoulder. 'I'm only—' 'Putting your best foot forward, Dorothy. I know, love. Come on, now, chop chop.' And out they would go into the lamplight on Regina Road, and a little puff of cold air would come in. 'Take your time,' his gran used to say. 'We're in no hurry to see you again. Are we, John?'

This was the face, today, as they left Deptford behind, and the hills rose and fell as the bus travelled south towards Lewisham. She had a job to do, today, and so did he.

And what now? He was a hale and energetic seventeen-year-old, as everyone was telling him nowadays, with his whole life in front of him, and the city in the sky, in Lewisham or Charlton or somewhere else, would be just a short period, a year or a couple of years, they said, before he pressed on into life and into London – but it was all he could do to keep his countenance, to turn to his mum with a smile. A big smile. That was his public face too.

'Look at the size of this place.'

It was impressive if you could only take a step back, take it all in. The machinery, the men, the scale of the works. And this just one of many such operations now being duplicated all across London. The money being spent, and the materials being trucked and shipped, and the whole machine at work, pounding and sawing and humming. The people being shifted around, as though they were goods on a lorry, or a boat, by the hundreds and thousands. It was – if you could only step back – truly spectacular. And he could step back: there was a piece of him that was able to understand the ambition that lay behind all this.

He slid a glance at his mother. She still had her face on, her public face, and yet she seemed shrunken this morning: though he supposed he did too. The very workmen appeared like ants and spiders, for – spectacular or not – there was an inhuman aspect to the whole operation. But his mother didn't seem like a spider or an ant – but like a tiny version, suddenly, of a normal human being. Oh, she was attempting courage: she had squared her shoulders, he had watched her this morning, as they left to catch their bus, looking at the filth pooling on Regina Road and the boarded windows and the empty houses to right and left and opposite. The tears – of rage and humiliation – had risen once more, but that was the last time. It wouldn't be Pepys and it wouldn't be Lewisham and it might be Charlton, who knows where it might be, in the end, but she had accepted that it was her fate to live in the sky, and there would be no more tears.

There was her public face.

She was shrunken, and that couldn't be helped.

Now, she smiled back. 'I know,' she said. 'Now, where's that dad of yours?' They had both been gazing around, at the armies of spiders and ants, looking for the familiar shape of him, the broad shoulders and chest of a river man now washed up in this dusty place. They identified him, high on a scaffold: a tiny figure, very high, an arm flung wide in greeting.

He descended slowly, carefully. He showed them around, and introduced them to all comers, and told them what was what; and after an hour or a little more, they went home again. An interesting afternoon, they agreed. It had set the seal on something; and now for a fresh life, a new beginning. They had seen one of these cities being built in the sky, in this very place.

This meant that his mind was able to track and watch it all, when it happened. His physical absence was no proof against his imagination, when, several weeks later, the news came one afternoon that his dad had pitched from the scaffolding on the ninth floor of the grey tower, had fallen through the dusty air, had fallen on his back onto the turned-over ground.

The sound, the dull *thump* of the body as it hit the ground. And imagining the sight, of what will happen to a body when it falls from a height.

The men doubtless knew what to do. It was not as though falls, and deaths, and a variety of horrors, were uncommon in such places. In his mind's eye, he watched as they screened his dad's body – with their own bodies, before a man came, at a brisk trot, with a length of dark canvas to lay over the scene, to tidy it away. But the dark canvas made no difference to John. He could see white bones, and redness, and grey matter where his dad's head was broken, and the small pool of almost-black blood that crept across the ground. He could see the scene a minute before: the set of his dad's shoulders, the shape of his back, a small figure high on a scaffold, sure-footed and nimble. The moment of imbalance. Would he fall? Could he catch himself, right himself, shake himself, shake off the shock, put down the hammer he was holding, laugh a little to disguise the sickness in his stomach?

Or would he fall?

Would the second pass, and the rightness never come, and would he fall back instead, back first, and then head first, and then his shoulders seeming to lead the way, and all in a matter of seconds?

He fell.

He fell backward: his back first, and then his head, and then his shoulders, as though in these few remaining seconds his dad was straining still to right himself, to catch himself, to fend off death. And then his head again.

John could see the fall, and the impact, and could hear it too. The doorbell on Regina Road, and the message, and there he stood, the blood rushing in his ears and his heart thumping fit to burst in his chest, all in a second before he set to managing his mother. He did not even remember hearing her scream.

The third man to die that summer, they said later. On that one job. A shame: but all part and parcel. It went with the territory.

His memory remained broken into pieces, as though it were itself a fallen body.

Mica

7

'It's a fact,' Roisin said.

Roisin had a head on her. She was *combative*, Miss Glackin had said to her parents right in front of her, as she stood looking down at the floor. 'I see it in the course of the day. Every day. She has too much to say for herself, far too much, for an eight-year-old. She's just like her sister was at that age.' And, 'opinionated,' said Miss Glackin. 'And we can't be having that.'

There was a knack. Roisin knew this. But she hadn't picked up this knack, whatever it was, and the proof of this had been Miss Glackin slapping her legs with her long ruler.

'What's the knack?' she asked Maeve. She brought up her school skirt a little, and her sister looked at the thin red lines that Miss Glackin's ruler had left on Roisin's legs.

'There is no knack,' Maeve said.

'But you said there was. You did say.'

Maeve frowned, and ran a hand through her red curls, and Roisin looked at her.

'You just have to not *say* anything, I mean. That's the knack. It's not really a knack at all.'

'What do you mean?' said Roisin.

'We don't want people taking an interest,' Miss Glackin had said, as Roisin looked at the floor, 'there, in the town.' Roisin looked up, as her mother shook her head. She agreed, so much was clear: she definitely didn't want anyone taking an interest in Roisin. That was the last thing she wanted.

And Maeve agreed too. When people took an interest, Maeve said later, it was a bad sign.

But Roisin didn't understand. She could say what she wanted, couldn't she? She could speak up for herself.

Maeve shook her head. 'No. Nope. That's what I mean.'

And now here was Roisin, standing in the school corridor where she had no right to be at this time of day, taking in Holy Mary.

For years – for twenty-something years, ever since the school had been built, they said, way back at the beginning of the 1950s, back in the olden days – the statue of Holy Mary had stood in the long corridor that ran from the classrooms to the assembly hall. The corridor was lined on one side with broad, rectangular windows that gave a view of the playground, and the handball alley, which wasn't worth looking at, at all. It had grey, rough walls, and bright green moss grew there winter, summer, always. On the other side of the corridor, the walls were lined by more windows, this time of frosted glass, and on the other side of the windows was the assembly hall itself, with its stage and its curtains of dark red velvet – 'like Hollywood,' said Maeve – and its polished floor.

Maeve knew about Hollywood. 'I know about *everything*,' she liked to say. She had a picture of Faye Dunaway pinned on the wall of their bedroom. The other girls told Roisin that she was lucky, that Maeve was the big sister they all wanted. The glamour of her!

Halfway along the corridor, a recess, a sort of notch, its walls painted not custard-colour, like all the rest of the walls, but brighter-than-bright white: and in this recess stood the school statue of Holy Mary, all blue and white and crowned in gold, her hands held out in, said the nuns, *benediction*. Roisin knew that for twenty years now the town's children had eddied past Holy Mary, day after day, on their way to morning prayers, on their way from prayers to their classroom, to and fro all day along. At the beginning of the school year, the waxed floor shone like a mirror, and squeaked underfoot; at year's end, the floor was dull, its wax worn away. Holy Mary herself remained unworn. She was dusted daily, she caught the eyes of the children, she was unmoving and unchanging.

Now, though, she had moved. Now she had changed. Now she had taken it upon herself to clamber down and walk the corridors of the school, in the evenings and by night.

And Miss Glackin had given Roisin her golden chance.

'Roisin O'Hara, come here please.' And then, 'I want you to run along and drop this note in to Miss Black. Go straight to her classroom and come straight back.'

This was her chance – though she knew to keep her eyes looking at the classroom floor. Head down, eyes low:

anything else was what her mother called *a red rag to a bull* – cheek, or the possibility of cheek, made Miss Glackin's face, her nose, go rag-red, and every girl knew it.

'Yes, Miss,' Roisin said, and looked at the floor.

How she would swank it over the girls, later.

She set off down the corridor, glanced at the custard-yellow shiny walls as she passed. She remembered what she'd thought when she first went to school – but of course that was ages ago, ages and ages, that was three years ago, she was just a little girl. She'd thought, then, that the paint, the walls, were made of seashells. They ground them up, the shiny seashells; maybe they stamped them into dust with big boots, and they mixed the dust with water, and Bird's custard powder, and the dust became yellow paint, the colour of custard. That was the way it was done.

Ages ago. That was on her first day in the school, and that evening, in their room, she'd said this to Maeve, about the seashells and the custard powder. 'It's just the paint they use,' Maeve told her, 'the shiny paint. That's all. So, they don't need to bother with seashells,' Maeve added gently, 'because the paint is already there, in big tins.'

Maeve knew it all.

Roisin had been glad about that, glad that Maeve had told her about the shiny paint before she said anything about seashells and custard powder to the other girls, before she'd been turned into what her daddy called a laughing stock.

'A laughing stock, you are,' he said sometimes, a lot of the time, to her mammy, 'in the town. A holy show. Mooning around like that.'

Roisin walked and walked down the long corridor – and now here was Holy Mary, standing on her stone that sparkled a little in the light from the windows. A *pedestal*, said the nuns, shining with diamonds. She stood in front of the shiny stone, the custard walls, and looked.

Only looked.

There was nothing at all that said that touching was *strictly* and *absolutely* not allowed, there was no rule – but Roisin knew. They all knew. Every girl in the school knew what was allowed and what wasn't allowed. None of them needed a set of rules.

A glimpse of Sister Immaculata's long ruler was all they needed.

Strictly and absolutely not. That was one of Sister Immaculata's sayings. *No, girls,* she'd say, and she'd fix her little black glasses on her nose, *strictly and absolutely not.* In the playground, in the corridors, when she rang her big bell from the top of the steps. *No running, girls! Strictly and absolutely not!*

How bold of me, how brave I am, how bold I am to stop just here. How *bad*.

To glance over her left shoulder, her right shoulder – the coast clear, the school silent, no clipping of a teacher's feet, no almost-silent pad-pad that indicated that Sister Immaculata was on the prowl. Sister Immaculata, they said, had her shoes made with special rubber soles, her feet cushioned in cotton wool, because that was the best way to catch a girl in badness. Red-handed.

Sister Immaculata's cotton-wool shoes were specially made in Rome, and sent to her by the Pope, they said.

But today, nothing at all. Sister Immaculata must be in her warm office, beside her hissing, clunking radiator.

The school was silent. Or almost silent: just a mist

of noises in the air, a times table recited, a chair moved, scraped for a second. Lots of faraway voices, rehearsing a hymn. *Christ all around me, shield in the strife.* It was strange to be in the corridors at such a quiet time, it was almost creepy.

And she was disobeying, too. Miss Black's classroom was in the other direction.

A holy show, standing there before the statue. Jars and jars of bluebells surround her, smelling of Heaven, and there she is.

Roisin hugged herself, almost. This will be something to tell the girls during break.

The statue wasn't wearing shoes – or none that anybody could see. Only a dress, blue on top and white underneath, reaching all the way to the ground. But Roisin had never studied her – not really. There had never been time, or any reason to. The statue had just been part of the furniture.

Not now, though.

Roisin looked up. Holy Mary looked – not stern, not cross, but not sweet either. Not gentle, the way she was supposed to look. She didn't much look like anything, did she? As though she felt a little bit bored, maybe.

But how could she feel bored, the things she had been up to lately? – and now Roisin frowned a little. This was confusing, this didn't really make sense.

She remembered Miss Glackin, she remembered Miss Black, she had to go. Holy Mary was bored. Was that it? Was that why she was doing what she was doing?

The sparkle caught Roisin's eye. Holy Mary standing on her bit of rock – and the rock shining. Maybe the little girls were right, maybe there were little diamonds inside the rock – and the sun shining on them brought them alive.

Roisin stood for another long moment, gazing at the rock, the diamonds, the bottom of Holy Mary's long dress. She wanted to look longer, but Miss Black was waiting, and Miss Glackin was counting the seconds, was waiting to be cheeked. One more moment, one more look, and now Roisin stretched out her hand – and touched, not Holy Mary's long dress, but the stone, the *pedestal*, on which she stood.

It was cool, though not cold. It was rough, a bit splintery. But how did the glinting diamonds feel? She couldn't really tell: it was hard to tell. She moved her hand away, turned on her heel, scurried back the way she came, off to Miss Black's classroom. *Quick, Roisin!* Maeve's voice sounded in her head – on the beach last summer, running races. At Sports Day, in the field, in the sprint. Maeve's voice calling, the excitement of it. *Quick, Roisin! Quick, quick quick!*

Roisin won the sprint.

She felt – something, a difference. Back in the classroom, with Miss Glackin writing on the blackboard, tapping on her desk with her finger, tapping on Siobhan Reilly's head with her ruler: Roisin was thinking about a sparkle, about the statue of Holy Mary waking, and stretching, maybe, and stepping off her diamond rock.

8

'**D**on't let the food get cold,' said Philomena.

The family was at the table, and the meal had barely begun.

A statue of Mary, another statue, had been seen walking, and weeping, somewhere down the country. So they were saying.

'The country's full of them,' murmured Maeve. 'An infestation, like bedbugs.'

This moving statue had been on the news.

'Surely one statue is enough,' murmured Maeve.

This piece of news would have been enough for Roisin – without their own statue, Holy Mary up at the school, getting in on the act too, walking too, and weeping too. She too had been seen by someone, caught as she strode the corridors. It was, said Roisin, a fact. And she had stopped to look at the statue herself, today, she said, while running an errand for Miss Glackin, so she knew what she was talking about.

The girls, at break, had been 'agog', said Roisin.

Philomena listened, and said nothing.

It was a fact for her mother, too: Philomena had heard them yacking about it in the town. That day, in fact, that very morning: there were duck eggs for sale in Comyn's, so she took herself off to buy half a dozen; and as she waited to be served, she caught up with the news. A prospective land sale, which had caught everyone unawares, two fields, and one of them the good one, which meant money problems; a bridge table, just the previous night, come almost to blows at the Masonic Hall – and now the walking, talking statue of the Madonna up at Holy Cross.

It paid to be a daily Mass-goer – it had been on the steps of the church, following that morning's Mass, that she had heard about the duck eggs – but there could be no question of Philomena believing this story of their own Holy Mary on the loose up at the school. The girls were a bit hysterical, agreed the women at the counter at Comyn's: it was the way with girls, sometimes, for hysteria to spread like a winter germ; and old Patrick Comyn himself, over eighty now but still serving his faithful clients, agreed. Echoing Maeve, if he only knew it.

'One statue wandering around all over the place, in Tipperary or wherever it is: well, ladies, that's enough to be going on with, if you ask me.'

There was no question mark added at the end of his sentence – and Philomena, for her part, wasn't about to disagree with him. She had watched the news, had seen the foreign television crews, had listened to their English (on the jeering side) and American (indulgent; they found it hilarious) accents, had been mortified.

Had kept her counsel, needless to say. Instead, she smiled a little, an absent-minded smile, and looked up at the blue insect-repelling light that hummed above Mr Comyn's head, and down at the blue veins in her thin hands. She allowed the conversation to eddy around her, and listened, and said nothing. She wondered, her shoulders set and tense inside her coat, what Roisin would say to such stories. What Maeve would continue to say, whether Maeve would be sensible enough to say nothing at all for once. Whether the subject would come up that evening, as her family gathered at the dinner table; and if it did, whether it would lead to a row. It would of course come up. Nothing more certain.

A family of four: and this was strange enough. Philomena knew the way it went.

Very strange: these two girls, this family of four. Surely not the *Pill*, people thought: well, a little mental arithmetic showed that it might be the Pill – but no, surely Philomena wasn't the sort of woman to be so quick off the mark, to slide across the border to consult with some doctor or other, to have some obliging friend, some bustling, interfering Protestant it would be, to set the thing up. The notion was unthinkable, and anyway, Philomena wasn't the sort of woman to have Protestant friends at all – even in such a place as this, where they were thick enough on the ground. Philomena feared God, the right variety of God. That was obvious. So the wordless thoughts went, and were set aside.

So, it couldn't be the Pill.

But there were plenty of other reasons why a man and wife would find themselves with two children only: to do with pipes and tubing, perhaps, or to do with something else a little more on the grave side. Incompatibility raised its head – what did the priest know? – and more than one person yearned to be a fly on the wall of *that* confessional.

Philomena knew the stories, and recognised the glances.

The men, after a pint or two, might have commented that Philomena was the wearer of the slacks *there*, or so it seemed; that Cormac – in spite of appearances – was the sort of fella who did as he was told. The women, like Philomena, kept their thoughts to themselves, for Philomena was quiet-spoken and kindly, was popular in the town, was not the sort of women to be shredded by gossip. And she went to Mass daily.

Maybe the women also envied her: envied her her two children at any rate, though nothing else, perhaps, about her life. Perhaps she *had* been ahead of the game, they thought, gazing around and down at their own numerous broods: perhaps, in spite of appearances, she had been quick off the mark, with the Pill. Perhaps Philomena was the sort of woman who liked to take charge of her life.

It seemed unlikely though, didn't it?

No: much more likely that she had just had two children. Surely no priest would be able to quibble with anything to do with this marriage. It was more likely that, since Cormac was in any case a withdrawn sort of man, he'd got the timing right and had withdrawn here, too.

Philomena, at the counter at Comyn's, had looked at the blue veins running across her hands, and waited for her duck eggs, and thought of all the things that people were saying about her, about her family, about her daughters. She knew all of this talk, all of these words – how could she not, in a small place? – but better to say nothing.

Now, at her own kitchen table, she looked at her bright-eyed younger daughter, who spoke out. What had Bríd Glackin said, her lips tight, her forehead scored and furrowed with frown marks, what had she said? – *too many opinions, that girl*, and *too fond of the sound of her own voice*, and *too much*, and *too much like Maeve*. What was wrong with these two girls? What was Philomena doing wrong? – because she was clearly doing something wrong. So Bríd Glackin seemed to think.

But also: *be careful*. What happens to girls in Ireland who get uppity? – a list of possible outcomes, and none of them good.

Philomena watched Roisin, now. She had watched her in the incubator, then in her crib: Roisin had been premature – and the birth was dreadful, a horror of pain and fear, with nothing but death looming at the end of it all. She had – had she screamed? She thought she had, and they had made her sip water, and crunch ice that shattered at first like glass in her mouth. The crunching of pieces of ice: sharp, and then melting, as she bit down and screamed.

There had been no need for questions. The midwife's face told her everything: it was set, professionally motionless, until the worst was over. Then, as the ice began to melt, the baby was given her start in the world, and the midwife's face melted too, and sagged with relief and tiredness, and she changed her tune, saying soothingly that it hadn't been so bad after all. Had it? 'Think about the baby you have,' the midwife said, as she must have said a thousand times before. 'You'll soon forget about the other things.' The cracked tooth, the red rips in flesh. 'And this little one: she'll be fine now, she'll soon put on the weight, you did well.'

Cormac was at home minding the elder girl. Men, the midwife told her, were beginning to attend in the hospitals, the odd man at any rate, it was the modern way – but Philomena said, no, not this husband; and the midwife said nothing more, and got on with it.

No, no Cormac hovering in the delivery room. Imagine. Philomena could not imagine, and she was relieved about that, one thing to feel relieved about, anyway. She could stand many things, including excruciating pain and fear, and blood, and torn flesh, and the cracked tooth: these all came with labour. But not that: not Cormac at her side, at such a time. She had the room and the baby, to herself. And now she nodded and smiled at the midwife – mildly enough, given what she'd just been through. This wasn't it at all.

This was the last time she would have a baby, and she needed to take it all in, to remember it. That was all.

She closed her eyes and felt tranquillity, opened them and felt her cracked tooth with the tip of her tongue; looked at this tiny scrap of a thing, this second daughter, touched her tiny cheek.

The next day, the midwife told her that she had spoken,

had done what she considered to be her duty. Had drawn Cormac aside, in the Jeyes-smelling corridor. 'She needs a bit of support, but she'll be fine. Don't be worrying, but support her, and she'll be fine.' What had Cormac said? – the midwife didn't say; but very likely nothing, not a word, just stood there and wondered (his eyes looking down at the floor) why this busybody woman was talking to him in this fashion, very likely wound up the conversation as fast as possible. Philomena listened as the midwife reported on the conversation, and smiled, and watched the midwife contemplate the strangeness of husbands and wives, the flatness and sluggishness of people in the face of the miraculous.

You don't know him, Philomena thought.

Later, in those first weeks when the family was safely together under the one roof and the routine re-established, she waited for Cormac to go to bed at his usual time, and leave Philomena to sit up, hour by hour, and watch the tiny baby's chest rise and fall. She could never again go through something like that labour, that birth. She looked over her shoulder, looked back at death, and looked away. Cormac would just have to understand.

Now, Philomena sat at her table and watched her daughter. The meal was not very modern – shepherd's pie, a heaped white blanket of mashed potatoes – though with sweetcorn and greens on the side, for Philomena was anxious to boost her family's intake of vitamins, to stave off the cancer and the blocked bowels (for herself, not least) for as long as possible. Comfort food, though she herself was not feeling comfortable.

Philomena was light, pale. Two daughters explained the slicing frown mark: danger, rape, molestation and thuggery scraping to get in, a curved animal claw glimpsed scrabbling into the space below the door – daughters were no laughing matter. Nor were sons, of course, people said, but in a different way; after all, it's a whole lot easier to rape than to be raped, if it has to come to that. But at least Philomena's blessing could now kick in again: only two daughters and not three or four or five or more than five, like everyone else. Only two to fret about. She could see how people got hold of the ideas they had about her.

And also, Roisin and Maeve seemed like nice girls. Or nice enough, anyway.

There was a touch of – of something there, and people, not only Miss Glackin, liked to gesture towards this, when the subject came up. Philomena: a good egg, but she'll need to keep an eye on that Roisin; Maeve has a way about her that she'd do well to get the better of, and Philomena will want to see to it that her Roisin doesn't go the same way.

So they liked to say, in the town, and Philomena knew it. They meant spirit, that Maeve had spirit, and Philomena knew this, too. She had high hopes for Maeve: higher than Maeve had any notion of.

Philomena looked at the yellow cube of corn speared on a tine of her fork.

And little Roisin, holding forth with seeming confidence. She spoke of facts, and Philomena listened. She saw her elder daughter listen to Roisin, the shepherd's pie and greens and sweetcorn cooling, taking a back seat. The conversation made Philomena nervous.

'A fact?' said Maeve, and Philomena saw her husband stir in his seat.

'Let her speak,' Cormac said.

9

'What's it called, Mammy, when a bit of rock, when it shines, when you see it shining?'

'Shining?'

She watched her mother set her fork down carefully on the edge of her plate.

In Roisin's head, in her mind's eye, the bit of rock on which Mary stood shone and sparkled: she wanted to know if what the little ones said was true, if there really were diamonds hidden inside the rock. She'd had the girls' attention that day, at break: she had told them all about her visit to Holy Mary – up close, she was right there, with her nose on a level with Holy Mary's shoe, or where her shoe would be if she were wearing a shoe, she was closer than any one of them had ever been, since this had all started.

'I'll tell Miss Glackin,' said one voice. A nasty, spiteful voice – but Roisin knew she'd not tell.

'You'll not dare tell,' she said. She didn't even look towards the voice; there was no need to look.

Had the statue moved?

'I think I saw her move. I think her eye moved and looked at me.'

A breathing, in the little crowd of girls, like one breath. How excited the girls had been.

She hadn't said anything about the shining rock, though. About touching it, about feeling the rough, cool stone. Why hadn't she said anything? – it was hard to describe why she was excited, why she found it exciting. It wasn't just about the diamonds. Although—

'Like there are diamonds in the rock. The statue is on a rock, is standing on a rock, and the rock has a shine in it, like diamonds. Are they diamonds? In the rock?'

Daddy said, 'It's called mica.'

They all looked at him, Philomena and Maeve and Roisin: when he spoke, they listened, that was the rule in this house, and they all knew it. 'Mica is a sort of mineral,' he said.

'A mineral?'

'Not that sort of mineral.' Maeve tittered bravely. 'Not like Club Orange. Daddy means mineral like the shiny bits you saw in the rock.'

A pause, and Roisin looked up at the top of the table, and he spoke again.

'And you get shiny bits, as your sister would say, shiny bits of it in granite, that's what the rock is called, granite, and it makes the granite shine. That's what those hills are too, outside the window.' He waved an arm towards the kitchen window. 'So that's what you call the shine that you can see: it's called mica.'

Cormac had already cleared his plate, and set his knife and fork down neatly. He did not look at his younger daughter.

'Mica,' Roisin repeated.

So that's what it was, the shining. It was *mica*. And she'd seen it before.

'I saw it before,' she said, 'on holiday. In the field. With the donkey. Do you remember, Maeve?'

Maeve nodded. 'I do remember,' she said, 'the old donkey in his field,' and Roisin sat back happily, and looked around at her family, sitting there at the table in the kitchen. The kitchen that, her mammy told her once, wasn't very nice. The yellow of the walls was not a nice yellow, 'wipe-clean' was what her mammy called it.

Or, 'bird-shite yellow', Maeve liked to call it, when their daddy wasn't around. And *bird-shite yellow* was a better description. You got a lot of that particular shade of bird-shite yellow round about, their mammy said once (she didn't mind bad language, so long as their daddy wasn't around to hear it): and it was as well to blend in, she said, so they had gone for it too.

Why was it as well to blend in? Roisin had asked – but no reply worth listening to. 'Oh, it just is.'

And the kitchen was a bit gloomy, maybe, with all those cooking smells, and a bit dark too. The light on all the time. 'A man's world,' their mammy said, 'and a man designed this room and this house, and that's all there is to say about it.' And the sooner Maeve and Roisin passed their exams and got away, far away, she said once, the better.

Roisin ate her sweetcorn and looked out of the window. A rock that sparkles, a magic rock.

The bungalow looked out across the fields. Away in the distance, the fields stopped and the granite hills began. On frosty mornings and before rain, you could see every tree and every bush on the hills, you could see the trees planted there specially for wood and growing in a perfect square. But on rainy days, the hills vanished from sight, like magic.

She already knew that this was bad country. There were rushes growing in the fields, like tiny forests, and there was clay underneath the grass, blue clay that would turn your spade. And the water lay on the grass, for days and days, sometimes. It couldn't drain away. These were fields that kept people sad, and kept them poor. It was easy to know this; you didn't need to keep your ears wagging. Nothing for potatoes in these fields, nothing for cows. Almost nothing for sheep, here.

She wouldn't be poor, when she grew up, and neither would Maeve be. Their mammy had said so.

And little enough to see in wet weather. Just the vanishing hills. On grey days, wet days, stormy days, Roisin saw her mammy standing at the kitchen window and looking out: into mist, into the rain lying on the rushy grass. She said once, 'What're you looking at?' – and her mammy turned a little from the sink and said that she thought, some days, that she could see the grass turning blue.

Turning blue?

'I mean, the clay coming up through the grass, the blue

clay.' Then she'd given herself a shake and said, 'Ignore me, I'm talking nonsense,' and went on about her business. Roisin had stood there, then, on tiptoes, where her mother had stood, and she too had looked out at the fields.

Mica, mica.

Sparked by a thought of – of what? Of… and that was it, of sunlight on a craggy coast, a holiday in the west. Ages ago – such a very tiny girl, she must have been. A lighthouse, white-painted, black-striped, perched on rocks above a curve of yellow beach. The rocks are the black of – *basalt*, her daddy told her, and she isn't much interested in basalt. *Basalt* is too black, is dull, it's like a black, black night. But there are more colours than black, and more rocks than basalt. The beach is backed by hills, grey hills like home.

Granite hills, she knew now. She sat very still at the kitchen table, and looked at her mashed potato, and her yellow sweetcorn. It was something hard to remember, and to stay remembering. It was easy to forget.

Granite. In which diamonds are caught, as though the hills are a fishing net. A sparkle, catching the eye, catching the sunshine that catches on the waves on the ocean, and on the hills at home, and on these hills too.

Roisin sat very still.

Granite, and *mica*, and granite hills and mica mountains, right here at home, in the distance, over the boggy fields, and now she knew the words and names.

And now Holy Mary.

Maeve said, 'Can I have more sweetcorn?'

And now the family is on holidays by the sea, and the picnic is over. A small holiday house, a bungalow, on a slope above the beach, the lighthouse; a bench against the wall of the house on which Roisin and Maeve sit, in the sun, looking down on the beach and the sea. Brown legs and arms, and the rub of one toe against another toe, comfortably, and they discuss what they have seen and done: a crab in the deep rockpools on the far side of the beach, a bold crab that seized a stick in his claws, a stick that Maeve pushed at him, and he took the stick and dived into the depths of the pool.

'Put your hand in, Roisin,' says wicked Maeve. 'Go on, put it into the water. I dare you.'

Roisin shakes her head.

'Cowardy custard,' says Maeve.

'You put it in yourself,' Roisin says, and she leans over the pool and looks into the black water. Black kelp like a tongue, and silver-and-brown barnacles clinging tight to the rock, and the crab, down there somewhere, holding the stick. And Maeve's face behind her, reflected in the pool, reflected against the blue, sticking out her tongue: Roisin turns quickly, she looks over her shoulder – but Maeve has vanished, she is gone. Roisin looks over her other shoulder: Maeve has moved faster still, she is settling herself on a warm, flat slab of rock nearby. 'You didn't dare,' Roisin says, and Maeve smiles.

'I asked you first,' Maeve says, summoning the sacred rules of the game; and Roisin sits back on her heels, vanquished by this cleverer elder sister.

Maeve is not wicked. She loves Maeve more than anyone in the whole world.

And then a voice calling them. Up at the house, their mother has already sliced baps and ham, cut red tomatoes, cut bananas into the tiny slices that Roisin likes, fetched the tea leaves, filled a flask with hot water, and fished the red lemonade out of the tiny fridge. They'll have their lunch on the grass outside the house, then the girls will take a nap.

'Girls, come on up now.'

For another moment, Roisin looks at her brown toes. During this holiday, their toes have grown into the rocks; they can run and scamper, almost, as fast across the black rocks as they can across the sand.

'Come on, then,' Maeve says, and Roisin's toes hit the grass. The picnic is ready. They are starving.

And now.

The baps gone, the red lemonade gone, the banana skins tidied away neatly, Roisin watches as Maeve pushes her luck.

'Mammy,' Maeve says.

Their parents' eyes are closing; Roisin can see. The sun is warm, the grass smells green.

'What is it, Maeve.'

'Can we go and see the donkey?'

For – you can forget the lighthouse, and the rocks, and the sea, and even the fierce crab with its stick – they have discovered the best thing, the most exciting thing, right there in the very next field. Maeve discovered it on the first morning of their holiday. A donkey lived, all alone, in the little field just over the hedge: a friendly, placid donkey, that swished its tail, that blinked its eyes to show long, pretty lashes, that closed its eyes when the girls, having wriggled their way through the dense fuchsia hedge and discovered this silent field – this silent, sunken field, in which even the wind did not seem to blow, this field with its hedges dripping, said Maeve, with purple fuchsia flowers and open red roses, this field with a great rock of grey granite swelling up through the grass – and approached timidly, and held out their hands timidly, and then, emboldened, scratched him under his chin. He blinked, he liked that, he liked being scratched.

They have come every day since. All three days. The donkey likes apples, so they feed him apples; and he likes Crunchies, so they shared a Crunchie with him, once, a quarter of a Crunchie for Roisin and a quarter for Maeve and a half for the donkey. They have come every day – and now Mammy says they can go again. She will fall asleep on the dry grass, in the sun. So will Daddy. 'Off you go,' Mammy says, 'and stay in the field.'

They squeeze through the gap in the hedge, and the ground falls away a little, and then they are in the field, their own field. The sun is warmer, the wind is less, the air smells as green as grass. And the donkey, surely the donkey is pleased to see them. They have no Crunchies today, and the donkey doesn't like bananas – but Maeve has saved up half an apple, and now the donkey takes the half-apple carefully into its mouth, and its long brown teeth crunch into the apple. The donkey blinks.

'Maybe it's donkey for thank you,' Maeve speculates, 'the blink.'

'Should we blink back?'

'We should.'

It might be rude, the girls think, not to blink. So they blink.

This is where it began, thought Roisin, sitting very still at the kitchen table and looking down at her sweetcorn, and remembering, remembering, quickly, quickly, before it all went away.

The great granite rock in the middle of the donkey's field is warm in the sunshine: it wells with the sun's heat, and it glints and gleams like tiny jewels, like – yes, diamonds. The girls sit against the rock, and the donkey browses the grass. He pulls up long, juicy stems of green grass by the roots, and crunches them down, while the girls listen. This is their own warm, silent, safe kingdom. Roisin, and Maeve, five and eight years old, together in a small, still, grass-smelling bowl of green.

This is perfection.

10

Something to remember, then: a glint in a rock, to catch her eye and her memory, and bring her back to a green field, and a full stomach, a warm sun, and the smell of the sea.

And here was another time, now arrived. She had put away her white dress, what Maeve called her wedding dress of First Holy Communion. All the parties, and the excitement: all that was over, which was sad – no more money – but now there was another chance for excitement, and for God to be magical, and for Roisin and all the girls to whirl in excitement, and Miss Glackin not able to stop them.

First of all, a statue of the Madonna, in some place two counties away, or three, or four, walking, and weeping. People claimed to have seen it, to have reported their sightings to the priest, to the authorities. The television cameras were sent from Dublin, first, and then from London and from all over the place. 'Laughing at us,' said her father, 'and what have they to laugh about?'

Laughing, the news said, at the Irish and their ways. What, they said: it walked? And wept? – did the tears consist of blood, perhaps?

Well, they could jeer all they liked.

Roisin listened to the girls whisper in the classroom. She whispered herself, about this walking, talking, moving statue. Not in their own county, which was a pity: their own county would have been best. It was somewhere else, some other county. But still, it was good enough – now it emerged that their own Holy Mary, their very own statue standing, that had stood always, white and blue and gold, in the long corridor that led down towards the assembly hall: she too had moved? Had she whispered and wept? Did she clamber down from her pedestal and, weeping, did she walk the long white corridors of the school after dark, when the girls had gone home, and the place fallen silent?

She did, the girls whispered, in the classroom, at break, over their sandwiches at lunchtime.

She did, they told each other, and she had.

'Enough, girls!' said Miss Glackin, and fingered her ruler. 'Enough whispering,' said the teacher on playground duty, 'get out there and run about!' But there was nothing they could do; and there were no boys to break up the girls' huddles with fists and footballs and clods of dirt; the news spread unchecked.

Someone had seen their own walking, weeping Holy Mary: nobody knew who had seen her, but someone had. A fact was a fact.

And now these facts could be related by Roisin, too. She had seized her moment, she was now a witness. She had studied Holy Mary at her leisure, and watched her eyes, and taken in the granite pedestal, and the mica in the granite winking in the clear light from the windows. The sparkle made anything possible. It made her think of happiness. And now.

'It's a fact,' she reported. The shepherd's pie cooled.

She was going to stand her ground. She didn't know what was going to happen, but she could see Maeve already squaring her shoulders, getting ready to be sharp, to laugh, to tell her to catch herself on. But that was alright. Roisin knew better: she knew with her own eyes. And there was more. It was bluebell season now, and Holy Mary, on her glinting pedestal, was enjoying her May altar. Surrounded by glass jars of bluebells (though it seems a shame, she'd heard one of the nuns say to another of the nuns, a shame to pick them when they wilt so fast), jars of bluebells picked up in Carter's Wood, blue to match Holy Mary's too-long, sadly drooping blue cloak.

Bluebells, and whispered stories, and her own eyes: they'd stand her in good stead. They'd fire her up, Maeve squaring her shoulders or not. She could face up to her big sister, with her mouth tight and her eyes like slits sitting over her shepherd's pie, and sweetcorn and greens.

Maeve will surely go to Hell if she isn't careful. There'll be no bluebells for her, not down there.

She watched Maeve glance at their daddy, she watched as Maeve opened her mouth.

'Would you ever catch yourself on,' Maeve said.

Boldly, too bold.

'She's probably right now banging her stone head against the stone wall at the thought of how stupid you all are,' Maeve said.

What a sin.

Roisin said, 'That's a bad thing to say. A sinful thing to say.' Because she knew about sin. Miss Glackin had made them draw a picture of their souls, last month, for Religion. And Roisin had drawn a big circle on her page, the shape and the size of one of their own plates, at home, and she'd taken a black crayon, and drawn smudges inside the circle, all across the circle, and she'd smudged the black crayon marks with her finger, and Miss Glackin had taken her page and held it up in front of the class – she was in a good mood that day – and given Roisin ten out of ten for her soul, and a gold star for her table, and had pinned the picture of Roisin's soul, with its black-smudged sins, in the Art Corner.

So yes: Roisin knew about souls, she knew about sin.

If their parents were not right there, she knew what she would do, she would start a fight with Maeve – and smudge her soul some more, but it'd be worth it – but she couldn't start a fight, because there Daddy was, which meant loud voices were off the table.

'That's right, Roisin,' said Daddy.

Daddy must be on her side today. He wasn't on her side every day – it was so hard to tell – but today he must be.

'I suppose she has to pass Eternity somehow,' said Maeve, later, as they all sat in their front room watching the news. 'Holy Mary, I mean. She has to put in the time somehow.'

So, there was a knack. And now – look, Maeve had forgotten it herself. Roisin watched as their parents glanced across at Maeve, Daddy in one way and Mammy in another:

and then Daddy crossed the carpet and turned up the volume on the television, and Roisin saw that Maeve saw this for what it was, a last and final warning, and remembered the knack, and kept her mouth shut.

Later though, when she and Roisin were in their narrow beds in their bedroom: later, Maeve tried again, more daringly. 'Statues don't move,' she said into the darkness, to the beloved little sister whom she would move heaven and earth to protect. 'They just don't, Roisin.' Maeve felt caught, tormented, by the moral rectitude that emanated like gamma rays from her true believer of a sister. Maeve had been there herself, once. There is enough of this already in this bloody country, thought Maeve, without having it blast its way in through the front door of their own house too.

Yet she could see that there was no talking to Roisin, not at this time, not for the moment. A walking, weeping stone Virgin, with added bluebells, was more than a match for Maeve's disbelief, her unbelief. That much was crystal clear. She would just have to wait and be patient. Roisin would wise up.

But she couldn't just stay silent.

'Would you have a bit of sense,' she told Roisin. 'A bit of bloody sense. Who believes,' she said, 'in this stuff? Who believes in it, anyway?'

But Roisin believed that she believed. Fervently, in the semi-darkness (for the May twilight lingered outside, and the bedroom curtains weren't lined) she renewed once more her belief. Maeve could feel it.

'I do,' Roisin said, and she meant it.

'Then you're an eejit,' Maeve told her, beginning to drowse, for it had been a long day, and a weight of truth and knowledge weighed her down, these days. Eleven years old, and more and more she was weighed down.

'I wish you'd let me help you.'

Silence.

'An eejit,' Maeve repeated, in low tones: now her eyes were closing, and sleep beckoned, and – or because – Roisin was safe enough, for now.

Roisin herself lay awake for several more minutes, and her mind studied sparkle, and the glint of tears on Holy Mary's cheek. Maeve didn't really understand – but Roisin did. This was the road to happiness. She saw this road stretch in front of her feet. Smooth and straight, without a hump, without a bump. The donkey in the field, the sun pouring down like melted butter, and now Holy Mary and her tears and her bluebells – they were all the same. Maeve would see this too, in the end.

It would pass. It would never do to have a sister growing up and behaving like that. Not many did, not any more. Though – well, no, this was hardly the case; there were plenty of them still, more than enough. Later that night, as Maeve woke and looked into the dimness, she knew that there was a good deal of this rubbish around. And maybe that was fair enough.

Just not for Roisin.

And besides, it was also the case that the world was speeding up, was moving on in the last few years, and this was a good thing, for Maeve. The world could not move rapidly enough. They were in Europe, now, the world was coming to get them. She never looked back, she was never tempted to do so. Onward, onward. What use is there in looking back? There is no use. She could not wait to move on and grow up, she could not wait for Roisin to move on – especially from this tiresome present phase – and grow up. She would whisk her away, to a wide world, to safety. They would go abroad, maybe, to London, or France, or America. Faye Dunaway looked down patiently from the wall. Maeve turned in her narrow bed, and closed her eyes, and slept again.

11

Maeve looked.

School was over for the day: and usually she was part of the crowd flowing out of the school gates, and away. But today, she stood in against the hedge and watched them stream ahead of her. They seemed loud, boisterous in a way that she hadn't noticed before. Branches and twigs nudged her back.

A few weeks previously, the boys, across the road in their school, had been lectured about self-abuse. This was the news they told, as they left school, and mingled with the girls. They had even been asked by Mr Carney, the French teacher – but also the Religion teacher – whether they'd indulged in it, indulged in self-abuse.

'What, just like that?' Maeve had asked. They were walking towards the town centre, a gaggle of boys and a gaggle of girls, trailing towards town and home, as usual.

The school buses had departed, whisking away the country ones; the crowds were thinning as pupils beat a retreat. 'What did you say?' What, she thought, what *would* you say?

Michael Clancy shrugged. He was her pal – her 'chum', as he said, and a fruit, which everyone knew, and nobody seemed to care about, Michael himself least of all. He shrugged. 'I said, *Yes, sir, of course, sir, would you like a demonstration, sir? You can join me if you like, sir. Would you like that, sir? I think you would, sir, from the way you're licking your lips, sir.*'

Mr Carney, with his daddy-long-legs limbs, and his sharp-ended nose. She laughed. 'What did you say, really?'

'Oh, you know, I let on I didn't know what he was on about, so I made him explain it to me.' Michael sniggered. 'Right down to the last detail. *I don't really understand what you mean, sir.* It was good craic, so it was, seeing him go red like that.'

'What did the other fellas say?'

'The same. Sure, you wouldn't miss a chance like that. It'd be a *disgrace*, a waste.'

The two schools faced each other across the road, and it was almost as though the two were one. So Maeve liked to think. She knew every detail of life in the boys' school, and Michael Clancy knew every detail of life in the girls' school. They even shared sports pitches, though the boys and the girls never used them at the same time: what Maeve had heard her Maths teacher call a 'complex algorithm' had been formulated to prevent such a thing. They shared nothing else – and the schools, their principals, the nuns and priests on the staff, some of the parents: these conspired to keep boys and girls separate during school hours. It was better this way. Maeve knew that her father agreed with this; she wasn't too sure what her mother thought.

Her father and the others – the authorities, the clerics, the other parents – they all thought that it was a pity that the schools had been built facing each other in the first place. All that *contamination*, as Maeve heard her father call it. Oh, it had been a foolish move. Maeve knew that this was the general consensus. That it had happened at all had something to do with a piece of land that a farmer had donated to the Church in the olden days – in return for a swift progress through Purgatory when the time came. This piece of land had become the sports ground: it was cheap and convenient, it was the reason for the otherwise undesirable sharing.

Today, the authorities would change things if they only could, as Maeve well knew – but such changes being impossible, they went for the next best thing, for the 'complex algorithm'. 'Sure, in South Africa they'd call it apartheid,' said Michael Clancy, 'wouldn't they?' But the best that they could do was to make sure that Our Lady of Victories and St Joseph's existed in separate universes during school hours, and that was that – and what a pity, they sighed in various quarters, that such segregation could not be maintained after school too. All this Maeve knew.

She herself could not agree. School was not her thing: the basketball she did not mind, but the best part of school was walking home after it, part of a crowd, listening to Michael, crisps and a bit of chocolate from the shop to keep them going until they got home. News swapped. Some male company – high-smelling and spotty company, that was true, but beggars could not be choosers. And whoever said that the boys weren't gossips – well, they didn't know what they were talking about. And it wasn't only Michael Clancy, either: all the chunky boys swinging their hurleys, they were a crowd of old women once you got them going.

Which meant that now, a few years into Our Lady of Victories, she was well up on all the news, the politics, the scandal in St Joe's. She knew its teachers as well as if they had taught her themselves, she knew the problems, she knew the politics. The Latin teacher liked the fists from time to time; the Maths teacher liked to pick his nose and roll the snot into little balls on the palm of his hand, as though it were Plasticine, before flicking it onto the floor; the Geog teacher was a skinflint, and the boys liked to glue pennies to his desk, or his chair, or the floor, and watch him pick with his finger, or flick with the toe of his scuffed shoe, and try to ease the penny off the chair, or desk, or floor, and into his pocket.

Michael had her in stitches, telling her all this. St Joe's sounded like a bit of fun, a bit of craic.

It certainly sounded better fun, better craic, than Our Lady of Victories, where the only thing to catch the eye and raise a laugh was the turn in Sister John's eye. Who was Sister John looking at when she asked a question? – God alone knew; it could be anyone. 'Me, Sister?' 'Who – me, Sister?' That was OK as far as it went: but it didn't go very far, not really. And so many of the girls right bitches. At least you knew where you stood with a boy. He'd break his hurley over your head, and you'd have to get someone to pick the splinters of ash out of your scalp with a pair of tweezers, but you could be friends afterwards. The girls did it differently, and some of their splinters were embedded for good.

This was the usual way of it. It was a pity that just at the moment, she had other things to think about.

All this flowed through Maeve's mind as she stood in from the crowd, as she let them pass, as she began walking slowly home. No Michael today: he had music practice.

She was on her own.

Which was for the best, when you had a problem to solve. It had come to her that Roisin might have some angle on her problem, that she might have some facts and figures gleaned from one of her library books that could help find a solution, had even mentioned to Roisin that she had some news for her; but – no, that would be a mistake. No way. It was her job to shield Roisin. It had always been her job.

'Sure, nobody'll know,' the boy had said. The pebbledash of the youth club wall was cold and unpleasant against her back, the dusk was coming down and the damp too, it wasn't what you would call romantic. 'I wouldn't tell anyone, would I? And you won't either.'

Hardly.

'I'll be careful,' he said, but Maeve had no idea what he meant. Maybe there was a way of being careful, and then she realised she was about to find out, for he took her silence for agreement, and off he went. He had set his hurley propped against the wall, and after a minute he must have kicked it with an excited foot, for it fell with a clatter; and after another minute it was all over. Zip up, and shirt tails tidied away; and she supposed the pain would pass in another minute. Nobody ever mentioned that it hurt. And how had he been careful?

'Not a word,' he said, 'from you or from me. And sure, maybe we can do it again.' She didn't hear a question mark.

Something else to tell Roisin not to do. Roisin would be OK. It came to Maeve – as the boy took up his hurley, mumbled a goodbye, shuffled off into the dusk – that her part in life was to do things first and report back to Roisin, to give Roisin the thumbs-up or down, to act as a, what did that hymn say, a shield in the strife. The boy had vanished now: his father was a holy joe, and scary too; so there'd be no playground boasting going on, at any rate. She was safe enough. She would think what to do with her knickers later. She slipped away in the opposite direction, made her way home.

Roisin looked over her shoulder. There was Maeve's gang behind her, though of Maeve herself there was no sign. Roisin didn't walk home from school with Maeve any more, and that was fine; it wasn't the thing to do, once school had ended for the day. There were rules in teenaged life, in secondary school, and both of them knew what these rules were. Roisin was in her element now at school. Good at lessons, good at basketball; and the art room, the biggest classroom in the school, with its big window looking north, where she was spending more and more time. Maeve had no turn for art, either, she had painted a blue sky with a dark blue paint, a paint so blue that it was almost black, and she had, besides, ladled the paint on to such a degree that the paper tore, and Mr Cooper went through her for a shortcut – offended by just about everything that Maeve had gone and done – and that was an end to art for Maeve, there and then. Maeve didn't mind: she'd laughed until the tears came, as she told the story – 'it sagged down in the middle and then just tore in two, and the face on him!' – and Roisin had laughed too. The two of them, laughing their legs off.

Roisin smiled at the memory, checked herself. Because it wasn't so funny, not really; it was another thing that Maeve wasn't any good at, that Roisin was. 'Nice work, Roisin,' Mr Cooper had said the other day about a little watercolour she had put together, the colours watered and paled down to virtually no colour at all, just as an experiment, to see how it would turn out, but – Mr Cooper! Who frowned so much, who had a face on him, who was so hard to please! – 'very nice indeed. You have an eye, Roisin.'

There never were two sisters so unalike.

Maeve heard the watercolour story not from Roisin, of course, but at school. She glowed, she looked at the watercolour in the bedroom they still shared, she exclaimed with pleasure. 'The loveliness of it,' was what she said. She kissed Roisin. 'My talented sister.'

And that was good, was one thing not to feel bad about. She didn't have to feel guilty about her sister, which meant she could concentrate on feeling guilty about her mother, guilty about spending as little time as possible around the house. She was leaving her mother behind: but sure, wasn't this the thing to be done, what everyone had to do?

'Don't feel badly about it,' Maeve told her. 'Sure, isn't it what she's trained us both to do? To get out and away? You're only doing what you're told.'

Yes: and at least she wasn't leaving Maeve behind. True, they didn't cook up plans any longer to move to Hollywood: but London was still a definite possibility, with Paris for a weekend. They'd find a flat, they'd see what was what. 'The hell out of here,' said Maeve, 'and Mammy can come and visit us.' What would Maeve do? – for Roisin might have her heart set on university; but Maeve would have to find something else to do. The teachers were complaining about her. No academic bent: but, so what? Maeve didn't mind her absence of academic bent: that was clear. 'The whole world to choose from,' she said, and her eyes sparkled. So there was no particular reason for Roisin to mind either. It would all be grand, in the end.

On this late spring day, as she walked towards home with her friend Aisling, Roisin thought again about her mother. Aisling was complaining about her own mother, which was a surprise: to Roisin, Aisling's mother had seemed to be sound, as mothers went. But apparently not: apparently she didn't want Aisling to go on to university, when the time came. She wanted her to get a job as soon as the law allowed, to begin to earn. What's the use of all that study for a girl, anyway? – seemed to be Aisling's mother's attitude.

'I don't believe it,' Roisin said. It was true: Aisling's mother seemed so sensible.

'I don't believe it either,' Aisling told her flatly, 'but it's true all the same.'

'Where does she think you'll get a job? Does she think there *are* jobs? What, would you go into the creamery?'

'The abattoir, maybe,' Aisling said, 'making glue.'

'Dog food.'

'Cat food.'

They laughed, shoved the problem aside. But it put Roisin thinking about her own mother. Of course there'd be no university problems there: her mother was so hungry for her daughters to better themselves, to get an education, that Roisin could almost hear the stomach growls. She was – good that way, Roisin thought, though she knew better than to say it to her friend. Her mother was not the worst: Roisin suspected that her mother harboured thoughts that were not in the Catechism. She suspected that her mother had no great regard for Ireland, where they buried babies in the fields, where bishops ran amok and belted their parishioners across the head with croziers of solid gold. 'My lord' here and 'My lord' there. They were all still living in the olden days, right now, in this country: and Roisin suspected that her mother wasn't too pleased about it all.

Her mother, though, she kept her mouth shut. You had to read the runes, to study the stars wheeling slowly in the sky, to get a sense of what was going on in her mother's head. She kept her thoughts secret, and she passed the lesson on.

'Glue!' Roisin exclaimed, and Aisling laughed aloud. '"Excuse me, modom, may I borrow your prize wolfhound? – we're running a little short of glue, don't you know."'

Roisin knew to keep her mouth closed, out in the world. She had learned from the best. She lowered her eyes, nowadays, when she passed one of the nuns, or a priest: and she supposed they thought she was doing it out of courtesy, out of respect. But she knew better. She knew she was doing it out of the contempt she was beginning to feel for such people. She lowered her eyes so that she wouldn't have to look at them or talk to them. And that was the right thing – but of course better to keep her thoughts to herself.

'She'd make a grab at your tits,' Aisling had muttered the other day, as they passed a nun (obviously a nun, you didn't need the sight of a habit to identify them, the short hair, and the tight lips, and the odd fashion choices, all combined to give them away), 'given half a chance. You just have to keep walking, keep away from them.' They both laughed – but they both kept walking, too. You couldn't be too careful.

She glanced over her shoulder once more. There was Maeve's gang. Laughing their heads off, bags of crisps; the purple wrapping of a Dairy Milk cast away onto the pavement. No Maeve. Maeve wanted to talk to her: she had something to tell, she'd said. 'A bit of craic, just; tell you later. Something to manage.' So many thoughts to think, so many of them to be considered silently: Aisling's mother and her strange behaviour; and her own silent, secretive mother; the future, and the past, sister and father and mother. It was best to sail on, to stride forward, to never look back over a shoulder, to make the past dead and keep it dead. Aisling cracked a joke – a dirty joke, a bishop and a nun, a joke that would set the fires of Hell burning around your feet and racing up your skirt – and Roisin smiled, but now she was only half listening. She was tracking a future course.

Of course there were a lot of problems. Their house was falling apart, was one of them. Which was a worry – though she hoped she'd be well away before that particular problem would have to be solved. *Mica.* Causing the house to crumble. The irony of it: and her mind flitted again to the sparkling rock in the donkey's field. How it had gleamed, how warm it had been from hours of soaking in the summer sun, how green the air had been, how gentle the donkey's brown, lash-fringed eyes had been. How she had laughed and Maeve had laughed, in that bowl of warm green. And how – contaminated that memory was now; yes, that was the word for a memory that she ought to be able to look back upon with pleasure and delight; a child's dream that was laced now with poison, with mica, with the horror of a disintegrating house.

She and Maeve would have to get out of the house before the roof fell in on them.

And the donkey, most likely, turned into dog food by now.

Well, and they would get out. The parents would manage, would swim, would not sink, each in their own way. She had a life to live, and she would live it far from these damp fields.

She looked over her shoulder. The school crowds were thinning now. Still no sign of Maeve.

12

Philomena was at the shop. This was her usual beat, her midweek beat: when Maeve and Roisin were younger, they had liked to accompany her, to cruise the aisles, to slip forbidden objects – Oatfield Emeralds and Angel Delight – into Philomena's basket. They knew, even as youngsters, that this was the time, these were the places, when Philomena was at her most relaxed – the bungalow with its mould and its damp and Cormac, safely out of sight. Sometimes they would go to the cafe beside the shop and feast on sardine sandwiches (for Philomena) and jammy buns and squash (for them), and Philomena would let her hair down, a little, and smile. Even laugh, sometimes, for it was difficult not to laugh when Maeve was around and Cormac was not. At such times, Maeve laughed and laughed.

But those days were over. Of course, and she wouldn't wish them back: her children wouldn't be seen dead with their mother, wandering the aisles; and quite right, too. Philomena suspected that Maeve would, in fact, have been glad to take off to the supermarket with her mother – but imagine what those friends of hers would say if they caught her at it. Out of the question.

Philomena focused on the list. Washing powder, and apples for Roisin, and chicken. And – she shouldn't have married him. Scanty comfort to know that most of the women she knew felt the same about their husbands: who had seemed at least tolerable as fresh-faced, unlined young men of twenty-two, twenty-four, all with a bit of knowledge of the world, all more or less tolerable. Toilet tissue, which this family seemed to eat, to judge by the way they went through roll after roll of the stuff, and beans. Or so it had seemed: now, the women seemed to be saying, their men had slipped to just the other side of tolerable: thick about the waist from chips and grease, red about the face from beer and spirits, narrow in the brain, and getting narrower with every passing day. Which reminded her: oil, for the stuff in the chip pan needed changing. That's what men did: they got narrow, there was no changing their ways, not a jot nor a tittle, not after a certain age.

Philomena listened quietly to all this stuff. She agreed with it all, too. She had reached these conclusions years ago, long before her peers. She didn't say much, and the other women didn't probe. They knew that her Cormac was a case apart. Thick and red and narrow, and all these things – but there was something else going down too, with Cormac.

Chicken: she'd make a casserole, later, and freeze it for during the week; and another chicken for tomorrow's dinner, with roast potatoes, and cauliflower and peas.

Cooking apples for a crumble. She nodded at a familiar face pushing a trolley, but she didn't stop to speak. No idea who it was; it would come to her later. (Philomena looked pale, she looked failed, thought the acquaintance, she should make more of an effort with the poor woman. She would, next time.) Philomena thought: I might pop into the cafe next door, if I have time: I might get myself a sandwich and a milky coffee, it might put a pep in my step.

She had met Cormac – where else? – in the pub. The pub was in Galway, where she was visiting friends, and he was visiting as part of a stag weekend. He caught her eye across the room, he nodded, and she nodded back after a moment; later, he appeared at her elbow, and her friends melted away. He wasn't a stranger, exactly: that was the point. They knew each other to see – same parish, same fields, same church on Sundays, and now here they both were in Galway, city slickers for the weekend – but had never exchanged so much as a word, the age difference of seven years having put paid to that kind of intercourse. The other kind, rather to Philomena's dismay, took place that very night in Cormac's hotel room on the edge of town: having bought her a number of drinks, he seemed to expect that this was pay-back time, and she hadn't liked to resist, to seem ungrateful or frigid or a user or any of those things. (She knew how men talked about women, she had heard her brothers talk that way when her own mother was out of earshot; and she didn't want Cormac to talk that way about her.)

She hadn't enjoyed any of the different forms of intercourse on offer, because Cormac was a bit lacking in the small-talk and charm departments; and, as it turned out, in the sexual department too. Surely it should have amounted to more than this – though it was difficult for Philomena, given her own profound inexperience, to reach a conclusion, and she didn't want to think unfair thoughts.

Maybe this was the way it was with everyone. Maybe it was a conspiracy of silence. She heaved the chicken in on top of her other groceries.

How amazing, though! – that an unsatisfactory evening on the Headford Road could lead on, with seemingly unstoppable, inexorable haste, to marriage, to a white wedding, with Cormac's belly bursting out of his shirt, to a rambunctious, drunken reception, and a pregnancy hot on its heels, and the lot! So rapidly! – and without so much as a by your leave! Philomena stopped in her tracks right there in the supermarket aisle, with pure astonishment – even all these years later – at the package she'd ended up holding.

Like a chicken, heavy and plucked and nothing much to look at.

And now a house, a bungalow, with mould on the walls, a house that would – just watch and wait and see – eventually fall down.

Her daughters were the only good thing to have come out of this bloody mess. At least Philomena had that. Something – some dignity, some substance – to hold on to, though by the very tips of her fingers.

Saturday, again. By the middle of the afternoon, Roisin had her homework done for the following Monday, and her reading up to date, and all set for the week ahead. Maeve had been out all day; her mother was in and out; her father was out somewhere, the further the better. She would go to the Vigil Mass, and her Sunday morning would be free for something that was not Mass. Ten minutes' walk would take her there and ten would take her back; and she was sure of seeing Aisling and some of the other girls there too, for a bit of craic afterwards. I wonder where Maeve is?

'Not important,' Maeve had said. 'Some scandal I was going to pass on, and that I'm now not going to pass on. I'm turning over a new leaf. I am Virtue Incarnate, from now on: just you watch and see.'

'Right,' Roisin said, 'we'll see how that goes'; and she laughed then at her heavy irony; and Maeve smiled but did not laugh.

Mass passed in a daydream, which was the only way to get through it, and thank God for rote, so that she knew when to stand and sit and kneel and speak and stay silent; and thank God too that the new priest with the agonising stammer knew to keep the homily short.

She had a bit of a laugh afterwards, with the girls, on the steps. Then it was time for home, for Saturday-night lasagne.

The next bit – she realised later, for there were years and years still to pass – she would never really leave behind.

The best feature about their church was the stone grotto, off to the right. You turned into a crazy pathing that ran between tall shrubs – it was not a shrubbery as such, because most of the shrubs and trees that had once grown in the church grounds had been grubbed up and cut down on the orders of the last-but-one parish priest, who thought that they were a nuisance to keep clipped and tidy; better to give them the chop; and he had spared only the tiny patch of planting that screened the grotto, and laid a sea of inky asphalt instead.

Roisin liked the grotto, though this was a fact she would not have admitted to anyone. She'd left her religious phase behind her now, that was years ago – but maybe this phase had left some sort of trace. For Roisin liked the gold and blue statue of the Virgin framed by the gleaming white stone arch, and the modest acreage of mosaic-work, gold-glinting on the walls behind the Virgin. The mosaic reminded her of the illustrations of Byzantium in her History textbook: so decadent, so lustrous. The gleam and glitter and colours that stirred associations of long ago.

Summer, and sunshine, and the green smell of growing grass.

She wouldn't make a *habit* of going to the grotto, of course – it was nothing like that – but she liked its environs, and the glint of gold that had such associations for her now, for good or ill. She also liked the expression on this particular Virgin's face: it seemed right, wise, clever, neither too sweet nor too sour. She could see that this was a superior statue to the Holy Mary which had strode the corridors of her primary school, long ago. This one was better-looking, and she wore better clothes, a better cut and fit; she seemed less downtrodden, she had an altogether better sense of herself, in Roisin's opinion. She had style.

Their mother had brought them there, she and Maeve, from time to time after Mass, when they were tinies; and she liked these memories.

On an impulse, on this mild Saturday evening, Mass over, and the sky still bright, she turned onto the crazy pathing and slipped in behind the screen of shrubbery. The grotto appeared: a bar of late sunlight fell across the white arch, so that it fairly dazzled; and onto a band of mosaic-work, so that the gold gleamed too. It didn't fall onto Maeve, who was sitting inside the arch, against the mosaic, nor onto the blood that flowed from between her legs and across the ground. Not a thin trickle of blood, but a lot of blood – pooling like a shadow, like a patch of darkness there on the shadowy ground – and the straightened wire coat-hanger on the ground, enveloped by blood.

Maeve was very white. And when Roisin touched her, she was very cold.

Roisin was above the scene now, suddenly. She had risen above the ground, the grotto, the gleaming rock, above the body of her sister sitting there in a pool of shadow, amid a flowing of dark blood. She was looking down from a height, from a place of safety. She split herself from the scene, from the sensations she was now able to observe as from afar – the last light of evening, the glistening sheen of the rock, the thin breath of wind sighing through the enveloping trees. She floated, and watched, and that was enough.

Nobody could sustain the loss of such a lot of blood, they said later, and besides, though Maeve was tall for her age, she was skinny too: she was, as Philomena used to say, 'only a rickle'. When the ambulance came – for the other Roisin, there on the ground, did all the right things, she didn't waste a second, she didn't fuss around after realising that there was nothing she could do, that a doctor needed to be here – when the ambulance came and Maeve was moved, and slid into the vehicle: when all these things happened, there was still a moment to spare. Roisin stood, and looked at the ambulance, at the two ambulance workers, at the young, stammering priest, summoned in haste from the sacristy and standing there now on the crazy pathing, slipping his little round case of oil back into his pocket, looking still and shocked. At the grotto now slipping into darkness, at the wire, and the deeper darkness lying pooled there on the ground. 'Come with us now, love,' said one of the ambulance people, a woman. 'Come,' and held out a hand, and Roisin, moving stiffly, clambered into the ambulance to join the cold body of her sister.

She was driven off. She left herself behind.

Falsetto

13

They moved in the darkness, together, and now Martin sighed in his sleep and rolled away. Nothing woke him, or so Ward used to think – not a traffic helicopter overhead, not a car alarm right outside the house. Not bottles being slung into the bottle bank at the end of the road – slung and smashed at two, three, four in the morning, by God knows what selfish, antisocial shit. Just some of the infinite varieties of noises emitted by London at night, so many of them terrifying, if one was of a mind to be terrified.

Ward lay awake and looked into darkness.

The worst of this array of noises: the animal sounds made a few months ago by that young guy, screaming as he was stabbed, not ten yards from their own front door – though granted, this was highly exceptional.

And granted too: Martin had woken for that one.

Though not for their very own house alarm, which in the first weeks after they moved into this house – 'taking up residence,' as Martin put it, 'I'm Queenie arriving at Windsor for her Easter hols' – had worked not quite as it ought to have done, shrilling at three o'clock, four o'clock in the morning, three, four nights in a row, shredding Ward's nerves.

Shrilling and screaming, alarms and aircraft and stabbings and car horns. Enough to bring the dead to life. But Martin would sleep on and on, more dead than the dead.

'When I die,' he had said the other week, 'I want to be buried in wicker, a wicker coffin. I want you to arrange that for me,' he'd said, stirring his coffee meditatively. 'Will you promise?'

'They wouldn't allow wicker at Westminster Abbey,' Ward told him. 'You do want your send-off to be at the Abbey, don't you?' This, a glance at Martin's preoccupation with the royals, which was something Ward could not begin to understand, much less approve of.

Safe ground, or so Ward thought. Martin had spoken lightly, airily; and it was, besides, impossible to make a drama out of wicker. So: 'You won't need wicker,' Ward continued, 'I'll just roll you in the duvet and stick you in the boot of the car like that, and deliver you to the undertaker myself.'

'The still-warm duvet. Efficient,' Martin said, pursing his lips, taking a sip of coffee. But now the cleft on his forehead appeared, like a line run in black ink. 'Before rigor mortis has set in. Always so efficient. And you're right, of course: wicker might be better than nasty old polished wood, but a duvet's better than wicker. No extra expense, for one thing.'

Another sip and a frown. The cleft remained – but it seemed that the jocular just about worked, this morning.

Or perhaps not. The cleft deepened, and Ward felt the temperature plunge, and braced for the chill. Nothing new about any of this.

'You know,' Martin said after a few minutes, 'it would be nice to think that you would actually pay attention to my wishes.'

'I was joking,' Ward said, 'it was a joke,' and Martin shrugged slightly. 'It might be better,' Ward pursued, 'not to talk about coffins over breakfast.'

A silence, after that. Martin excelled at silences.

Later – three days later – in the throes of a clear-out of bathroom cabinets, Ward heard a rattle, stirred the stew of Disprin boxes, tubes of hotel moisturiser, fished out a small brown bottle of pills. Sleeping pills, which explained the sleep of the dead. 'I didn't know you took sleeping pills,' Ward said, later.

A shrug, again. 'From time to time. Nothing to worry about.' Three days, and this wicker-sparked coldness still endured.

Three days, in fact, was nothing.

'What do you need sleeping pills for?' – and a stiff, reluctant few words. Just from time to time; it was nothing, Martin intimated, to worry about. It was none of Ward's business.

And, Ward liked to reflect, there *was* nothing to worry about. Martin's mood changed as the weather changed. A few days later, and all would be well.

There were no pills tonight: Ward was almost sure of it. And true enough: when the phone a few minutes later emitted a tiny beep and buzz; when at the bottom of the bed, Felicity arched her back and sat up for a moment before settling back again into the nest she had made in the duvet – when these things happened, Martin's breathing changed: he sighed in the darkness, cleared his throat. Ward watched in the dimness as Felicity's large, dark eyes turned to gaze at Martin. She blinked, purred for a moment, then stopped and slept. Outside, in the darkness, London too inhaled and exhaled.

Ward reached for the phone before its light died away. A text message, from work. *A theft. A Sandborne. And an assault*, Charlotte wrote. *Ireland. Request you call the office at your convenience.*

Mrs Sandborne.

Ward looked at the screen for a moment, then turned the phone off, set it down gently. Martin was very obviously now awake, but it would not do to behave in too ostentatiously wakeful a manner oneself. And it was only five o'clock: murders and Charlotte would have to wait, for two more hours at least. Ward burrowed into Martin's warm, smooth back, felt Felicity sink her considerable cat weight, heard her tiny cat snore, felt Martin relax, a little, slept.

When the alarm went off, after two more dark, silent hours – the two of them spooning, moving, sleeping soundly – it was Martin's turn to reach out and silence it. He had an old-fashioned alarm clock on his side of the bed – a Disney model, with Pluto's arms doubling as the clock hands, a long-ago gift from his little sister and now deployed ironically. Certainly it stood out when set against Martin's capsule wardrobe, with its blacks and charcoals, anthracites and sharp whites, and the collection of thin, slippery socks (unpleasant socks, Ward thought privately) that Martin favoured. A forbidding wardrobe. But the clock was manufactured specifically to be bashed satisfyingly into silence – and now Martin reached, and bashed, and they lay together for another moment, naked in the darkness.

This moment tended to establish the temperature for the rest of the day. A good day? The very foulest of days, with a wind ripping down from the north-east? Martin – Ward imagined this was the way it worked, though really, who knew? – took his own temperature, and then assigned this temperature to the world. So: frigid, or balmy, Siberian or subtropical: it all flowed from this moment.

'Who sent the text, the nocturnal text?' And then, before Ward could reply, 'I wish, I really do wish you would turn your phone to silent. It's almost as if you do it to piss me off.'

Piss me off. So, a frigid day.

'I meant to,' Ward said, 'but I forgot.'

At the foot of the bed, Felicity sat up again.

'And so my sleeping patterns are messed up. Well, nice.'

'It was Charlotte. A theft in Ireland, I assume Dublin,' Ward repeated, with a renewed sense of dismay. 'Some sort of assault, too, she says.'

'Really,' Martin said. 'Novel.'

'I assume Dublin,' he repeated, underscoring his own sense of dismay. 'Most likely I'll have to go over there.' Back there.

Ward was aware of speaking just a little too fast. This was a mistake, a detectable floundering, amid the undulating white cotton-and-goose-down foothills of the duvet. Martin detested nerves.

'Weren't we going to Southwold for the weekend?' He spoke softly, with the apparent gentleness that in other contexts cast such a spell over Ward's friends. A voice echoed in the memory: *He has lovely manners, doesn't he?* – exclaimed a clearly dazzled one of them, months ago now. *I didn't think people had manners like that, not these days. You really did land on your feet.*

Strange, how manners can have the edge of a sharp blade.

'Southwold,' Martin said again. 'Haven't we been looking forward to it for weeks?' The soft voice continued amid the foothills. 'Sea air, fish and chips, a paddle in the water, even: didn't we say that it would set us up? I seem to remember' – and here Martin's voice rose a notch towards falsetto, the beginnings of a mocking lisp – '"Thouthwold. I love the thmell of thalt in the air, don't you?" But perhaps I was the only one looking forward?'

Ward flushed in the darkness.

'I'll check with Charlotte, of course…'

'You did *book* the time off, didn't you? I mean, you did actually *book* it?'

'Of course I booked it. What I mean is, sometimes these things happen. I get a sense from Charlotte's text that they'll need me, that I'll just have to suck it up.' And now a rally, a call to moral order. 'And it's a big theft.'

All at once, Martin threw the duvet off. 'Something and someone unknown to me. Big deal. And, what, suck it up? It seems that *I'm* the one who has to suck it up. *I'm* the one being messed about here. Which always seems to be the case, with you.' He vanished into the bathroom. 'Oh, but I forgot. What is it? – oh yes, a vio*lation*, common *pat*-rimony,' he said. 'The empty *frames*,' he said, and closed the door.

There was a meeting at the clinic, early – too early, in Martin's opinion. This was, Ward realised now, never going to have been a good morning: this early meeting had been a point of bitterness for several days. No meetings until after noon: that should be the rule, Martin said, to allow the partners to come within touching distance of their humanity. 'And make the right decisions, as opposed to the wrong decisions.' Ten o'clock in the morning was, he said, stupid. 'Stupid, stupid,' he had said. 'Everyone and everyone: why is everyone so stupid?'

On other mornings, better mornings, they would lie together for a few minutes after the alarm sounded, there in the darkness and the warmth; and at such times it was easier to imagine that all was well, that the world was in a state of equilibrium. 'Not yet, not yet,' Ward would say, and cling to the warmth, 'two more minutes' – and then Martin would be gone. 'I have made the transition,' he would say over his shoulder, 'I have crossed the Styx. You go and make me some coffee.' He would throw himself in the shower, into the day. *I have made the transition, I have crossed the Styx*: his good-morning catchphrase. That was the way of him, on good mornings.

No catchphrases on this bad morning.

Ward lay for another moment – then up, downstairs, putting on the coffee, Felicity padding silently behind.

The kitchen looked south, over the little back garden, over a fragment of skyline. Rooftops and chimneys of the street below their street on this steep London hill, and a glimpse of the Shard, bright today, and acute against a slice of blue: a new Chartres Cathedral, some critic had said; though, what would the Qatari owners make of this parallel? Ward moved automatically through the morning routine: coffee ground and set up and flame ignited, raisin bagels slid into the toaster, butter and honey. *And a bowl of oranges too.*

The raisins burned easily; you had to watch them.

The thought hovered: what would Daddy have said, about the raisin bagels, coffee like this coffee, the spare Heal's table and chairs, all blond ash wood and not very comfortable to sit on? And Felicity there on her chair?

Daddy had liked to drown any kittens that crossed his path.

And the early sunshine pouring sideways – *like butterscotch* – into the kitchen? Their whole set-up here in this house?

'You wouldn't prefer *cane* furniture, would you?' Martin had asked, as they shopped in Heal's that day. 'They have some nice stuff in cane, nowadays. You like cane.' He glanced. 'Only joking,' he said, 'just my little joke,' and he pointed with a gloved hand. 'Look, there's what we want, over there.'

Daddy often hovered. Often stepped into the frame, though long dead: what would Daddy have made of this, or of that? The bagel, the coffee grinder. Daddy, Daddy, you bastard.

Daddy had crossed the Styx long ago. But he was like Martin, he seemed to have no problem crossing back again, and again. Some people must have special passes.

A plane slid across the slice of blue, and after a moment Ward heard the groaning note of its engines. The city stepped up a gear: a refuse truck passed along Despard Road, to empty the green bin left tidily out by Ward the previous night (watched by a sleek fox, its bushy tail a testament to good living); the high note of children's voices, walking along early to school. Upstairs, Martin was out of the shower: a board creaked, a door slid open and closed as he clothed himself from his capsule wardrobe for the land of the living.

A silence that overlaid all this bustle, that he seemed to push, again, down the steep stairs and into the kitchen.

In Ireland, a theft and an assault. In London, Charlotte to be contacted. In the kitchen, early sun like butterscotch, the toaster radiating heat and a note of burning, and popping. No Southwold, very likely, no salty air, no fish and chips: his instincts were clear. And a reckoning to come: but for a few more minutes, it was possible to hold the world at bay.

There was a new Julia on the scene at the clinic: this, as though to add to the offence, to the list of grievances. That was what Martin called them: the administrators, all of them, in the pecking order in the clinic. The Julias. They held the real power, they could muck it up for anyone if they felt like it; this was, Martin said, the first lesson to learn about administrative staff. They kept the diaries, they knew about the finances, they burrowed like ticks into the stuff of the clinic to find out the secrets. There had been an actual Julia once, a couple of years ago: long blonde hair, as Martin described her; a fondness for black coats, on the shoulders of which motes of dandruff lay strewn – 'an Alpine scene,' Martin had said at the time, 'snowy, a Narnian scene.' An identikit Sloaney type, really, he said, and in Martin's opinion not very good at her job.

Now all such, men and women alike, were referred to as the Julias.

And this new Julia was worse than any of these predecessors. This Julia had arranged the ten o'clock meeting. To discuss the clinic's financial situation, to discuss relationships with private health providers, who were cutting back on the counselling slots they were prepared to finance.

This Julia was a man.

Now Ward heard Martin's light step on the stairs, and he appeared, in anthracite today, his long dark hair (a unique selling point, the hair, or so Ward understood; if you were a counsellor of a certain stripe, it seemed more important to look the part than to be good at your job) still damp, still smelling of his orange-scented shampoo. Sometimes he sloughed off his mood on the stairs – had he, today? 'Julia awaits,' he said, and rapidly he polished off his bagel, drank his coffee. What would he say about Ireland, about the rapidly vanishing Southwold?

'Perhaps it's a good thing. I mean, we could each of us use some space,' he said, almost in passing, almost over his shoulder, almost as though he did not now very much care about Southwold, about the weekend, as though the scene upstairs, amid the billowing bedding, had never taken place at all. 'I can catch up with a few things, I suppose.'

'What things?' Ward asked. Without taking a moment, a second to frame a response.

Martin pushed forward his smoothly shaved chin, he pushed his orange-perfumed hair back. 'Me things,' he said. 'I might go down to Kent,' he said. 'To Nigel. You can crowd me, you know,' he said. He had begun, lately, to deploy this phrase. 'Keep me posted, if you can be bothered, I mean,' and now he was gone without another word, and the front door banged, the panes of yellow and green stained glass juddering in their frames.

How long might Ward be in Ireland? – Martin hadn't asked.

Ward imagined Martin's movements for the next few minutes: his long legs making short work of Despard Road, quickly down the hill; cross at the lights, down the steps and into the bowels of the tube, to be whisked to Bloomsbury, and to the exacting, tick-like Julia. An easy commute, by London standards: as easy as pie.

Ward had met the original Julia, and had liked her. Warm, a touch of vivacity, anxiety to do well. With dandruff, yes, but she couldn't help that. She presumably used anti-dandruff shampoo, did her best. 'I thought she was nice,' Ward had said, mistakenly.

Martin replied, quite lightly, 'Perhaps you're not much of a judge of character?'

Julia had left London, in the end, for a job in Bristol.

The new Julia was a different kettle of fish. He didn't take prisoners, this Julia – so Ward had deduced. He was a results man. He couldn't be analysed in passing, and pulverised. He liked numbers, targets and order.

So did Martin – but the new Julia was, it seemed, a match for him.

Martin had brooded and fulminated over his coffee.

Daddy had liked his coffee instant: Maxwell House, powdered, mild blend.

Ward read Charlotte's message again. *A Sandborne. And an assault. Ireland. Request you call the office at your convenience.* The famous Dublin Sandborne then, it must be. In the early hours: well, at least she hadn't actually phoned. Charlotte was an awful bitch, but she did at least know when to call and when to text, did have some basic sense of boundaries and manners. A theft accomplished was a theft accomplished, and waking up Martin as well as Ward, and forcing Ward out of bed and into an actual conversation in the middle of the night: none of this would magic back a stolen painting. At least Charlotte knew this.

It was time to ring in.

But shower and dress first.

14

Ward was – they both were, he and Martin – tall and lean. They could have swapped clothes, had either been inclined to do so. Many of Ward's gay friends were ill matched in this respect – little with large, willow with gym-and-steroid-pumped beefcake – and Ward was aware of the assumption that he and Martin were in this respect a blessed couple: the stars smiled on them, in that they could go off shopping together, whirling through the West End picking out clothes, selecting for one another in congratulatory unison. Such perfect amity. 'The unbearable smugness of being,' one of the boys had called it. This was – the assumption continued – a win-win situation.

So Ward picked up.

And of course he and Martin did, sometimes, go shopping together; and did, from time to time, wear each other's clothes. Many's the morning (not this morning) Martin had vanished along Despard Road wearing Ward's straight, dark jeans – smart, perhaps looking smarter on Martin than they did on Ward. So Martin had said, once – though he denied it, later. 'Nonsense, you said it yourself. Or implied it, anyway. Negative body image, is what this says to me.'

Sometimes in the past, when Ward felt he needed a touch of gravity, he had worn some item belonging to Martin. Maybe I should wear black today, he thought as he stood dripping from the shower: and he stood in front of Martin's half of the wardrobe, the doors of which Martin had left open. Martin's clothes. Black and charcoal and steel-grey: but his fingers hovered only for a moment before he selected a soft cotton shirt, his own nice heather-green fine-gauge merino sweater. 'Smug gits,' his friends liked to say, automatically, without noticing that Ward's taste in clothes differed from Martin's taste, as day differed from night; and Ward would smile back, and say nothing.

Mrs Sandborne.

All these jobs and heists were big deals, of course, by their very nature: but Emily Sandborne was especially big just now, and the media would take an interest. This was never good: the only thing worse would be a murder, which had happened only once, and tastelessly. 'Murder, murder on the wall,' Martin had lisped, falsetto, when the news came through of that incident, 'whoth the deadetht of them all?' Ward had left the room, then: murder didn't lend itself to raised voices, far away. Now he pulled the green sweater over his head, went back down to the kitchen, sat down and at last dialled Charlotte.

'A robbery gone wrong, it looks like,' Charlotte said. No

preambles from Charlotte, no *hello*, no *good morning, how are you?* 'A young man, throat cut.' No softening of the facts.

'Throat cut?' This was almost Neapolitan. In the only other case, a man had been coshed on the back of the head, which seemed, somehow, preferable. And what about the art? 'Oh dear.' Ward liked to play up the campness, sometimes, because he knew Charlotte didn't like any sense of Kenneth Williams in their serious job. 'Who is this young man?'

Also. He didn't want to go to Dublin. He wanted this job to go to someone else; he knew that his fate in this regard was already signed and sealed.

'Nobody – nobody in particular. It was at the National Gallery – not the actual one, I mean, the one you apparently have over in Ireland,' said Charlotte. 'They came in to steal a Sandborne, they tell me. *The* Sandborne: that famous one, hang on.' Here she paused, and there was an audible rustling of Post-It notes. 'Here it is.'

'*The Jewel*,' Ward said.

'That's the one,' Charlotte said briskly. 'The one with the story.'

'So, they came to—'

'Yes, take this Sandborne – and this chap, I mean this man was there with a woman, both gallery members of staff, of course, and—'

He allowed Charlotte to quack on for a moment or so, and then said, 'I'll come in. I'll be with you in an hour.'

'If you *could*, Ward, that would be wonderful.' This was Charlotte's one and only concession to that incontrovertible fact that Ward had booked today, and the rest of the week, off. He was off – and now suddenly he was on again. No Southwold: now, this was clear. 'See you in a while, then.' The line cut.

Also. Charlotte had voted Leave, and had been brazen about the fact. And Ward had to work with her.

Ward cleared the table, cleaned the kitchen, stacked the dishwasher, filled Felicity's space-age range of timed-opening dishes with kibbles, and treats, and fresh water. Martin would, and frequently did, leave jars and spoons and dirty dishes right there on the table, but Ward had a horror of food left out. It attracted the dead, as well as flies and microbes; and life had enough hassles.

Daddy might feel he was being encouraged to come back. It was better to put everything away.

He went upstairs, and bundled the usual items into the overnight bag which stood ready and open – Felicity liked to sit in it, and its insides were sometimes infested with cat hair – in the bottom of the wardrobe, brought it downstairs, said goodbye to Felicity, who was still settled in the sunny kitchen. 'You're in charge,' he said, and placed his forefinger on her soft head. She closed her eyes momentarily, opened them, looked up at him.

It was time to go, and he went. But still not fully engaged. A near-murder, and he should be: but his mind was on other matters. On the past and the present. On *The Jewel*. On the dead, and on the living.

He followed Martin's path along Despard Road, down the hill, down the steps, skirting the homeless people, into the tube. Not quite skirting: fatally, he caught the eye of one of the homeless people. Young, dark, a scant beard. Too young. Not that it was ever right, but it was less possible, somehow, to blank the very youngest of these people, the ones aged seventeen or nineteen, the ones kicked out of the house, most likely, for some reason or other. Ward stepped onto the escalator and descended to the platform, where a train had just departed. He stood by the curving tiled wall, closing his eyes against the dirty air that churned in the train's wake.

On one occasion, some years ago now, entering the station at Tufnell Park with Martin, he had caught the eye of another such homeless man, also unacceptably young, a scanty beard, a sleeping bag, the usual accessories. No dog. A moment's meeting of eyes. He had sidestepped, and they had jumped into the antique lift as its doors slid closed, descended to the platform, had made their way to its end to await the train, and then—

'Wait, where're you going?'

'Just wait a second. I'll be back in a second, OK?' In too much of a rush even to look over his shoulder at Martin, Ward had retraced his steps, threading the crowds, issuing apologies in the face of glares, gained street level once more.

Pushed a tenner into the young guy's hand, his heart beating like a hammer.

He'd heard no mutter of thanks, for which he was grateful. He wasn't waiting about to nod or to smile or to receive a nod or smile from this poor guy, whatever his miserable story was.

Just take the tenner, and do something with it.

The lift descended once again. Martin was standing in

the same spot, the very same, and he seemed determined to if possible outstrip the rush and churn of foul air generated by a just-departed train. Ward closed his eyes against the gale.

They had been together for six months, meaning that the time for niceties and manners had passed.

'What the hell was that about? What, did you have diarrhoea?'

Ward flinched at the coarseness. He tried to explain: the homeless man, practically a boy, the lock of eyes for a second, the personal history that would remain unknown but that could be guessed well enough. Martin's expression barely changed.

'And you think a tenner will set him up for life, do you?'

No.

'Because it won't. I get enough bloody drama at work, day in and day out, without things like this happening in my time off.'

This was the first time Ward had experienced in its totality how Martin could hold and nurture a grievance, and how he could weaponise silence.

How he could require space, and walk away into the London evening, and return to the flat very late in the night, with the smell of another man on his dark clothes.

'I just walked,' he told Ward. 'And I'm tired now. Go to sleep.'

Ward had phoned: three, four times. Each time the call had clicked to voicemail.

Another gale of warm, foul air on the platform. Martin had avoided the worst of the rush, but Ward hit it, as he opened his eyes and shook himself a little, and moistened his mouth with his tongue, and elbowed his way onto the train: armpit city, as the train rattled south towards Camden Town and Euston amid a whirl of morning fragrances. But he knew his commute, too, was easy. He emerged from the underworld at Warren Street, went around a corner from the station, and he was there.

His building – put up in the nineties, all occluded glass and bright metal, six storeys of it – was, he thought, delightfully anonymous. It could have housed anything from one of Her Majesty's spy cells to a firm of quantity surveyors, and no passer-by would have been any the wiser. It in fact housed – as a discreet menu in the lobby proclaimed – several smallish legal firms, and a medical-something company drawn to the area, it was to be supposed, by the magnetic allure of University College Hospital across the way.

And Ward and his friends, who did whatever they did from their offices on the top floor.

'What *do* you do?' a young man, an intern or student of some kind at the clinic, had asked him plaintively one evening, in a Fitzrovia bar. 'I couldn't quite make it *out* last time we met.' Ward had been waiting for Martin, examining his nails against the marble-effect tabletop, when this young man, this boy, appeared at his elbow. They had met before, he claimed, at a seminar, several months ago now, had Ward forgotten? A seminar? – but no matter: the young man introduced himself again; told him that Martin was running late, was in a meeting, could not fish out his phone in front of board members – '*you* know how it is,' the young man said, and Ward blinked with dislike at the cod-intimacy

– and had ordered the intern to trot around the corner and offer his apologies.

And of course to keep Ward company, to join him in a drink, to flirt a little – because Ward knew he was nice-looking, what with his height and his nice clothes, and no paunch (yet), and sallow skin and white teeth and a full head of glossy, well-conditioned, not-yet-receding hair; what a lucky couple he and Martin were – until repelled by Ward's refusal to flirt back. Ward would have preferred to be left alone: to drink a nice glass of white, to look at the talent swirling around him; plenty to look at – but no.

'What *do* you do?'

Ward explained, in as few words as possible. He lost the young man's interest and attention very rapidly: that was all too evident, from the way in which his companion began looking over his shoulder at the hairstyles and shaped eyebrows drifting past their table; and it was satisfactory too. Ward preferred to close down discussions of exactly what it was he did; there were various methods of doing so, and he was a dab hand at them all.

'I'm a sort of civil servant,' was one of his special methods. That was usually enough to head off any further questions, because nobody ever wanted to talk about what civil servants did and did not do. 'I work on Warren Street,' he might add, so as to seal the deal. Sometimes, if Martin was there and listening in to these conversations, he might – depending on his mood – collaborate, turning the chat into another channel. Or – in order to stir things up a little – he might interject, hard. 'He fights crime, he catches criminals, is in fact what he does. *Warren* Street isn't much of an explanation, Ward, is it?'

It was not always easy to tell how Martin would respond.

But it was true: he could not accuse Martin of telling lies. Ward did fight crime, though he would not have quite put it this way himself. He fought crime, and so did Charlotte (who had voted Leave); and so did everyone else, in their own way, and all part of their generously funded, well resourced, well regarded *unit*. They all did their best. Ward disliked talking about what he did, but that was just him – and the fact was that he was proud of his job, and of his results. It was an anchor in his life.

A necessary anchor, now that the other anchor was dragging along the seabed.

And even Warren Street, anonymous though it essentially was, had come on in the last few years. There was a craft beer place in situ now – where the doctors from the hospital went at the end of their shift, to, Ward supposed, pick over the day's salvations and medical misadventures, and conspire about how best to cover up the needless and accidental deaths – and a nice Italian bakery place on the corner, where Ward liked to stop to pick up his second coffee of the day and josh with Giorgio, the handsome owner.

It was bakery time, now.

Giorgio knew his usual order, and this was gratifying: it made Ward feel as though he were part of an actual community, improbably on Warren Street.

They would talk politics as the machine ground and hissed behind him: Giorgio had lived in England for twenty years, he knew all the idioms, but he had never taken citizenship. 'Will they give me the boot, the old heave-ho?' he had said, once the initial shock of Brexit had, not faded, but rather developed into an even greater shock. 'After all my taxes? Will they do that?'

'They won't do that, Giorgio,' Ward told him, thinking at the time that they would, that Giorgio would be told to sling his hook and take his foreign coffee machine with him, that instant would be fine from now on. 'They wouldn't be so stupid.'

Today, Giorgio seemed perky: perhaps cheered by the clear sunshine, London's bustle, the queue going back to the door, the jingle of money and the soundscape of electronic transactions filling the air. So perky that he slipped a couple of zaleti into one of his green-white-and-red *Giorgio's* paper bags and handed the bag over with Ward's espresso and a wink. 'We need to enjoy life, my friend,' said Giorgio. 'Have a good day.'

Ward said, 'I will,' and for a moment he meant it. 'Thank you, Giorgio.' He stepped around the corner and into the glassy, bright atrium of his office building, said hello to Security – always wise to keep in with these guys – touched his fob, passed the barriers, entered the lift. There was more security, now, on the sixth floor too: this was something new, a sort of beefing up suggested by Charlotte and nodded through elsewhere, a precaution to deter a passing opportunistic terrorist. This security person sat at his newly installed desk: burly, muscly, but here it was, not even nine in the morning, and already he looked bored out of his tree, because it would take a determined terrorist to get as far as the sixth floor, and this guy knew it. However.

'Morning,' Ward said, and received a curt nod in response. He touched his fob again, and now he was in.

Ward had worked here for five years now, and the place seemed never to change all that much. Except for the art, of course: this was changed on a regular, virtuous three-month rota. In the waiting area now, a block of red on the wall that might have owed something to tapestry, except that it consisted of a sheet of hard shiny plastic – grooved and notched for maximum tactile effect, might have been the idea, though it was art, and thus not to be touched. It had cost – 'a fucking fortune, I mean for God's sake,' Charlotte had said when it first appeared, a week or so back, 'we're supposed to be concerned about art, could we not have got ourselves something a bit better than that?'

Ward knew, everyone knew, that this – this swirl of pieces from the four corners of the world – was one of Charlotte's grievances. And in the shocking aftermath of the referendum, she had become increasingly vocal in her objections. What a waste of money, what a fuss, what was wrong, in an English office, with English art?

'British,' Ward said once: and for a moment feared she would deck him.

'*British*, then,' she spat. 'What's wrong with British art?'

Because they weren't a British organisation – but he knew better than to take on Charlotte.

This expanse of red plastic was Portuguese. By a 'plastics artist', the little information note unnecessarily said, who was based in Porto. Ward liked its boldness, its pillar-box redness. True, he thought, I wouldn't have it on the wall at Despard Road. Also, he had to admit that it didn't add much by way of calm to the waiting area here in Warren Street; it reminded him a bit of blood.

But sure look, you couldn't have everything.

Charlotte could be glimpsed through a window in the wall of her lair, her corner office at the end of the corridor to the left. A few more private offices, a few larger meeting rooms, a kitchen, loos – but most of the sixth floor was open-plan: white desks and walls, and already vibrating with the hum of activity. Floor-to-ceiling windows that looked west and north, glimpses of the trees in Regent's Park, the Telecom Tower, the roofs and satellite dishes of Fitzrovia. It was good enough.

'Ward catches criminals,' Martin had said recently. 'Imagine.'

Martin called him Ward, the same as everyone else.

'Does he?' said the person on this occasion – the woman, someone long since messed up by psychoanalysis, Ward surmised, from the way she was focused completely on Martin, from the way she didn't so much as glance at Ward, in spite of the fact that the exchange was supposed to be about him. 'Fight crime?' They were talking about him as though he wasn't there. Does he take sugar?

'We advise on tracking and recovering stolen artworks,' Ward said evenly, goaded to irritation by this sensation of invisibility. 'On counterfeiting. If a gallery or a dealer or a museum comes across a suspect piece, they ask us for advice – so, is it the genuine article, or a counterfeit? That's mainly what we do.'

She looked at him.

'And because it's big business – counterfeiting, forging

– it was decided to set up what you might call a centre of excellence.'

'Counterfeiting?' she said.

It was more and more difficult to tell a forged painting from a real one, he told her: it was a huge international business – 'huge, huge,' he said – with vast amounts of money at stake. So it was decided that a body needed to be set up to advise. He said, as he always said, 'To offer advice on provenance, you know? Think Unesco, without the resources,' and now she nodded, as they always nodded, once they saw a label attached. 'And after a heist, after a painting or artwork gets stolen, and that also happens all the time, the local police will ask us for advice. Because if you think about it, there are only so many people who can afford to engage in this kind of theft; and part of our job is to maintain a database, to advise on likely subjects.' And now he paused, inviting her to think about it. 'And that's it. That's what we do. Possible forgeries, and thefts, and we offer guidance, and insights. It's very much below the radar.'

He stopped, and she nodded again, and Martin raised an eyebrow. 'Imagine,' he said again. 'Isn't that clever of him?' he said to the woman. 'I do think that's awfully clever of him.' He had stepped sideways from his neutrally middle-class educated-English accent into something fruitier. 'Really awfully clever. Lots of European cases, you know – but hush!' Martin tapped the side of his nose. 'We don't like to make too much of that side of things, not nowadays. We don't want him strung from a lamp-post for being thought European, not really.'

The woman blinked. 'European, how? Are you, like, French?'

Ward shook his head. 'No.'

'Are you based in Brussels?'

Another shake of the head. 'No, here in London. London is a centre of the global art trade, and unfortunately it's a centre for the global art theft trade too; so it was decided to establish it here. And we go where the crime goes, no borders. But we're not a police force,' he added with a smile that she did not see. 'I mean, we're art historians, we don't carry *guns*. We discreetly offer advice, and guidance, and leads. That's it. Did you,' he said, 'ever hear of the Gurlitt Collection?' She shook her head. 'You should look it up,' he said. She nodded.

'No *borders*,' Martin said. 'Or if there were, he could just cross them as though they weren't even *there*. Imagine the privilege of that. We'll all be stealing his passport soon, and using it ourselves.'

'Sounds great.' The woman's gaze swivelled back to Martin.

It was – *great* was perhaps not the word, Ward thought at the time. But it meant something; it brought satisfaction in its wake. And standing now in the waiting area, noticing that the light was slightly ruddy from the slab of crimson plastic on the wall, looking about him, even with Charlotte crouching in her den just over there, and a slashed throat as well as a stolen painting awaiting him in Dublin – he felt a wash of relief, a sense of security.

Something that resembled the security that other people assumed he had already claimed for himself.

Because he was already sorted – that was what people thought.

He had his job, and he had a house off Highgate Hill with stained glass in the front door, close to the park, and the tube, and even the hospital, should Ward stub his toe and need attention. True, Ward himself said he lived in Archway, while Martin said, 'Highgate, darling!' and scoffed at Ward's careful reverse snobbery. But the fact was that they had a lovely house, with its little south-facing back garden, and enough room to swing Felicity.

'You want to wise up,' Martin had said.

15

And for ten years now, Ward reminded himself, they had had each other.

They had met the best way – through mutual friends who had organised a Saturday evening meal (a big meal, lots of people, safety in numbers) at a Spanish place in Farringdon. A night in November. He hadn't known it was a set-up, though Martin had, and had arrived preened to within an inch of his life. They had clicked – Ward tried to remember this, during the bad days, the silent days – over the patatas bravas, and the tangled mess of octopus tentacles soused in garlicky oil, and the olives black and green. They had left together, just the two of them, gone for more drinks, and at the end of the night they had gone home together – to Martin's home, which at that time was a bit of a dive on the top floor of a run-down house in Tufnell Park; but the bed was big, and that was all that either of them had at that moment cared about.

These memories were worth retaining, worth treasuring, surely they were.

The next day – in fact, the next evening, the winter darkness already settled onto the streets, the whole day gone – Ward had left, with Martin's number stored safely on his phone, and had made his way back to Gipsy Hill, and phoned Martin as soon as he closed the front door behind him. No playing of games, no hanging about until Tuesday evening before making the next move, he was thirty years old now, life was too short for elaborate and unnecessary games of Twister – and Martin had answered on the second ring; and they had met to go to the cinema on Monday, and met again on Wednesday; and within a month Ward had given notice at Gipsy Hill and moved in with Martin. And two years later, they had cashed in their chips, and bought the house on Despard Road.

No marriage yet, but surely that would come.

So. House, partner, clothes, south-facing back garden, cat, job.

But the house was the thing. He had said something like this – perhaps not quite wisely, but it had to be said, his heart was swelling and bursting – to Martin a few months after they had moved in. That the house was the centre of it all. It might have gone wrong: surely Martin was the foundation, that was the way it worked, a house was just a pile of bricks, when it came right down to it? A little frown mark, then, a cleft, on Martin's forehead, but on this occasion quickly smoothed away: he understood, he said. He could see where Ward was coming from.

Because Ward had had his demons, said Martin's expression.

And Martin knew all about them, now.

And oh, how Ward had loved that house, from the first moment. They had viewed it on a Saturday morning, an autumn morning, a touch of gold in the air and light: and they had stepped into the narrow London hall, and looked up the narrow London stairs, and there was the sun shining through the windows at the back of the house, through the squares of yellow glass on the corners of the generous window on the half-landing, into all the back rooms. Not much of a view – but high enough to see a wide arc of sky.

Ward clocked another couple, a straight couple with a small boy in tow, arriving on their heels. The adults nodded warily, the estate agent handed out brochures. '1860 or thereabouts,' she told them, riffling distractedly through her notes. 'It's down on its luck at the moment,' she went on, eyes down, lashes curling back almost 180 degrees, reading from the brochure in front of her, 'but a very little investment and you'd have a home to be proud of.'

Martin took Ward's elbow, pushed him into a light-filled rear sitting room. 'Right, you look downstairs, and I'll look upstairs, and I'll see you in the garden in a minute.' This was their usual operation, after weeks and weeks of looking: it saved time; you could tell if a house was right inside of two minutes, the property pages told them, and they had realised that this was the truth. So Martin took the steep stairs two at a time, and Ward slipped into the kitchen, from where iron steps led from a back door down into the garden – there was a tiny little basement too, with direct garden access; the house had everything. They met in the garden. 'Two good bedrooms,' Martin reported, 'and wainscoting in the bathroom, this is it,' and 'this is it,' Ward repeated, and the two men turned and kissed – on the lips, this was no time for anything uptight – and the sight of the kiss caused the other people, now heavily descending the iron steps, to turn sharply and retreat back into the kitchen, shepherding the little boy in front of them – and yes, this was it. The decision made: other people were arriving to view the house, and others again behind them; but the house was theirs. The first home Ward had ever had – and he could see that Martin knew this, and knew too that, for now, there was no need for frowns.

'Well, good morning,' said Rob, glancing up from his screen, stretching, cracking his knuckles.

'In early?'

'Ish. I was supposed to have the kids this weekend, so plans to be made, you know.' He was expat New Zealand, married-and-divorced with a brood of children; Ward liked to pretend he couldn't remember exactly how many children. 'Since Dublin seems like a foregone conclusion: Charlotte says,' Rob added, 'that she wants us in asap, as soon as you're settled, she says. Good holiday?' he added and Ward rolled his eyes. 'Bummer, I know.' A pause. 'How's Martin about it?'

Ward shrugged.

'This one,' Rob continued after the briefest pause, 'sounds, well, not all that nice, really. Cut throat. Poor guy. Still, at least he's not dead. Not yet, anyway.'

'I know,' Ward said, and blew out a long breath. 'Well, come on. Let's do this.' As he bustled for a moment, picking up and putting down pieces of paper, he caught the edge of Rob's cologne. Woody, an acrid tincture of sweat, masculine. He glanced at Rob, but Rob was intent on his own papers, mess, screen, and he did not glance back.

Ward watched Charlotte, seated behind her desk, watching them the length of the corridor. The corridor seemed to lengthen the moment you set foot on it, Ward always thought, like a mile-long monstrous something you'd expect to find at an airport. Also, there was Charlotte herself, and the way she made you feel. Made Ward feel, and made Rob feel, anyway: they had talked this over many times over pints of red beer and bags of designer cheese-and-onion crisps in the craft beer boozer. 'Like you're the biggest fool she's ever seen,' Rob sighed. It wasn't a sexist thing: they were both sure it wasn't that.

No, it was Charlotte herself.

Charlotte as a human being, Charlotte the Leaver, Charlotte who had been pretty awful before the referendum, but who since then was beyond the pale.

'Beyond the beyond,' Rob said that day, gazing into the supernaturally red depths of his glass of craft beer.

They knocked, entered.

'There you are,' Charlotte said. 'At last. Sit.'

They sat.

'We're a little late getting this off the ground,' Charlotte went on. 'We were alerted at five o'clock this morning – of course, you both got my text.' They nodded, naughty schoolboys. 'So now we have a little catching up to do.'

'You could have had someone else on a plane to Dublin at eight o'clock,' Ward pointed out. He looked over Charlotte's shoulder at the clock on the wall: nine ten. 'They would have been there by now. You didn't need us.'

Charlotte shook her head. 'You're the right people for the job. And you're Irish, Ward: I thought you'd jump at the chance to do some field work, you know, on home ground.'

'You were wrong about that.'

'Well, wrong or not, you're on the job: so let's make a wrong into a right, shall we?' She rustled some papers together: her desk was a mess too. Ward's own desk was a shrine to order; and he didn't believe in paper. 'I'll need you in Dublin by lunchtime.'

'Ah, Charlotte, for fuck's sake.'

This was one thing he appreciated about Charlotte: just the one. She didn't dislike salty language; indeed, she embraced it herself. The rustling got louder. 'Don't you fuck's sake me,' she said. 'I need you on this job, Ward; this is Victorian, this is your patch; and I want *you* with him, Rob; and that's all there is to say about it. If you don't like it' – well, she *had* voted Leave – 'you can fuck off back to Ireland, or New Zealand, or wherever it is you came from. And take me to court if you like, for saying that. Now. Take this: read about it, come back in an hour, ready for the off.' She gestured at the door.

They did as they were told, of course: retreating down the corridor, feeling Charlotte's gaze on the backs of their necks, ducking into one of the meeting rooms to digest and discuss, all in an hour.

'So,' Rob said, settling himself. 'Tell me about this Sandborne.' Victorian wasn't his period: but Rob had a knack of making connections, of putting a fact to a name, and dragging the name from the agency database. They had all seen it in action, again and again.

'What, haven't you covered it?'

'I've looked at it, mate. But I want you to tell me about it.'

Ward rolled his eyes – but of course he was pleased, too. Rob liked to listen to his stories. He sat upright now, waiting. 'Emily Sandborne,' Ward began, slowly. '*Mrs* Sandborne, they used to call her. Well, it's a sad enough story.'

'OK,' Rob said.

'OK. Where to begin.'

Where to begin. The crimson grooved plastic wall panel in the lobby cast an oblique ruddy light even here: refracted from one wall and through a pane of internal glazing to fetch up, he noticed, as a rosy patch on Rob's smoothly shaven right cheek, and conflicting with his green eyes.

Emily – Mrs – Sandborne.

'Mrs Sandborne. They called her this, for years. Very old-fashioned. Kept her in her place. She was English,' Ward said. 'One of those Victorian lady painters who weren't really taken seriously in their time, and weren't really taken seriously for years and years afterwards. Not in mainstream quarters, at any rate.' A curled lip – he imagined – and an eye raised to the heavens when the name cropped up. *Sandborne: oh yes. Mrs Sandborne. Emily Sandborne, didn't she kill herself? So many of them did.* A just imagining, probably. Feminist scholars have done their best with her, he said, and with whole generations just like her, but too few female curators, and too few female scholars, still.

And the men, 'You know, they blather on piously about resurrecting lost painters and rediscovering forgotten stories and dissolving the canon – all without ever actually intending to do much about it.'

'Too many old farts,' Rob said, 'who just aren't interested.'

'That's it. You know how it is.'

Rob nodded.

'The thing is,' Ward went on, 'she's incredibly good. Incredibly vivid: the colours shine like they're on fire. I've never seen anything like her use of colour' – by anyone, he thought, from any period – 'and nobody seems to know how she did it.' Those beautiful colours, as though lit from within. And her versatility: oils, watercolours, pencil drawings and chalks, the lot. Though not some gigantic body of work, either: she took her time, and she got it right. And was essentially ignored for her pains. 'Some pieces at the Academy summer shows,' he went on, 'but in general, the gents didn't take her seriously. And her work didn't sell, not that much anyway, and she was always sidelined. Ruskin wrote something about her, what was it—'

'I know this bit. I have it here, somewhere,' Rob said, and he riffled through the papers on the table. 'Here it is,' he said, and read aloud, his Kiwi accent conveying the words oddly: '"If art is greatest, as I say it is, when it suggests to the mind of the spectator, the greatest number of the greatest ideas: if this is so, then I declare that the ideas conveyed by Mrs

Sandborne are poor and pallid things. For while her work glows and shines like stained glass, it in the end signifies nothing. The glow and the shine soon fade: and the ideas fade too; and they become little and womanish and in all ways incapable of exaltation."' Rob blinked. 'God, what a bitch. Ruskin, didn't he have some, what, some issue with, what was it, women's pubes? Couldn't stand the sight of them?'

Ward paused scrupulously. 'So they say. Might be an urban myth. Let's not talk about pubes. Sandborne's husband had money, and she had a little money,' he said, 'so she was never, you know, starving in some frozen garret. She did OK. But she became a little eccentric in her ways: reading between the lines, isolation, lack of—'

'Affirmation,' said Rob. 'Getting kicked in the head by the likes of Ruskin.'

'Right. She—'

'Retreated into herself,' said Rob. 'Christ, it's just the same story, over and over. Called mad.'

Doing nobody any harm, Ward thought, but the word went around that she had gone mad, and people didn't like that: and she probably thought that they'd be coming to lock her up. 'Besides which, her husband went and gave her syphilis, probably on her honeymoon. In the true Victorian style.'

Rob nodded. He clearly knew this bit too. 'Nice,' he said. 'Stylish.'

'So she came up with a plan,' Ward continued. 'To paint, as she approached the final stages of her illness, her last piece, and bring it to the grave with her.'

'Yeah,' Rob said. 'That's what Wikipedia told me.'

'A sort of a shroud idea. A distemper piece, painted quickly, and sealed, and wrapped, and brought with her when she—'

'Realised she was dying,' said Rob mournfully. 'And that's *The Jewel*.'

'Yeah. Which was forgotten about for years and years.'

Eighty years, he thought. They opened her coffin in 1919, just after the First World War. Word got out that some painting had been buried with her, her vulture descendants applied for permission to open the grave, and the distemper piece was found – untouched, unfaded. The descendants took one look and flogged it off – to an eagle-eyed curator in Ireland, and she treasured it, and stored it, and told the story to whoever was interested. And her gallery exhibited it once a year, quietly, for a month.

Good old Ireland, he thought. Nice job. 'Let's have a look at it.'

Rob unrolled a reproduction. Even here, the colours sang.

'And let's have a look at her.'

Because it was the artist herself who caught and held his eye. Sad, the books said; a solemn witness, said the catalogues. He waved an index finger. 'What did the biographer say about her expression there?'

Rob said, 'Oh wait, I have this, too: "Sandborne's grief and anger are caught in her eyes; and the watchfulness, the alertness of her form indicates the transgressive nature of this piece – of a female figure controlling this tableau, upright and vigilant and wary of danger, here in a public place where no woman should be."'

Well, perhaps: but to Ward's eye there was a pull upward in the set of her lips. The slightest indication of a wry smile.

Who can tell what I'm thinking, who can tell how I made this piece, who knows how I mixed my colours and set them to last? Nobody. Nobody knows me at all. So, put that in your pipe and smoke it.

Good on you, Mrs Sandborne.

And now her time had come: now, the scholars had become interested, and the word had got about, and this piece of linen valued and found to be essentially priceless – distemper pieces never lasted, always faded, *The Jewel* was one of a kind. Now, Sandborne was – *iconic*, the art websites said, and *emblematic*.

Found, famous, appreciated, at long, long last. The biography revised, and the Dublin gallery, which had kept faith with its curiosity decade after decade, unable to believe its luck.

Bravo, Mrs Sandborne. Too late for you.

'Fuck's sake,' Rob said. 'The bloody waste, mate.'

And now, here I am, Ward thought, despatched to Ireland. Thanks a bunch, Mrs Sandborne.

Rob had fallen into this job more or less by accident: so he explained once, long ago, over yet another pint of bright-red beer. He had worked at Te Papa back in New Zealand, had taken a year's leave to do the whole OE thing, met his Englishwoman in London and married her in short order, and had to magic up a job in England. This was Rob's story, packaged by him into the plainest possible Kiwi box.

As Ward now knew, there was a bit more to it than that: he had taken a degree in art history in Wellington before joining the museum: and all in all, he and the agency made a good fit. And now Ward knew that he was a bit of a bloodhound – good at sniffing out the story, the clues, the lies. He loved the forgeries, Rob said – and it was true: a mere month after he joined, he had spotted that the green pigment in a German Expressionist piece had not in fact existed when Erich Heckel was alive and painting: the painting a forgery, the dealer and the august gallery saved. Rob's discovery made discreet waves; additional funding was secured – and he became a minor hero. More results followed: he was bloody-minded about getting a result; and he loved his pigments. He was possessed of a sort of professional morality that burned. *Fuck's sake*. The waste of it. But he kept this side of himself carefully hidden from the likes of Charlotte.

And he was your typical laconic New Zealander: he didn't like talking about himself too much, and Ward knew this also; the two of them had a good deal in common.

And divorced, now, from Jane, though you'd hardly know it.

So: pigments, and Victoriana: so Charlotte had a point, putting them together.

'Shall we go through the paperwork, then, mate?' he said now. 'Or, do you want another coffee first?'

'I've had my two. Let's go for it.'

'So, *The Jewel*,' Rob said, leafing through the file. 'I had a good look through this morning. There's a good chance it's left the country already, the Irish police say: bunged onto a waiting craft and' – he shuffled a page – 'it's probably over here somewhere already, they think, ready to be processed.' He said *processed* with a raised eyebrow: this was Charlotte's catch-all phrase for a catch-all phenomenon; a painting could be kept hidden quietly for a while, before being moved on; or it could be sent straight to its client by various means; or it could be held for ransom, for as short a time as possible. It all depended – and *processed* it was.

He paused. 'So that's the thing,' he repeated, 'but now, here we have a not-quite-dead person too. So, male, twenty-two years old, Irish, unlucky to have been there. A professional job, our turf, so can we offer any insights, is there a match with any knife-wielding maniacs in our systems, which there isn't.'

'No.' It was hardly likely, Ward thought: murders cropped up from time to time in this line, and they knew their stuff about them; but presumably so did the police in Ireland. Probably, he added to himself, they knew more. 'Is there anything?'

'Definitely not on the systems, no way,' Rob said judiciously. 'But.'

'But,' Ward said.

There was a pause.

'Let me take a bit of time,' Rob said, 'and we'll see what we see.'

'OK,' said Ward, 'right,' he said, and the two men began to look through the notes spread out across the table. Charlotte was waiting.

They munched through their files in forty of their allocated sixty minutes. Not, thought Ward, that there was much to be absorbed in the way of facts: Sandborne, the gallery, a man and a woman and a slit throat; that was it, really, and the Irish police had, not unreasonably, gathered little more information in the few hours since the crime had been committed.

'Colours,' Rob mused at one point, 'and fabric.'

'Anything?'

Rob moved his head – though difficult to tell whether it was a nod or a shake. Ward knew to leave him alone.

With twenty minutes left, Rob called Jane again, to finish setting up the new childcare rota; Jane was still cross, Ward surmised, if Rob's defensive tones, his flushed neck were anything to go by. Ward left a message on Martin's voicemail, to be collected when Martin emerged from his budget meeting with Julia. Ireland was definitely happening: talk later; and all delivered in the businesslike tones that Martin liked at such times. This took a couple of minutes, ten minutes to check email and look at headlines – the news of the stolen Sandborne had now been released, Ward noticed dispassionately, the journos were hauling stuff out of storage about Poor Emily – and then, with five minutes to go, he gathered himself, prepared to meet Charlotte once more.

'Come on then,' Rob grunted, and snapped shut his laptop. Less than half of Ward's mind was on the Sandborne, files and notes and slashed throat notwithstanding; more than half was on Martin. I'll text him from Heathrow, he thought; it'll be fine. I have to think about the work.

I have to think about Ireland.

I have to deal with Charlotte, now, in a couple of minutes; I have to avoid being dealt with by her.

I have to go to Dublin, and stay there for a while.

I have to work to find *The Jewel*. And, he thought, I need to put this top of my list of priorities.

He blinked, and saw Rob's eye on him.

'I was thinking about Martin. He said he was thinking about going down to Kent for the night.'

'Oh yes?'

'His friend Nigel lives there.'

'Nigel. Nigel who lives in a converted oast house, that Nigel?'

Ward nodded.

'His ex Nigel, that Nigel?'

Ward nodded.

It was evidently all Rob could do not to roll an eye. But instead he said, 'Well, it's out of your hands.' A pause, and then, 'What about Felicity?'

But Felicity had her dining plan all set up. She'd be fine, he told Rob, fed and watered as usual.

'That's good,' Rob said. 'I like Felicity. She's numero uno.' He got up. 'Come on, then. Ake ake.'

16

The truth was that Ward did not much like crimes that melded, mingled one into another. Robbery and murder: they should occupy different worlds. Robbery was one thing: they were trained in such a matter. Murder was another, and they were untrained. Murder was bad. He and Rob had seldom had to deal with murder and the like: just the once, in fact.

And the once, for a variety of reasons, had been enough.

It had been a prominent affair. Munich and a soap-opera crime: a high-profile theft, an accompanying murder. The museum – its quality, its starry status – and the painting – the Blaue Reiter school, Gabriele Münter – heaped glamour on the case. The Germans had heard about Rob: this was more German Expressionism, they wanted him on the spot. He had gone to Munich, Ward had tagged along, and they dealt with lots of German people, also glamorous, very professional. Ward had eaten a good deal of heavy Bavarian food, potatoes and dumplings and fragrant salami, and masses of cakes, and returned to London several pounds heavier than he had left it. (Rob, who was a disciplined eater, had stuck to veggie fare, and had stayed just the same weight.)

Later, Martin had complained about this extra weight, during sex. 'Get off me, I can't breathe, you're squashing me flat.'

Martin had not had to complain about any other aspect of this trip to Munich. He had never guessed about any other aspects, or so Ward assumed.

Of course, it was most likely a mistake to make such assumptions. Ward knew this: on the other hand, Rob was so very straight-as-a-die. Who would ever guess?

And it had only been the once, really, more or less the once, and long enough ago, now, that it had become just an element in their friendship. As a tree grows around and about a nail embedded in its trunk, and makes the nail a part of itself – so Ward liked to think: it was like this.

A woody scent, a touch acrid, under the Munich chestnut trees.

After a long day in the Lenbachhaus, he and Rob had walked slowly back to their hotel in Lehel. Dusk was settling over the city. The gallery, in this warm spell of May weather, had stifled them – the office areas increasingly stuffy as the day had worn on, as the meetings had worn on, as tempers had risen steadily under a carapace of German calm – and now, as they walked through the Hofgarten, they shed jackets and ties, opened shirt buttons, tried to slough off the tension and exhaustion.

'Christ,' Rob said. The case was sensational: the media was crawling all over it. It was tasteless, and violent. It was everything that it should not be. 'Let's sit for a moment. I need to fill my lungs with something more than dust.'

They sat, amid the radiating paths and pruned trees, facing the ugliness of the Chancellery building. Surely this painting would never be located or returned: it was evident that the Germans they had met thought so; and this explained the frantic atmosphere inside the gallery.

'Christ,' Rob said again.

Ward shrugged. 'Let's go down to the river, get some fresher air and a bite to eat.'

They walked on slowly. And by the Isar, the air was indeed fresher; and the tall candles of chestnut blossom, white and pink, shone above them. Rob breathed deeply, breathed in the woody, acrid chestnut aroma that now filled the air. 'Fantastic.'

'It reminds me of sweat,' Ward said, 'that smell. At the gym.'

Rob said nothing. His divorce had been settled, that very week, once and for all. He felt – it was difficult for Ward to judge how he felt. Delicate, he sensed, bruised; relieved, also. A page turned.

They ate outside, within earshot of the river, still running fast with spring rain and cold and green with melted snow. One, two, three good German beers, and now the tension of the day did slough away, and they laughed at rubbish, at ribald jokes, at gossip from the Warren Street office; and maybe it was not especially surprising (Ward thought later) that when they returned to their hotel, a few streets back from the river, and when the doors of the lift had closed, maybe it was not especially surprising that Rob should turn to him and, just like that, kiss him. Full on the lips. A proper kiss, and a response, and more kissing as they stumbled down the third-floor corridor, and more kissing when the door of Ward's room closed behind them.

It wasn't all that surprising. Not really.

Rob needed to unburden himself – and besides he knew about Martin, about that patch of unhappiness in Ward's life that was now like a seam coming apart, the stitches unravelling one by one.

And so maybe they both needed this; certainly they both wanted it, each taking advantage of the other, and of the situation.

In the morning, when Ward woke, Rob had already gone, had slipped away in the night, had left the smell of himself on the white hotel sheet. When they met at breakfast – a gargantuan buffet, of which they both also took full advantage, eggs and salami and cheese and pickles and gallons of weak German coffee ('well, we worked up an appetite last night,' said Ward) – they were very grown-up about the whole thing, they discussed what had happened, they agreed that it had been fun, that it shouldn't happen again. It would be unwise. Rob had appeared unfazed; and when Ward checked in with himself, he too realised that he felt a – a calmness, more than anything else. Quite unfazed: a good thing to have happened. But it probably shouldn't happen again.

And it hadn't, really. It had hardly ever happened again.

And Martin didn't know about Ward's lapse, and had almost certainly not guessed. It would have been punishing, had he guessed. Ward could imagine the forms of punishment that might be meted out.

Martin wasn't taken with Rob: thought him hardly worth thinking about, or talking to. Rob barely registered. Which was as well.

But the point was, not that there had been a lapse in Ward's personal life, but that the case itself, this Munich case, had been disagreeable in the extreme. There had been a good deal of media attention: the murder had been part and parcel of the crime, and had been ritualised, involving a hanging carried out right there in the gallery – tastelessly elaborate, Rob complained, like something from a Dan Brown novel. This meant pressure, of course – how cross the authorities were about it all – but yes, it also meant a dash of glamour; certainly there had been envious looks thrown in Ward's direction and Rob's direction and even one or two catty comments from among the ranks of his colleagues.

The assumption that the 'boys' had enjoyed it. When the opposite, for the most part, was the case.

Ward had caught one of these catty comments. In the craft beer place around the corner: he was settled in one high-backed booth after work, waiting to go on a bender with Rob when he finally arrived (this was how quickly everything had settled down to a sort of normality) and quite invisible to the little gaggle of his colleagues gathered in a neighbouring booth for a bout of the usual post-work gossip, bitching and slander over a beer. He heard enough, quite enough: he heard that he was too smug, too cocky, too much of the Paddy about him; while Rob, well, what did a Kiwi know about crime, anyway? Apart from sheep-shagging, obvs.

'What does a Kiwi know about art, like, full stop,' said one of them, to titters. He sounded like Martin.

'Nice, guys,' Ward said, surfacing like an orca above the top of the booth wall. 'Agency solidarity. We can never get enough of comments like these.' And ignored the cries and bleats of regret, headed out into the night, rang Rob as he reached the corner: he fancied a change – what about walking towards Marylebone? – he'd see him on the corner.

And the agency was just this sort of place: a bit bitchy, incestuous, like a university department, like the Borgias in the matter of rivalry and career development. No wonder, Ward sometimes reflected, no wonder they were all pursuing a career in crime – or the solving of it, which was just the other side of the same coin: they all had the criminal's eye for the main chance. He didn't exclude himself from that description, either – though he did exclude Rob, who had something of a homespun, scrubbed-clean air that certainly wasn't Borgian.

Rob was alright. And their friendship was weathering well, in spite of everything. And Rob had been instrumental in locating the Münter. The reams of information held on the agency database had come together under his eye and formed a pattern, in a way that seemed miraculous; and the thief – the killer – apprehended two days later in the Munich suburbs. The agency congratulated, again, and more funds released.

★

'All set?' Charlotte asked: then, without waiting for a reply – her usual method – she began rustling through the heaps of papers on her desk. 'Only, you know, time running along, and all that.'

'Quite,' Ward said.

Charlotte did a little more shuffling and ruffling. 'You're booked on a noon flight, Sandra has the details, and so you should be at the gallery around two o'clock, they tell me. Dublin: I haven't ever been, but of course you have, Ward, so you'll be on home ground. In a manner of speaking, I mean.' She smiled briefly at Ward, switched the smile off. 'At any rate, it's good to know that you'll understand local ways of doing things, local sensitivities, proclivities, the usual. It'll all be very helpful, I'm sure.'

Rob said, 'What proclivities would those be, exactly?'

Charlotte said, 'Ward will fill you in on the local colour, Rob, I'm sure. Won't you, Ward?'

Ward nodded. 'Oh yes, sure I will,' he said.

'So,' Rob said in more businesslike tones, 'what sort of sense do you get from the Irish police?'

'Sense.'

This was another thing about Charlotte. She had a way of making questions sound in some way foolish. Ward knew what Rob meant, Charlotte knew too, it was a reasonable question: were they panicked, did they have things under control, were there leads, were they all at sea? Would there be resentment at the mere sight of them?

Resentment was the worst scenario, as all three of them knew. Sometimes the local authorities were excessively protective of their patch, would sooner a crime wasn't solved at all, than see it assisted by outsiders. They all knew this: would Charlotte then, Ward thought, not just cut the crap, and get on with it?

It seemed that she would, that she was now thinking better of annoying them. 'I think you'll find a certain relief. This theft, this Sandborne,' and here she glanced at Ward, 'isn't exactly good news anyway – but in this local context it's even bigger, Ward, am I right?'

'You *are* right,' Ward said, tilting back his chair a little. Charlotte said nothing more, so Ward glanced at Rob. 'This is the bit you wouldn't have seen in the files. Ireland has had a couple of notorious break-ins, art thefts; so they'll be super-touchy about yet another one.'

'Touchy,' Charlotte echoed. 'Yes: exactly – I got a definite touchiness on the phone.'

'OK,' Rob pursed his lips. 'Anything else?'

She shook her head. 'The man, the young chap who almost died: there doesn't seem to be any extraordinary story there. He was working late: wrong place at the wrong time, just bad luck, really. You saw in the notes that there's a witness: an older woman, a big cheese in the gallery. They haven't said much about this side of things.'

'And the painting itself?'

Charlotte shook her head again. 'Do they want money, was it a bespoke collector's theft, only two choices, and we don't know which. That's for you to find out.'

There was a short silence, and then Ward and Rob stirred themselves to leave. They were nearly at the door when Charlotte spoke again.

'Do tread carefully with this one: it really will be ballet

shoes all the way. OK?' She looked at them, looking at her. 'I hope you've packed your ballet shoes, Ward. We don't want any rows, any quarrels, so be careful.'

Ward said, 'Careful with ourselves?'

She laughed. 'I don't care about yourselves. Just be careful with your language. That's all I mean.' She waved them away; and that, Ward thought, was an end to that.

Be careful, be careful. Ward thought about Charlotte's warning all the way to Heathrow in the taxi, all the way through security, all the way over on the short flight to Dublin. Be careful, be careful.

Charlotte had not infrequently demonstrated this sort of – sixth sense, or ability to place a talon on a soft piece of flesh, on a scab, on a wound.

Run the talon along its delicate, reddened, painful surface. Its barely healed surface. Withdraw the talon, having caused just enough pain. Return to business, with a feeling – presumably – of satisfaction.

Be careful. Of causing annoyance, of inflaming sensitivities: that was all that Charlotte meant. No use taking all this seriously, personally. It was – Ward thought as they banked a little at thirty-six thousand feet over the Mersey and began the long, slow glide across the water to Dublin – hardly a warning in any case. It was more of an admonition. A professional admonition; Charlotte was just doing her job. Probably she said this at the beginning of every new project, and he had never noticed before.

Be careful. Watch your mouth, your back, watch everything. Mind the long wounds on your body – healed now, but still visible as thin, vertical scarring. All the sorrows that a body can bear.

Charlotte hadn't meant anything out of the ordinary.

Ward ran a hand across his eyes. He thought: don't be a drama queen.

Rob had the window seat: and after having left Ward well alone for most of the journey, he poked him now between two ribs.

'There's Llandudno,' he said, pointing out of the window and down. 'We went there for the weekend, once.'

'Not us, you don't mean.'

'With Jane and the kids; a few days away,' Rob went on, ignoring him. 'Ice cream, the beach, the Great Orme.'

'The Great Orme.' He had been on the Great Orme too. He had gone walking on the Great Orme with Martin once. A weekend in Snowdonia. What, God, six, seven years ago already. 'That sounds nice.'

'It was nice. It was a lovely few days.' He paused. 'And now look at us.'

Ward said nothing.

'I sometimes wonder what the hell I'm doing, mate,' Rob went on. 'I move to the other side of the world; I get married, I get divorced, I don't see enough of my kids, I just keep moving and moving.'

Ward nodded. 'I know.'

Rob sat back in his seat; the Great Orme drifted away below them.

A pair of cabin crew, a stewardess, a camp steward, appeared with their trolley, and began to clear away the empty peanut bags, the plastic cups and glasses; the steward looked at Ward, raised an engineered eyebrow, looked away.

Ward was too old for these ruthless, fascistic boys even to waste time, to waste a moment looking at, these days.

He saw Rob watching, smiling briefly, looking away.

The young guys these days, they plucked and preened at themselves far too bloody much – so Ward reflected now, as the ruthless young steward passed on, as the tray tables were stowed all about him, as the cabin warning lights illuminated and the aeroplane began a new sort of vibration, and slipped through dirty grey clouds.

The Irish coast was approaching. Grey too at first, and obscured here and there by grey cloud, and then as the plane flew lower and lower and the coast grew closer and closer – suddenly green, as though in a film shifting from black-and-white to colour. *The Wizard of Oz*. Truly emerald too: a green coast, backed by green hills that faded to purple on their upper slopes, and then vanished into a haze; and the pincer arms of Dún Laoghaire harbour to the north, and now houses and estates, and a slicing motorway, as the mass of south Dublin spread out below. *Come out, come out, wherever you are.* His memory flashing a scene – from long ago, when he was still living unhappily in Dublin, clad in a transparent plastic poncho and seated in a downpour to watch a public screening of *The Wizard of Oz. Come out, come out, wherever you are*, said Glinda, and she waved her long magic wand, and all the gays in the audience tittered appreciatively. *Only bad witches are ugly*, she said, and a long trickle of rain flowed coldly down Ward's neck and spine, to join the puddle of water he was sitting in, poncho or no poncho. *And meet the young lady who fell from a star.* The rain was falling as though a high-pressure hose had been trained on them. *The house began to pitch,* the Munchkins squealed, *the kitchen took a slitch.* 'I thought we could go for a pint after this,' he said through the rain, through the poncho, 'just the two of us.' But Briain shrugged. 'Well, let's see what the lads are at, will we?' Ward opened his eyes as the wheels of the plane thumped onto the runway, and the engines roared. How had the evening ended? – not pints with Briain, not pints with anyone, he had gone home to change out of his soaking clothes, to have a shower, to go alone to bed.

He was aware of Rob glancing at him, glancing again. A growing bustle as their fellow passengers began to stretch, to organise. 'Here we are,' Rob said, an eyebrow quirking up; and Ward nodded, said nothing. No wish to be back. He had put Ireland behind him, and thankfully he was in a line of work in which Ireland figured infrequently; and he had always managed to wriggle out of any dealings with the place. He had become an adept. But not this time. A stolen painting and a lonely, ignored Victorian lady artist were dragging him home, and a slashed throat into the bargain.

Ward blinked as the plane vibrated noisily around him, and then gave up and closed his eyes. Melodrama he hated: give me underplayed, unspoken, he would say, any time. Of course he was aware of it; he wasn't completely stupid. The irony, that he should end up living in the house on Despard Road with Martin, who was adept at a mocking falsetto, who liked to tell dramatic stories with gusto, who had a taste for the dramatic life. This had been one of the attractions, at first. A certain kind of drama, mingled and blended with what Ward took to be comedy, and signalled by that falsetto voice.

'OK?' said Rob.

Martin had slipped into falsetto that very first night – later, when it was just the two of them, in the bar with the heavy, uncomfortable iron chairs, their stomachs filled with Spanish food, their minds and emotions on the tingle for what was still to come. Martin had been mocking some work colleague or other, mimicking this guy's accent. What had it been? – his Essex tones, it had been all about class, as usual, overlaid by a freakish shrill voice. And drawing attention to the red splotch of birthmark on the man's neck. 'It's a second mouth,' Martin shrilled. 'I have a second mouth, when I get tired talking out of my main mouth, I just switch to secondary systems. I'm very lucky in that regard, me.'

Ward laughed, sat forward in the heavy chair, laughed again.

'Moron,' added Martin, switching back to his own pleasant tenor. 'Anyway, that's work, that's what I do. Tell me more about you now.'

That was then.

Now, he mimicked Ward's lisp, the little issue he had with the *th* sound.

Only sometimes though.

Behind his closed eyelids, Ward felt the beginning of tears. 'Yes, fine,' he told Rob, and opened his eyes.

They retrieved their cases from the carousel, elbowed their way out into the arrivals hall, and into a taxi. Dublin blurred past: it was mizzling, and the windows of the car were smeared with wet grime, and the outskirts of Dublin were, Ward thought, not exactly Florence; and the combined effect of low skies, grey light, dirty windows and a surfeit of pebbledash made his heart sink.

'Focus up there, mate.'

'I am bloody focused?'

'You're the opposite of bloody focused, Ward. I need you to translate.'

Point made: and Ward focused up, or tried to; at any rate, he had his mind on the matter at hand by the time the taxi had inched its way into the city centre and dropped the two men on the street. The place looked much the same: clean eighteenth-century lines messed up by modern shop fronts, the busy intersection, a bus here and a bus there, crowds of pedestrians, and tourists bound for the Book of Kells. Neither smart, in spite of the Georgian brickwork, nor especially scuzzy, but rather carefully middling.

And there it was. There was the gallery.

Pauldron

17

And the funeral was something else. All of Deptford turned out, and the exiles returned from Eltham and Charlton. The church – that his father had never attended – was full, the sun shone yellow through the stained glass, and his mum listened as the vicar spoke the words she understood. 'We brought nothing into this world, and it is certain we can carry nothing out. The Lord gave and the Lord hath taken away; blessed be the name of the Lord.' She nodded at that. 'Comfort us again now after the time that thou hast plagued us: and for the years wherein we have suffered adversity. Shew thy servants thy work: and their children thy glory. And the glorious majesty of the Lord our God be upon us: prosper thou the work of our hands upon us, O prosper thou our handiwork.' She bowed her head.

An accident on a building site, John told Stella. 'They rang and told us. I don't really remember the details: I didn't ask too many questions.'

'That's terrible,' Stella said quietly. 'Poor you, and your mother.'

He nodded.

A numbness as the vicar ran through the liturgy. The man of the house, they said to him. Which was laughable: but it would have to do.

'I suppose,' and Stella was silent.

This was in the Prince Regent – which afterwards was filled to the brim. John walked from group to group, *thank you*, and *thank you*, and the old men told him that he was the man of the house now. *What house?* – he wanted to say. *We'll have no house, soon, for God's sake.* His mother stayed at the centre of the pub, amid a tight group of women. A sherry sat on the table, but she did not drink. 'I'm sorry for your trouble,' said the old-time Irish; the English touched her elbow and her shoulder and said little; the party broke up late.

And when the funeral was over, they made his mother move to a city in the sky. Theirs was the last house on Regina Road to die; within weeks, the houses were scoured away.

'We'll make the best of it,' his mother said, and she rolled her hands in her apron, and looked out at the sky and the distant horizon. 'That's all we can do.' At first she went back to Deptford from time to time: a bus and another bus and you were there. But the buses were a nuisance, and the second one was hardly frequent; and with each visit, there were fewer and fewer faces she recognised. The glue was being picked away, and they were being painstaking about it; the old community was scattered across south London. Soon enough, she stopped going, and stayed in her city in the sky, and looked out at her view. There was quite a prospect up there, all the way to the South Downs, and London was green, and filled with the waving crowns of trees. It was pretty, she said, which was as well, because there was precious else to do up there but look, and wait for the day to pass.

Days passed, and time, and a line was drawn, and now she never went back to Deptford. John did, though, just before the wrecking ball went to work; and then again afterwards, to see the scouring for himself. For a long time, they parked cars where Regina Road had once run; there was a long delay in the building process, they told him, on account of the seam of heavy blue clay that ran underneath the houses and down to and underneath the river. Eventually – though this was years later – they built new council houses. So he heard: he never saw them for himself. After he saw the car park, and the pools of rainwater lying on the rutted ground, he too never went back.

The banquette squeaked and juddered. The place was so dark: John did not think he had ever seen the actual shade of the plush velvet with which the banquettes were upholstered: a very deep shade of red, he imagined, and set off by golden paint, a gilt look, as though the banquette was in itself a framed piece. Or it might have been a thick black,

Coca-Cola black. Who knew? – Mildred was an odd bird. But one thing was for sure: the place was as she wanted it to be, it looked as she wanted it to look. Mildred ran the tightest of ships.

The banquette squeaked and juddered. Stella had bounced to her feet, the banquette bouncing with her, and gone along to the little girls' room. 'Just off to powder my nose,' she would say. Or, 'just off to the little girls' room.' Or, 'Oops, a call of nature!' It was the way of her, to speak thus, to speak in her squeaky little-girl voice, to veil or armour herself, to give the appearance of being what some men called a dolly bird.

Stella was no dolly bird. It was amazing, the sort of ideas men would accept.

'The girls are coming with me,' she'd say. Or – standing in front of her swinging wardrobe door in her tiny terraced house at World's End, which was squashed between shops selling incense and candles and herbal teas – she would glance over her shoulder and say, *faux* judiciously, 'Let's see, let's see. I'm not planning to be upstaged by the girls tonight.'

The girls were her breasts – ample, generous, the very best of breasts, in John's opinion. Voluptuous. John liked to stay away from the clichés, but in this case, only *voluptuous* would do. The girls completed her, they didn't upstage her. Though she was only joking about this battle for attention between herself and her girls. Stella and her girls, he could see, had the happiest of relationships. They got along just fine.

Stella's careful act fooled the men – or it fooled most

of them, the foolish ones who looked no further than her yellow hair and her short skirts. They could or would or did not hear the tick-tick-ticking of her brain; or see the glint in her eye as she in a trice sized up a situation. Men, as she was fond of pointing out to John when they were alone, would not know a suit of armour if it fell on top of them.

They were fools, really.

'Not you, obviously.'

What a great act she had going. And it began with her name.

Her name wasn't even Stella.

'Begins with a V,' she said, on that very first evening, 'see if you can guess.' This was in his Camberwell digs: a thin, omnipresent scent of gas from the penny-fed fire; an oilcloth on the enormous table which filled the room, which squeezed his narrow bed against one wall, his cheap tin sink against another. 'I'll sit here, here's lovely,' she said, on her first evening, making the best of it. He had suggested scrambling her an egg, and now he apologised for the place, and asked her to comfy herself up as much as possible.

'It's lovely,' she said. 'But, two eggs, if you have two.'

Scrambling her an egg? They laughed about that, afterwards. Stella hadn't been a pick-up job in some bar, some club. She had been around the college for some time: at any rate, he had been noticing her for some time, though he wasn't sure that she had been noticing him. It was the yellow hair, and the girls, that did the job. The other students, the other women (because after he met Stella and talked to her for a little while, a matter of minutes, he could never use the word 'girls' again) had black hair, black out of a bottle, offputtingly black. Stella's yellow hair had help from a bottle too, probably, but it was a good bottle if so. Her hair stood out as though it were lit under a lamp.

Just noticing, first.

Then he had – after weeks of this – walked up to her one afternoon, in the college lobby, and asked her to go for a coffee with him.

'Would you like to go for a coffee with me some time?' had been his pick-up line. He hadn't even remembered to introduce himself, which was an indication (he admitted later) of his flurried state of mind.

Yellow hair glimpsed, again and again, in the corridors and studios of the college. Dark-clad, like all the other students, albeit with a bust that ensured she caught his eye – but she nevertheless seemed quite ordinary, just another girl with a chest, dressed in black. There was no shortage of such types. He looked away.

It took a little while for him to perceive the glow she seemed to emit. Nothing sexual, nothing particularly to do with her attractions. She was wholly self-possessed, or seemed to be so: and this was unusual among such a throng of the ambitious and the image-conscious as they moved through the college. Her ambition and vision seemed to be elsewhere: she seemed happy to drink her coffee on her own, and her eye was not continually on the rove, glancing over shoulders and out of windows for a sight of a better companion or situation. She was just herself, with a steadiness and an almost tangible rootedness, and she shone a little as a result.

'Would you like to go for a coffee with me some time?'

She looked at him, and raised her left eyebrow. This was one of her tricks: not everybody could master it. She said, 'I will – though you'd better tell me your name, first.'

A blush. 'I'm sorry,' he said. 'My name's John.'

'John. But there must be more than that. I'll need a little more than "John".'

'Irwin,' he said. John Irwin.

'That'll do,' she said, and laughed. 'Though I knew that already. How do you do, John. I'm Stella.'

'Stella.'

She smiled. 'Stella. Stella Wakeham. Well. Shall we go now?'

They went to the cafe all the college students patronised, on Camberwell Green. It stayed open half the night, and it ladled out a sort of chicken stew, or they claimed it was chicken, day and night. It catered to all comers; the chicken stew, at two in the morning, did the job, was a life-saver, set you back on your feet if you were half-cut.

Now, at three in the afternoon, the cafe was almost empty. They sat in the window, and drank reeking black coffee out of inch-thick mugs. Red buses passed by, endless traffic; the Green was hardly green at all.

They sat there all afternoon. The reeking coffee created consternation in their stomachs, but there would be enough time afterwards to worry about that. Then, with the light fading outside, he asked her back for a bite.

'A bite!' – and this time she laughed aloud, laughed her head off.

'I could scramble you an egg.'

Peals of laughter. 'Go on, then. Have you bread?' He had

bread, too. 'Go on then. A scrambled egg and toast will set me up for ever. Have you butter?'

He had butter. 'It isn't much, my place,' he said, already half regretting his offer.

'Whose is? You have bread, and butter, and an egg. Two eggs, if you have them. As long as the eggs are well scrambled, I won't mind a bit what the place is like.'

Well, at least he had managed her expectations. Slowly, they walked up the hill together. The street lamps shone through newly opened plane leaves; late spring and London at dusk, at its most gentle on this mild evening, and the plane leaves were a bright, startling green in the lamplight. 'As long as you don't expect a palace.'

'A palace,' she repeated, and looked around at the great houses that lined the hill: one or two shabby still, with decay all too evident in sill and frame and lintel. More had been restored, beautifully, grandly; a few windows lit softly, already. 'I'm not expecting a palace.' And a pause, and then, 'In fact, I don't want a palace. A palace is the last thing I want.'

He thought that she might have lived in a palace, or the next best thing. Her tones, her accent, the way she carried herself: everything implied that she was posh. There were a lot of posh, confident girls in the college, but here was a poshness of the sort that he hadn't encountered all that much. So: 'Have you ever lived in a palace?' he asked her, and she shook her head, as though it were a serious question.

'Never.'

Veronica, he guessed, and again she shook her head. A silly guess: too Spanish, too Catholic. You most likely didn't get too many nice English girls called Veronica. 'Those awfully strange Spanish statues with great manes of actual human hair,' she said, 'have you ever seen one of those?' He shook his head. 'No, well, I haven't either, but I've seen pictures of them, and they always give me the chills; and I always imagine they're called Veronica.' She shook her head decisively. 'St Veronica, wiping away. So, no.' Vanessa, he guessed: no, but getting close, now. 'I know *so many* Vanessas, darling. You've no idea.' Virginia, he guessed, and this time she nodded her head seriously.

'That's me.'

Virginia.

'It's a terrible name, isn't it?' she said, and pressed on without waiting for a reply. 'Though Ginny it was, mainly. I insisted on that,' she said, and she lifted the heavy coffee cup and sipped. That was where the wicker and the gingham came in, he realised later: for the moment, he only had the name to go on. Ginny. And her fine disgust. That was enough.

Easy to see why she had shed the lot of it.

'From Virginia Water?' he asked.

She laughed. 'My parents aren't as literal as that!' A pause, and then, 'Although no, they are. They're completely as literal as that, what am I saying? Not Virginia Water, though.' But near enough: deepest Berkshire, though she was finished with all that. She was Stella now, and people could take her or leave her.

Stella took the smell of gas and the smallness of the room in her stride: she was a trouper that way – and besides, it was just a place to sleep, wasn't it? One could sleep or not sleep anywhere, was Stella's way of looking at it. 'Not that I'll be sleeping here tonight,' she added, 'because I'm not that sort of girl. Next time, maybe.' And that was a good oilcloth on the table, she said, and ran an appreciative hand across its surface. She was a practical girl – and this gas-smelling room on Camberwell Grove wasn't Berkshire, and that was a good thing, was the bottom line.

'I'm twenty-five today,' he said.

18

He had a name for himself – or rather, he was beginning to acquire one, as he turned twenty-five: for his work, his art, but also for his life. He lived in squalor, the gossip went, in a nasty little place up the hill from the college. In a bedsit, it might be called, though bad even for a bedsit. It was supposed to be bad; he never let anyone near the place, except for the girls he brought back, and sent packing early the next morning, before they could take an inventory of the place. They told tales in the college and in the clubs, about the gassy smell – though this was all water off a duck's back for him.

So he understood. He heard the tales, they were repeated back to him, by the men who were envious of him.

He did a little teaching in the college, to supplement his income. He had a studio there, too, which he filled with difficult, troubling work. He sold a painting here and a painting there; he acquired a few patrons, never women, always men, queers, usually, who were then only too pleased to parade him for their friends. He was fine with the queers: you'd want to be fine with them, in the art world, so that was lucky for him. And the college teaching tided him over – and it was lucky too in another way, as he reflected after he had scrambled Stella her eggs and she had eaten them, and stayed on chatting, and then a little kiss, and then a walk back down under the green-shining plane trees to the bus, and a chaste goodbye, because, she said again, she wasn't the sort of girl who would go to bed with a man the first time she met him: it was lucky that he was in and out of the college, because otherwise he would never have met Stella at all.

So he managed, just about, between teaching and the odd sale. And the fact was that he was pleased with his gas-smelling room on the hill at Camberwell. Deliberately unfashionable, and good to come back to, to close the door, and take a small coin from his pocket, and light the fire, and stay awake all night.

'Oh yes,' said Stella, judiciously on that first evening. 'I can see that. Though, don't be counting on staying here too long.' She gestured out of the window, glanced speculatively at the spruced-up house on the other side of the road. 'These are great houses: the size of them! Give it another eighteen months, and you won't find a run-down house left on this hill. That's the way it's going now, even in places like Camberwell.' She might have been an art student, Stella, but she had a good, smart head on her shoulders.

'Well,' John said, looking around the room, 'we'll see.'

He didn't look eighteen months ahead, or eight months, or two months. And he didn't, needless to say, give much thought to home, to any future home. He knew better, now. The Lord gave and the Lord taketh away, and that was the Lord's business, but when the council began to take tips from the Lord – well, then you were in trouble.

His mother had died early in the city in the sky: a cancer swept through her in a matter of weeks, and she threw herself into this new experience with something like gusto. The tower, with its wide views and gales and excesses of fresh air, had worn her out: it was 'too much, altogether,' she said, and she closed her eyes and went with the gobbling, greedy cancer.

She seemed to expect that her son would be fine, left alone. Regina Road with its starched antimacassars and its crisp pastry might just as well never have existed. The furniture came with her, but the antimacassars were washed and folded in tissue paper and placed in a drawer, never to be seen again; and the three-piece suite, naked without the antimacassars, filled up the sitting room in the sky, so much so there was hardly room to move. She didn't mind that, because she didn't move much, after a while. No pastry, either. Not much cooking, and John she left to fend for himself.

It was as though she had placed the entirety of her past life into the drawer with the antimacassars. It was as though he had been placed there, too, and his dead father, and just about everything that meant anything to him – and his disorientation was all the more dreadful for being silent.

She didn't want to know about it, and there was nobody else to tell. There was only this light-filled flat in the sky, and the wind that screamed on stormy nights, and whistled thinly, along with the water pipes, most of the rest of the time.

She seemed, in fact, to think that he would be well rid of her: all those hours spent trailing home, back and forth to their tower, up in the lift and down again: this time could be put to better use. He could get himself a place of his own (with what? – but this thought also didn't seem to occur to her) and get on with his life, without any irritations or distraction. None of this was said, and so he couldn't quarrel with any piece of it, but it was all perfectly understood, and none of it made sense.

And, get on with what, exactly?

But when she was gone – and it was a quiet crematorium affair for her, and no drinking in the Prince Regent to send her on her way; that was all definitively over, now – he did indeed leave their flat in the sky and return to earth. Maybe his mum had had some sort of premonition of what he might do, and what he might become: because he did feel a sense of liberation. Guiltily, with grief distilled inside these sensations of freedom he was feeling – yet liberation, just the same. It had been punishing (for him, though apparently not for her; at any rate, she disguised it very well) to see how cancer consumed a body from within, leaving skin stretched over a skull, thin skin and seemingly translucent, stretched across the knobs of his mum's wrist bones in a way that horrified him, that made him want to vomit. Like canvas stretched too tightly over a picture frame, so tightly that it might at any moment rip and burst apart, and expose what lay beneath. He had seen too much now of his parents' bones.

And yes: it was liberating too, after a fashion, to be completely alone in the world, to have nobody else to think or care about. Yes: his mum had been on to something, there, well before he had realised it himself.

Though, he wasn't completely alone, for there were grants, you could almost say that there was plenty of money – in his terms, at any rate: there was enough to live on, which constituted plenty. There was, he felt, guilt from on high that had to be assuaged: they had ripped up his community, and there were plenty of people in the same boat. There had been crimes committed, and they would have to be paid for, in cold cash. And John was pleased to seem to assuage this guilt by taking the money, by applying to art college and being welcomed in, by accepting the grants, by studying and acquiring his qualifications. They made him study photography and a little history of art; they made him look at daguerreotypes, and talk about Cubism – but not too much, thank God; he had an abundance of time to work, to paint, to layer his materials onto a bare canvas: cries of pain, at first, and then bones, grey and white, a slashing of paint onto black canvas.

Charcoal, sometimes, though now at least he didn't have to go scavenging the old bomb sites for bits of burnt wood. They paid for the charcoal, too.

The colour – this he kept tucked away, for now.

'Not everyone's cup of tea, John,' an uneasy tutor told him, early in this process, looking at the bones, the greys and whites and blacks, 'but look,' backtracking as soon as the words were out of his mouth, 'do what you have to do. And the technique is interesting, certainly.'

And to be sure, his pieces did not generally find favour: but this was London, and it was the 1970s now, and there were always eyes watching, and taking in the new stuff. A piece, a large canvas, large enough to fill a wide wall, was purchased quietly at an end-of-year show; then another and another. An exhibition in a small gallery, and then another: and so it went on.

And invitations: to dinner parties, with bad food but amusing company, in Chelsea and Fulham and Kensington – and sometimes further afield, by the pioneers who, just as they were tarting up the houses on the hill at Camberwell, had also tarted up what had once been hovel houses in Notting Hill and near the old cattle market on the Caledonian Road. Their gambles had paid off: their ropy neighbourhoods were ropy no longer, and now they gathered, in groups of ten or twelve around long dining tables, all candlelight and stripped and polished wood, congratulating themselves on the glorious Georgian and Victorian houses that they had saved from the wrecking ball.

He was an object of scrutiny and even a certain degree of fascination, and he knew it from the off. He knew about Bedlam: about the inmates being viewed, as animals are viewed at the zoo, by the rich seeking diversion and entertainment. These evenings were Bedlam too, and he was the lunatic, the tiger, and they were gathered to take him in. He was a feather in their cap.

'Oh, I know all about that,' Stella told him. 'I know all those people, even if I haven't actually met all of them.' She shuddered: not fastidiously, but from pure boredom. These people had infested her life.

'You don't think I'm being unfair?'

'Unfair?'

'On these people.'

'Heavens, no.' She shrugged. 'Well, who knows: London is full of people, and perhaps not all of them are dreadful. But on balance, darling, I think you probably have them just about right.'

One such invitation: a chief patron, on the scout for a new piece and happy to wait for it. Coming to view John's progress, to observe the dirty whites and greys standing up on each element of a new triptych, whipped like waves, like a dirty froth or scum on the beach, surrounding a dark void. The same thing again, and again, a compulsion. *Connective*, John called the triptych: the patron – Etienne – already had *Tissue 1*, *Tissue 2* and *Tissue 3*.

'His walls are many,' said Stella later, 'and his appetite insatiable.'

As Etienne was leaving, he asked John to dinner the following Friday. He was one of the queers, though he was at pains to be clear that there was no agenda of that sort.

'A mixed bunch,' he said, 'old friends and a few TV people; I think you'll find them amusing.'

John nodded. Why not?

'Super, wonderful. Shall we say seven thirty?'

John nodded.

'I thought I might make my beef-and-mango casserole,' Etienne said proudly. 'It's quite special.'

Etienne was Etienne Foster – the Etienne a nod to a French mother, another feather – and he lived off the Brompton

Road. He gave John copious, anxious instructions, right and left and right.

'I'll find it, don't worry,' John said. 'Can I bring a friend?'

'But of course you can,' Etienne said, extending his arms wide. 'A man?'

'My girlfriend. Stella.'

Etienne's face fell. A girl, London was full of them; when men were so much more interesting. 'Stella, lovely.'

Stella, though, was not pleased. 'Oh no, I'll have to pass on that one. Honestly, darling, didn't I say, wasn't I clear, entirely clear?' She stood with hands on hips. 'Absolutely not: these affairs make me want to dash my *brains* out against a wall, as you very well know.'

'I said you would,' he told her calmly. 'He says he'll make his special beef-and-mango casserole.' He had learned a thing or two from her about the husbanding of one's resources. And she was a stickler for manners, try though she might to shed her English middle-class rigours. She would go. 'Too late now.'

Stella was too pragmatic, he could see, to waste energy on an argument. But she drew a line. 'Oh, very well. But never *ever* again.' A pause. 'The Brompton Road, you say? Well, we'll see what's what.' Another pause, and then, 'Oh God, what a joyless Friday evening, to be spent with bores and prisses and Uranians. I do *hate* you.'

That was the beginning of the end, although John could not know it at the time.

19

I'll have to pass on that one, Stella thought. She set her mind to thinking of a way to wriggle gracefully out of an evening that surely would be not merely boring, but objectionable. She had in fact glimpsed this Etienne person on the lurk in the college, sniffing after a triptych here and a triptych there, and he had seemed hardly worth anyone's time or attention. But not so: full pockets commanded attention – even from John, even if he appeared to disdain the very notion of money. She had watched Etienne glance at some new work in one of the studios: pointing, waving largely, his finger wavering over one piece and then another. She had asked a discreet question or two about him: he hardly cared, she was told, about the art, he hardly looked at the art he bought. He was a collector – of art, in theory, but in fact of reputations. Of people, Stella realised, and their room for manoeuvre. He liked to flourish sets, as one might spread a deck of cards across a table, or arrange a tea service in a glass cabinet. His walls were many. Money, Stella thought. He collected money.

And he was busy collecting John Irwins, now: a full set of difficult, painful, jagged paintings, all white and grey against black. To convert into money, in time.

Nothing of the real thing. Her flesh crawled.

Now, she considered how best to protect John from such a person. By diplomacy? By a dropped comment, an aside? Would John even care? – money was money, after all, and a wall was a wall, and a collection was a collection. But surely he would care.

But – no. She couldn't quite say. She couldn't quite put her finger on what John might or might not feel about it. She sat, once again, with her disquiet.

He had drawn her portrait. She had sat for him, for an hour only, in his studio at the college, and he had quickly sketched her: a soft, crumbling white crayon on green paper. The room faced north, and its large windows let in a flood of clear, cold light – even on that misty morning. But the mist, though it had not affected the air, seemed to cling to the lines and edges of the portrait. John had fuzzed its edges with his middle finger, systematically; and the result was a cloud, a snowfall on a green field.

'Impressionistic,' Stella said, 'I like it.'

He shrugged. 'I was thinking about snow, and this is what came out.' He paused. 'Etienne likes the *Connective* sequence, he says. He says he wants to buy them, the lot of them. A good price, too.'

'Snow?'

An unfocused glance and another shrug. 'And ice. I was thinking about the ice on the river, that time, and then I began thinking about snow. That's all.'

She nodded.

'Are you going to let him buy the *Connective* pieces?'

She had to repeat herself: and now again he shrugged, seeming to haul himself back from some edge or precipice. 'I suppose I will.' She looked at him, and looked at the snow-burdened portrait, and said nothing more.

Now, she contemplated a dinner with Etienne, considered ways by which this might be evaded, thought about means by which she could distance John from this person, this collector.

'I might pass on dinner,' she said lightly, 'unless you mind awfully.'

'I need you to come,' he replied, in tones that brooked no opposition. Stella nodded. But she wondered what he did in fact need. Did he need her? Did he need Etienne? The latter, perhaps, for affirmation, and bread and butter. But the former? – well, she wasn't certain any longer about that. There was a gap there, she was realising, that could not, perhaps, ever be bridged.

'I've been working on something else,' he said.

'Have you?'

'Yes,' he said. 'Inspired by you, I should add.'

She raised an eyebrow, tried to shed her gloomy mood. Beef-and-mango casserole, had he said? That didn't sound like fun.

'A distemper piece,' he said.

She looked at him. Distemper? She said, 'Won't that – fade?'

'Yes. Fade. Exactly.' Though, not always. 'You remember Emily Sandborne?'

'Oh yes, poor Mrs Sandborne, that was sad. That awful husband of hers.' Stella paused. 'Oh – yes, that piece, that discovered piece. That was distemper too.'

'*The Jewel* – it didn't fade. Nobody knows why. So this one might fade, or it might not fade; I don't really mind what it does.'

'Well, good for you, darling. Plunge in.' She watched him. 'Nobody knows why it didn't fade?'

He shook his head. Nobody knew. Nobody had been able to find out.

'Gosh,' Stella said. 'So, she was cleverer than the lot of us, was Mrs Sandborne. Well, that must have been a comfort to her.'

She continued to study him.

He would have the cloth stretched tightly across the frame, as though he were some Eastern European artist with an eye on materials and how much they cost. Keep the price down. Use as little as possible. The linen would be stretched almost to breaking point, like his mum's skin on her temples, on the knobs of her wristbones. No need to explain.

In the cold, clear light of his studio space, he worked quickly, and the piece came together. A length of linen, bought – and not cheap, either – in the haberdashery department of Peter Jones, from a snoot who couldn't understand what a man was doing, wandering around looking for a good linen tablecloth.

'A wedding present, sir?'

No.

'A gift for your wife, perhaps.'

A gift for my life.

'No.'

Not too large and not too small: but he couldn't decide on the size, so the snoot would just have to take each tablecloth out of its smart, careful packaging, and show him.

'But, sir—'

'I insist.'

He insisted: and whey-faced, the snoot did as she was bid.

'That one.'

Beautifully hemmed and simple, thickly woven yet translucent, creamy-white but not white in itself. Perfection.

'I'll take it.'

He prepared and applied the size, he set the linen aside for the size to set, he waited impatiently – for there was never any time to wait, not once he had an idea – and now he prepared his colours. His hands trembled a little – but no: Stella was right. You could, if you wanted to, she'd said, and now his yellow shone like the dense brown-gold of the Thames in sunlight; and the silver had the sheen of the Thames shingle at low tide; and the blue was the washed blue of early morning, when two little boys went scrambling down to the Quaggy to see what could be fished from the tidewrack. And the green – not that anyone could be expected to understand this – was the pure, welling green that shone on the very edges of a polluted London sunset, viewed from his mum's living room in her city in the sky.

'Look, Mum,' he'd said, once, 'can you see that colour, that green? You don't often see that.'

She looked. 'No.'

It wouldn't last, this distemper piece – but that was part of the deal; and Stella understood this, too.

'Yes, I see,' she said – this, after a long period of silence, as she took in this single piece, this large piece, this cloth transformed into something that dazzled. 'Give it its time, and let it go,' she said. 'Is that what it is?'

He nodded.

'Yes, I see,' she said again, and smiled. 'It sets my heart beating,' she said, 'fit to burst. And not for public consumption.'

'No, I mean yes,' he said. 'Yes, exactly.'

20

'Why,' Stella repeated, and shrugged. 'Well, why not, really.'

A fresh afternoon on the Embankment. The pier, and pleasure craft, and in the distance a train rattled across Hungerford Bridge, striking out for points south. A bus belched past, and another. Noise and diesel fumes and traffic.

'Let's get away from the river,' she added. 'Let's go to St James's Park.'

They walked in silence. On Whitehall, he asked the question again.

'Tell me, though, why Stella?' He was not insisting on knowing: but there was a little curiosity.

She looked up into the lime trees, around at the groomed buildings. Nearby, Big Ben struck the quarter-hour. A shrug. 'I suppose you could call it a wish, or an invocation.' A pause. 'The pouring of a libation.'

A libation?

She laughed lightly. 'Did I ever tell you?' – but of course she knew she hadn't told him – 'when I was thirteen or fourteen, and a difficult, spotty, monstrous creature, I would take a glass of milk, or a glass of squash, and pour it into the ground in our garden, in our little orchard, as a libation. I read about libations in some book or other, in Daddy's library, God knows why there was a book like that in a place like that, but anyway, there was, and I read about libations in it, and off I would go, and make a libation of my own.' A pause. 'Several, in fact.'

A libation? He was impressed. Nobody had poured libations in Deptford, that he'd ever been aware of.

'No, you never did tell me that.'

Stella laughed again. 'I suppose you think I'm a fruitcake.'

'No, I don't think you're a fruitcake,' he told her. 'But—'

'Why?'

He nodded.

'Well, that was the serious thing.' She looked serious too: they entered the park, and she took a breath of the fresher air, and frowned a little. 'Very serious indeed. I read Swift's poems to Stella, you know, Jonathan Swift in Dublin, and Stella was his soulmate, his love, his noble, great-hearted love, and she seemed so sensible too, as well as love-inspiring, and he wrote all these poems to her, and I read them; and I had Daddy's damned book, and it occurred to me that I could pour a libation, or two, or three, and request help to get away from Berkshire, and away from everything, and meet a man, and have a love like Swift and Stella.'

She had spoken much faster than usual – or rather, she had sped up noticeably as the words tumbled out.

Embarrassment, or mortification, or – was it possible, in Stella? – nerves, and now she had to pause for breath.

On the lake, willows and swans and ducks, and a heron motionless by the water's edge.

'I don't know these poems,' John said. What poems did he know? He looked up at the fresh green of the willows. 'What sort of a love did they have?'

'Oh, well, I mean, the first thing to say, really, is that they had quite a complicated *life*; and there was another woman, a younger woman, and then Stella herself went off and died on him, to cap it all. So it wasn't much of a life. But the love.' Again she stopped.

'Yes,' John said. 'The love. What was the love like?'

The love was beautiful, she told him, then. The lake water shone suddenly, a sudden onset of what felt like grace: and she told him that the love that had caught her eye, as a sullen, trapped girl in Berkshire: the love was respectful. Mature. Paced and balanced and based in mutual delights, on a meeting of minds, on beauty and harmony. And Swift wrote poems to capture the essence of all this.

'And so you poured a libation to the gods, to bring you a similar love.'

'In our garden. In our orchard,' she said in her best Berkshire tones.

'Oh yes, you said that, your orchard.'

'I didn't *plant* the wretched orchard.'

He looked into the shimmering water. 'These poems. I'll go and read them for myself.'

Did he – she asked again, there by the lake – think she was a fruitcake? He shook his head. It was unorthodox, for sure: but then it was unorthodox to get down on your knees and pray in a church, or beside your bed, depending on how somebody looked at it.

'I was just a child.'

He nodded again. A libation was fair enough. Easier on the knees, too.

It all gave him a lot to think about. The nature of love, and the love that somebody might want in their life, and the means by which it might be acquired. He gazed at the heron and said slowly, 'Maybe libations will become all the rage.'

Anyone can pour a libation, Stella told him, anyone can make an offering. To the gods, to the dead, to the dear departed. You just needed a little bit of wine, or rum, or anything at all, and a candle, and an intention.

To the Devil himself, in his coal-black waistcoat.

He thought of his broken mother, and his pulverised and splintered father. He thought of his gran, long ago now, sick with longing for the North. Would he pour a libation, would he say a prayer, would he ask for their help?

And help with what, exactly? There was so much: he would hardly know where to begin.

And the nature of love. Was that what they had? Stella was observing the waterfowl, now, she was back to herself, she was looking at the heron that seemed to be looking back at her. And yet she was subtly different. Something had shifted, just a little. She had revealed something of herself, of her wishes, of the trajectory of her life that had brought her here, to this lake in the middle of London, and that had not yet run its course. She had told him something, she had trusted that he would not laugh at her childhood self. A libation? She had told him of her dreams. And that was good.

He slid a glance in her direction. And yet. She had relinquished a good deal, to be where she was today: and now, suddenly, he saw that she might travel further on, and that she might leave him behind. A verse swam suddenly into his head. It had been spoken in the crematorium.

Lord, let me know mine end, and the number of my days: that I may be certified how long I have to live.

Would she leave him for dead?

He knew, suddenly, what he ought to ask for. He also knew he could never ask for help: this was not his style.

They walked on, under the heron's eye, along the shining lake.

21

On the Friday, they came blinking to the surface at South Kensington station, and walked slowly through the side streets. They were late, as usual – Stella's timekeeping was even more atrocious than his own – and his bottle of cheap greenish Portuguese white, his usual choice, was warming in his hand. Not that any of this mattered – not to him, at any rate.

'Too bad,' he said shortly when Stella queried the cheap greenish white. 'We're impoverished artists, remember? We arrive cheap, they feed us well, and we sing for our supper, isn't that the deal?'

Stella nodded, angled her head in false sadness. Her parents had recently disinherited her, and had taken the trouble of writing to tell her so. The letter had arrived written on her father's headed cream-coloured notepaper ('he orders it from Bond Street'), and Stella had read it aloud to him, over the oilclothed table on Camberwell Grove. 'I'm beyond the pale,' she said thoughtfully, turning the page over and over. 'A python strike. Well, goodness.'

'Are you – are you alright?' He felt truly shocked, even if she did not. She looked at him: the buttercup yellow of the oilcloth was shining on the underside of her chin, as buttercups themselves were supposed to do, and she seemed to gleam a little in the otherwise dingy light.

'Oh yes,' she said. 'Well, no: but I will be, given a little time.' Family money came first, she had explained to him: and if she couldn't be trusted to marry well and bring the money with her into another generational safe haven – well, it would all go to her sister instead. 'Nobody talks about it, it's the height of vulgarity to even *mention* it, but that's the way it works, you know, darling, in that class. In my class. It's all about the money.' She set the page down gently on the yellow oilcloth. 'Money, money, money, money, money. Well, there are some things a girl should never do. Will you make me tea?'

He nodded, and moved silently to the tiny hob.

'Some tea,' she said, 'and I shall be quite my*self* again.' But his eye could detect the dusty film of grief in her eyes that night, and for days afterwards. A dry layer of sadness, like the dust on a wall. Money, money, money, money, money. Stella could do without money – but she couldn't live without love.

The house off the Brompton Road was very handsome. It was

one of a curving terrace of white townhouses, all columns and elegance, facing a private, gated park. Impossibly posh. 'No pioneers here,' Stella said as they moved slowly along the graceful sweep. No: the pioneers would be disgusted to live in a house like this. 'Gosh, what a thought I've just had.'

'What's that?'

'Just, let's pray my parents aren't here.'

They mounted the steps, she rang the bell. She knew this terrain. He, in spite of his careless bottle of cheap Portuguese white, knew it less well, and was in his heart less at ease. This was a long way from Deptford. The door opened.

'Welcome, John. I'm so glad you could come.' Etienne spread his arms wide; behind him, a wide lamplit hall, dark walls hung thickly, a graceful staircase ascending. 'Please, come in. And you must be—' and he beamed at Stella.

'Stella,' Stella said. 'Lovely to meet you, and thank you so much for including me.'

'It's a pleasure,' said Etienne, smiling even more broadly. Queers understood Stella: John had noted this over the months they had been together, and moving through London together, and been thrown together with all manner of people. Women were wary, by and large, and men liked to think of going to bed with her, you could see it in their eyes – and queers delighted in her company, they clapped their hands in delight, almost, when she appeared amongst them. What fun she would be, what style she had. It happened every single time. And, much though she liked to complain about the Uranians, as she called them, Stella was fond of them too: 'They love me, the Uranians, they really do. Why, I simply do not know.'

And now Etienne did clap his hands.

'Your coat, your bag!' he carolled, Stella's remarkable effect waxing now with a speed that was almost alarming. 'Let me take your beautiful wraps!'

'Well, not all of them, I hope, darling,' Stella said, reprovingly. ('They seem to want me to *beat* them, darling,' she had told John one evening. 'Nicely, I mean. I don't quite understand it. They actually *ask* me. They seem to think I carry a carpet-beater around with me, and that nothing would please me better than to flourish it, and then beat them on their bare bottoms. They act as though they would simply *love* it. It really is the strangest thing.') Her girls appeared as she shed her light jacket and her scarf and handed Etienne her bag. John was left to hang his own jacket (second-hand); he had half expected a butler to lurk invisible in the shadows.

'And you found us quite easily!' Etienne went on. Then he took Stella's arm, and John's elbow, and in another moment, they were in the drawing room. A mass of paintings, and more dark-red walls, lit with white beeswax candles and yellow lamplight.

'Friends, this is John Irwin, the artist I've been telling you about. You've all seen his work,' Etienne said with some energy, his arm still on John's sharp elbow, 'including in this very room: and now here he is! And – Stella!' he added, as though this were the Royal Variety Performance, and he the compère. 'This is Stella!'

Quickly now, Etienne introduced the room: a male television producer here and another one there, a male television personality whose face John recognised dimly. A pair of women, one older, all skin tanned like leather and hanging jewels, another younger and leggy with blonde hair, of the type he knew could be found on every Chelsea street and shop, and eclipsed, already by Stella's mere presence in the same room. Names gabbled rapidly by Etienne, names forgotten in an instant, drinks dispensed with miraculous rapidity.

Stella, as it turned out, knew both women – though not through her parents. An art college connection and another connection, leading from this pair of women to Stella: and now they greeted her warmly. 'Ginny, darling,' said the leggy, blonde woman, the eclipsed woman, 'come and sit right beside me.' She tapped the seat, as though Stella were a hound, to be brought to heel. 'I want to hear all your news.'

'No, no,' Etienne said. 'Stella's seat is here,' and he gestured at the empty space beside him. 'Come and sit beside me, Stella.' He was the host, after all. He could crack the whip when he really wanted a thing.

'Goodness,' Stella said, and she shrugged her shoulders and held aloft the palms of her hands in a theatrical gesture that John knew now, and loved, 'how one is torn!' But she settled herself beside Etienne, as instructed. Already she seemed to be having a good time, her terrors of boredom and a surfeit of bores and prisses and Uranians forgotten.

John himself was having a good time, although his version of a good time differed from that of Stella. He was having a good time by wandering the elegant room and taking in the material on the walls. The paint itself was – well, it was clearly devastatingly expensive, was the first thing to be noticed and appreciated. You couldn't get that chalky finish from any old paint. The red of the walls was rich and pure, and the paint added a depth that was marvellous, that set the blood racing a little faster in his veins. Some day, he thought, some day, I'll have walls like this. Etienne knew his stuff.

And what a collection hung on these red walls. He could see clustered there some of the most cutting-edge names in London – and he was not beyond feeling enormous satisfaction at seeing *Tissue 1*, and *Tissue 2*, and *Tissue 3* hanging in pride of place. He tried, and succeeded, in taking a mental step back from the wall, in looking at his paintings with something approaching dispassion. But the force of these pieces was palpable: their naked power, the roar of the empty spaces that filled each canvas, the layers of white and grey paint that rose up from the surface in a mound of bones, whirling around the empty space. The subtle differences that marked each piece, the terror that each inspired – surely – when placed together.

He remembered his colours, leaping like jewels from the linen cloth in his studio.

He looked across the room to where Stella sat with Etienne. With her latest Uranian chum. She gesticulated largely, delivered the punchline, laughed. Etienne laughed with her, already in thrall. Longing, John assumed, for Stella to lash him across his bare buttocks until he screamed. John blinked. Would she not look across, would she not glance over to see what he was seeing, to take in the triptych in what now seemed its natural, its inevitable home, against these deep and dusty red walls?

She would not. Already she had begun another story.

He turned again to the wall.

The two women rejected by Stella now sidled along the wall to meet him. 'She's a darling, Ginny, isn't she?' said the younger one, the most rejected one. 'A treasure,' she added.

'She is,' John said, and he noticed, as he always noticed, how a certain kind of person blinked and almost flinched at the sound of his accent assaulting their highly bred ears. *She is*: was all it took. *She is*: scored through with something alien and uncouth. Of course the flinch was wholly involuntary, and it was caught just a fragment of a second too late. Manners mattered in these circles: neither of these two would be rude just for the sake of it. But there it was, almost imperceptible, perfectly perceptible. 'Although to me, she's Stella.'

'Stella,' the younger woman exclaimed, and across the room Stella glanced and smiled. 'Of course, she's Stella now.' She didn't say it unpleasantly, or bitchily, or with any tincture of sourness. She sounded just a little nonplussed. 'Why *Stella*, I wonder?'

'She just liked the name, I suppose,' he said lightly, and his Deptford vowels crashed from his mouth and onto the polished floorboards.

22

'I suppose she did,' the blonde woman said. 'Stella: a star.
Well, it *is* a nice name.'

'It is, rather,' agreed her companion, gamely.

Now, he was not having an interesting time. Sometimes
he did, at these events (though this was a cut above; this
was the poshest house he had ever been in; he knew that
Etienne worked at ITV, and there must be money in that,
but surely there must be – think of the house – family
money there, too; and granted, seeing his own paintings
hanging on the expensively dusty walls certainly was a
help), sometimes he found himself laughing his head off,
against his better judgement; sometimes, he told stories of
Old Deptford, capitalised, which made them all listen and
exclaim, though none of them had ever been in Deptford
in their lives, needless to say, and never would go there,
not if you paid them. Deptford equalled, yes, Bedlam:

that was clear, and he exploited the fact. They adored the authenticity of his stories: the smells and the sounds and the sights, the lazy slap of the Thames on its shingle and mud banks, the market traders and the strange churches. They delighted in hearing about all that: it bolstered their sense of superiority, of having been blessed in the lottery of life. But it was important that he didn't go on about it all too much – which was fine; he had good judgement on that score.

Tonight, though, was different. Etienne seemed quite relaxed: almost too relaxed, almost as if he didn't care all that much if people were having a good time or not; he was laughing a lot himself and drinking a little too steadily (and still no sign of dinner), but he wasn't tending to the conversation as a good host should; John watched him over the rim of his wine glass. And the other men seemed mere functionaries, though the television personality had a thing or two to say, mainly about himself. And the women were no better, no more interesting. A *woman* leading the Conservative Party, they said: wasn't it *amazing*? Though, that *voice* of hers: wasn't it awful? She'd need to do something about her voice, or she could forget about winning a general election. It was all just a little boring: but it wasn't, of course, the boredom that was bothering him. Stella was too alive, too brightly lit, too vibrant.

Dinner, at last: a bright green soup. The blonde woman seated beside him, with Stella on the other side of the table. Heavy silver cutlery, scrupulously polished, and heavy, green-tinted glassware from Czechoslovakia, complete with air bubbles caught and held in the element. A tablecloth in a shade of oatmeal, linen – 'Irish linen,' the blonde woman sighed, and passed her hand over the cloth, 'lovely' – and candles in tall antique French silver holders.

Yes, he would like, some future day, for such things to be his, too.

Later, as promised, beef-and-mango casserole, held in a silver tureen, and complete with a jaunty silver serving spoon. Etienne dispensed the casserole, Stella passed the potatoes, the candles shone in their silver holders. The blonde woman looked at the tureen and pursed her lips.

'Didn't we have this last time too, dearest?' – and Etienne blushed a little.

'Did we?'

'Oh, I think so. I remember I liked it a lot: but you know what some people do, they keep their menus, you know, in a menu book, and cross-reference them, so they don't make these mistakes. You should try that yourself, dearest.'

'Now, everyone,' Stella said and she commanded the table, surveyed the room, 'I think we should all look at Etienne for a moment – just a moment, just long enough to allow him to reflect on this *faux pas*. Come on now: reflect – beginning,' and she glanced at her slender wristwatch, 'now.'

Etienne laughed and his flush faded. They all laughed, and the blonde woman sat back in her chair.

'It's lovely, darling,' Stella said now to Etienne, meaning the casserole. 'Delicious. You are clever. A star.'

'Star anise, don't you mean?'

'Do I?' Stella said and nibbled another little bite, the tiniest bite of casserole. 'Gosh yes, I taste it now. Where did you get such a thing? Even more clever, darling. A hunter, too.'

She was kind, Stella. Sensitive to the feelings, the needs of others. Nothing of the bitch about her. John had always seen this – beginning that very first evening in the gassy bedsit on Camberwell Grove. The oilcloth was attended to, the eggs praised, the gassy smell ignored. And tonight, she was being kind, being sensitive to a fairy. There was nothing here to dislike. Even the woman who had flung herself back in her seat: even she was smiling again. Stella was a good egg.

Perhaps it was the patter of this evening, the patter of all these evenings. *Darling*, and *dearest* and *gosh, yes*, and *I see, how clever you are* – it all ran in the air like water in the pipes. Like sewage in the drains, John thought sometimes, in his dark moments: filling and spouting and seemingly never-ending, the language of a certain English class effortlessly pleased with itself, self-perpetuating, hatchet-ruthless at asserting itself, at getting its own way. Open to newness – to the likes of John himself – so long as this novelty could be corralled, and managed, and controlled.

He ate his beef-and-mango casserole.

She hardly needed him, of course. Was that it? She had her own place: that little house at World's End ('bought by Daddy,' she said dismissively, before the estrangement, before the severing of ties) and a little money had been settled on her when she turned eighteen. Not much, but enough to get by, which was now just as well: she was not quite, then, an epitome of high-minded and courageous independence. Not that he judged her for that: a little money, a little stash in the bank, was what every artist ought to have. It set them free – from their families, not least. Good for her.

But yes: it meant that Stella hardly needed him. Not at all on a material level. And her attitude, and her quest for a specific kind of love, and her focus and her libations, poured out into the soil of Daddy's apple orchard long ago – taken together provided her with another kind of independence, the sort that frightened him, chilled and froze him.

In his darkest moments, he told himself that he was inadequate to her needs. At night, lying awake – sometimes she was lying beside him, in her house; sometimes he was breathing in the gas alone, in his little room in Camberwell – this thought would come to him, infrequently at first, and then more and more often. Their trajectories were different – but no, because paths and journeys can be replotted, can be rethought. Inadequacy is different again, and sometimes there is nothing to be done about it.

He took up his heavy, bubbled Czechoslovak glass. If he flung it, right now, at Etienne's dusty red walls, if the glass shattered and its shards flew into the tureen of beef-and-mango casserole, and into the potatoes, and into the linen tablecloth—

Well, it would cause a sensation, for certain: but it wouldn't make him feel any better. He sipped, and set the glass down on the linen.

The blonde woman, who seemed designated tonight as his bad fairy companion, said, 'Delicious, isn't it? Star anise, as Ginny says, and the mango is delightful. A treat, altogether.' Then she added, 'How did you meet?'

He gave her a version.

'Lovely. To find someone. You're so lucky,' she added, almost visibly comparing his Deptford tones to Stella's

Berkshire ones, her carriage and tilted chin to his, and his, her past and her present and her future to his, and his, and his. 'So lucky.' She sighed. 'I'm divorced, myself. Already divorced, at my age. Imagine! I can hardly believe it.'

No. It wasn't that Stella didn't need him.

It was that she couldn't have him.

It was that there was a part of him that he couldn't give to anyone, Stella included. It was that she understood this, now, or had been in the process of understanding it, that day by the lake, under the heron's unblinking eye. It was that she was seeing the end of the road.

And his colour, and his distempered cloth: they wouldn't be enough to hold her to him.

The room swam before his eyes.

23

'Mildred's?' She didn't in the least want to go to Mildred's. It was too late, she had eaten too much, and she had drunk too much of Etienne's good wine (she had given their own cheap, green Portuguese the very widest of berths; her head would be bad in the morning as it was, without driving a Portuguese axe through it), and she had breathed in a little too much cigar smoke.

No, she wanted to go home.

But. Etienne had never been to Mildred's.

'Haven't you? Never? Well, we'll remedy that tonight.'

She heard John's voice, his deep voice, his carrying tones. His decisiveness. That was that.

She needed, really, to go home. Alone, preferably: to lie in her small bed in her small house, on her own, and think through the evening. There had been a stickily damp orange cake, dense with almonds, to follow the beef-and-mango casserole, and it was then that this fellow had made his move. She had been aware of Paddy York's voice the entire evening, through the bright green soup and the beef-and-mango casserole: impossible, indeed, to be unaware of his voice, for he appeared not to need to take a breath, he spoke in great dense blocks of text, not even sentences, on and on and on. Not opinionated, not, apparently, needing to talk over anyone, as such, but rather talking as water might foam over a waterfall. Unceasing, unceasing.

The good Lord preserve her from the likes of him.

He was a personality: she knew that. In front of the camera, but also behind the camera, a good sound business head with a Cambridge education and a little black book growing, so they said, by an inch a day. Paddy York, Patrick York, with his own programme, his own programmes, his fingers in a thousand pies.

A house just around the corner too, newly purchased, and a housekeeper installed in the basement, tempestuous but a treasure, so they said. Of course all this was neither here nor there. There was more to life than tempestuous housekeepers and all the rest of it, as she well knew.

And she had to keep an eye on John, who seemed a little tense, a little downcast. He had been fine earlier, as they had taken their bus from Camberwell to Victoria, and their tube from Victoria to South Kensington, and their legs from South Kensington to this candlelit haven, this palace with its dusted walls. But – perhaps it was being placed beside what-was-her-name that did the mischief, perhaps she had bored him into a state of desperation, she was a sweet girl, they said, but not at all bright, and even her husband had given up in the end – he had seemed low all through dinner. Even the sight of the paintings, his own paintings, on Etienne's walls had provided only the briefest of fillips.

And glass after glass of wine.

She had been watching him throughout the meal, and she was feeling the strain. Her own sense of honour called upon her to laugh with Etienne, who was a sweet man, and listen to him, and joke, and spread some good conversation around the table, and she had done all of these things, while simultaneously keeping her eye, her third eye, on John.

How many eyes was a girl supposed to have? It was a strain: she wasn't a professional *juggler*.

With the sticky orange cake came a change in energy: chairs pushed back, for Etienne liked his guests to shift around the table and to bring their fine china plate, their orange cake, with them. Etienne himself moved off to the end of the long table, to fraternise with the industrialists who had established a bridgehead there. And then, as if the evening were not already as dense as the cake, Patrick York appeared beside her, just appeared as out of thin air, and the whole cycle began again.

There should be more to life than duty, and obligation, and good manners.

Weren't these just several of the many forces from which she was fleeing, or attempting to flee? She gazed at her elegantly thin wedge of orange cake, she took up her small, glitteringly polished dessert fork. She wasn't making a job of this fleeing, was she?

'May I?'

She had heard this voice coming out of televisions and

radios with, of late, ever increasing frequency. His own programme on the BBC, a slew of them, in fact, after a quiet start on ITV; also, a radio show, and another radio show somewhere else. And eye-catching charity work, on the side – and now, wasn't he doing something in America, too? His own production company. A young Turk, out and out, and criss-crossing the Atlantic. And she had heard him only the previous Sunday on *Desert Island Discs*: choosing classical, and some religious, Edith Piaf, and a Beatles number for the youth vote; Betjeman, and English ale. She couldn't fault his public side.

A voice that grabbed you, slightly too much pomade in his black, quiffed hair, sharply suited, tall enough but not too tall.

Yes, a faultless public side.

She nodded politely, patted the seat – the still-warm seat – that Etienne had just vacated. 'Please.'

'Thank you.' He sat. 'It can be hard to catch all the names sometimes. I'm Patrick York.' He extended a soft, yielding hand.

'Stella Wakeham.'

'How do you do.'

'I know who you are, of course,' Stella said. To please him. He must be expecting it. 'The talk of the town, you are.'

To her enormous surprise, he flushed a little: then, as he caught her startled expression, his flush deepened, spread along his neck.

'People who don't even know me,' he said.

She glanced – a reflex action – across the table. John

hadn't moved, in spite of Etienne's efforts to get him to shift three seats along: but the older woman, what was her name? – had slid into the seat beside him. She was less of a bore, so they said, and certainly John looked less cross. And the orange cake was very good. She turned back to her companion.

'Well,' she said, 'I don't even know you: not the real you. So you can count me among this throng. You'd better tell me about yourself.'

But again to her surprise, he shook his head. 'It might be better if we told each other about ourselves. Beginning with you. I daresay you could hear me,' he added, 'all through dinner. I'm trying to do a deal with that chap, he has money I need' – and he nodded along the table to the industrialist with whom Etienne was now engaged in earnest conversation. Was the industrialist perhaps a Uranian too? Goodness, they were everywhere. 'So that was the public *moi* you heard. I'd much rather listen to you – I mean, if that's not thoroughly disagreeable.'

An accent she could not place. In fact, no accent. Accentless. 'Very well, I can certainly try, or at any rate begin. But I'm afraid I'm rather burning to ask you one question. I hope you'll forgive my curiosity: but where are you *from*?'

At the end of the evening, John and Stella and Etienne left Mildred's together, hailed a taxi, deposited Etienne – very drunk, now ('It's a strain, you know, giving a dinner party; it leaves one quite exhausted') – at the front door of his grand house which glimmered white under the street lamps, took the key from his drunken fingers, said goodnight, bundled him into his hall and closed the door behind him. He could crawl upstairs to his bed, or he could lie in a heap there in his commodious hall; they had done their best. Patrick York had slipped away from Mildred's a little earlier: he needed to walk, he said, he needed to clear his head or he would never sleep; he would make his own way home.

Etienne deposited, safely or not safely – perhaps he would fall asleep on his back, and vomit up his good dinner and his cocktails, and die; but if he died, he died, they were not about to haul him up his broad stairs, there were some things that nobody should have to do – John and Stella walked together towards the King's Road. Under the plane trees on Sloane Avenue, they spoke softly to each other as they compared notes. They were gentle with each other, now, with John quite as gentle as Stella; and they discussed the evening, and Etienne's gentleman, for the industrialist was indeed Etienne's gentleman, though he had vanished at the door of Mildred's too, to return home to his wife ('Did you take him in? – that was a nice jacket, and he's not all that much younger than Etienne, thank heaven; that chap has a bit of taste; well, you would know that already, I saw the paintings, how proud you must feel, darling'), and the women ('it's more that I know *of* them; I tend to steer clear of women like that, though I'm sure they're very nice'), and the food ('no, not tinned mango; I'm certain it was fresh; I know for a fact that they have them in Harrod's'). A long walk.

At the door of Stella's little house, a scent of patchouli

drifting from the nearby clutter of shops, she fumbled with the key. Now he said, 'What were you talking about, Stella?'

She paused for a moment. *With whom?* But she wasn't the sort to disclaim, to play games.

'About myself, mainly. I'm afraid my tongue ran away with itself, rather. I daresay he found me an absolute bore.' She found the light switch, switched it on, stepped back in the little hall so that he could close and lock the door.

'I daresay he didn't, you know.'

She sighed. 'No, I daresay he didn't.'

'You talked and talked, and he talked and talked, in Mildred's.'

He could tell, even though the jazz was loud that night, almost to the point of insanity, and even though the velvet darkness of the place ruled out lip-reading, ruled out sight entirely, or almost. He could tell that they had talked and talked, and talked and talked. Mildred's jiggering plush banquette had vibrated with the sound not only of the jazz, but also of their earnest, confiding voices, of Stella's voice and Patrick York's deep bass voice, humming, thrumming through the thick fabric, and into his fingers.

'Yes,' she said, 'we did. We talked rather a lot.'

He said nothing more. They climbed the steep stairs quietly, undressed and went to bed, spooned tightly as they always did, slept at once.

24

That was an end to their relationship, just like that, and John knew it. A full stop had already been applied – firmly, finely, with the tip of a brush. And he knew too that he wouldn't fight to retain her. It wasn't his style, he wouldn't know how to clutch, to attempt to persuade; he shrank away even from the thought. No: she was going, she was going, she was gone, and it would be demeaning to think that this particular fate could be avoided.

How to cope with wordless distress? To keep busy, to go to this party, or that party, this opening or that opening. To paint? – not that. He tried once or twice, but gave up. He spent much time alone in gassy Camberwell. Stella was elsewhere in the city.

'He talks to me, you see,' Stella said. 'He talks, as well as listens. He opens up. And I like that.'

They met once or twice – for thick, black coffee; for a drink here and there. It was all highly civilised.

'I didn't realise what I was missing.'

Early one morning, he took a train and then a bus from Camberwell to Sloane Square. Very early: he walked the length of the King's Road, where traffic was still thin; Stella's little street was still in shadow, though the sun was just clipping the roof of her house; the sky was a freshly laundered blue.

'John, for God's sake.'

He didn't say anything. There was nothing to be said: he had tried to think, to rehearse, but the lines failed to come. He stood on her doorstep, mute.

'Come in, for heaven's sake.'

Although, there was one thing to say – or rather, ask.

'Is he here?'

Stella looked at him. 'No, John, he isn't.' What do you take me for? – her eyes asked him. 'We haven't made that progression,' she added primly. Not that she looked prim: her hair was standing on end, as though she were Frankenstein's monster, as though someone had administered an electric shock. She caught a glimpse of herself in the little round mirror that hung in the hall. 'Credit me with a little class,' she said, 'though, would you look at me,' and now she tried to smooth her hair flat. It wouldn't do her bidding.

They sat in her kitchen, where the sink was filled, right to its brim, with dirty dishes and pots and pans. It looked like a sink in a cartoon, John thought. Stella caught his glance and said, 'I know. I'm a slut, it's a disgrace, I haven't had much time lately.'

'I heard you were at the BBC.'

She nodded. Very civilised. Patrick was recording a show at the BBC, she said; she had been over to Lime Grove to sit behind the cameras and watch the scene unfold. A scream, she said, the set was just partition-board, it looked as though it could fall over at any moment. But serious too.

Serious?

'It's certainly serious,' John said. He didn't want to hear about backstage assignations, scenery and sets that trembled at the slightest touch; and Stella took the point.

'Oh John, what do you want me to say?'

He wanted her to say that he was all she needed, that he answered every need she had, that Patrick York was as flimsy as the stage sets that filled his professional life. That was all.

'One can't help these things,' she said. She was upset, in spite of her crafted sangfroid: there were no tears in her eyes, because she was not that sort of girl, but her skin was paler than usual. There were no tears in his eyes either: this encounter, their last, was to be tearless. So much was clear.

She made coffee, and they drank it as London began to bustle audibly outside, as the sun rose a little higher and began to track along the upper edge of the kitchen window. Stella looked tired, he thought, and not only because she had been woken at cockcrow: she looked distressed. He looked – much the same, he imagined. The mask held. It was the early rising that gave the game away, on this occasion.

'We might stay friends,' Stella said. But – no: not friends. He shook his head, and after a few more minutes had dragged by, he left. No lingering on the step, no kiss, no hug. He guessed from the silence behind him that she stood there on the step and watched him walk slowly up the lane towards the main road – and the guess would have to do.

He saw Stella just one more time: some years, twelve years into the future – though this long gap was not by melodramatic design. Their paths were never going to cross very much, was the mundane truth. She married Patrick York a matter of months after that conclusive meeting in her little house at World's End, in the Westminster register office: and when his burgeoning career took York off to America, a few months after that, she went too. They settled in Laurel Canyon, or so he heard: they lived *like Angelenos*, his gossiping source told him: 'You know,' this at a heaving West End opening, all warm white wine and cigarette smoke, 'swimming pools and beaches and Hollywood, *you* know. Real *Angelenos*.'

'What,' he said, as sour as the wine, 'is that it? I'm sure they do more than just sit by swimming pools and on beaches. Or what, is that all that people do in Los Angeles?'

'Oh, John, where's your sense of humour?'

They met again, just before his assignation in West Berlin. A call out of the blue, and a coffee, what about somewhere off the King's Road, old time's sake, did he know any places? They met at a pavement cafe; a striped awning, yellow and white, provided shade. Stella had the tired look that came with a hot climate – though at least there was no evidence of surgery. She had aged, and so had he, and he took her in, as she was doubtless taking him in. Her skin was tired, but so was his. But.

'You look well,' he said, meaning that she looked happy.

'You don't.' Further scrutiny. 'Why not, I wonder? You're doing well, they tell me, you're still selling. But you don't look well.'

Seedy, she perhaps meant.

Later, as he surveyed the afternoon, his mind's eye provided an alternative history. He explains to her what it is that he actually does, that provides the impressive flow of funds into his bank account. The niche he profitably occupies. He is frank.

'Do you remember the distemper piece I did, the piece on linen?'

She smiles. Of course she remembers.

'Well,' he says, 'I've a lot more of those now. On linen, on canvas, the works.'

Stella smiles again. She isn't surprised to hear that: the colours sang, she remembers; impossible to forget them. Though, the colours on that first piece, they must be faded now, she says, and he nods.

'Fading, anyway. I take it out sometimes, and look at it. Fading fast,' he says. 'But I still work using distemper,' he says, 'and with more lasting colours too, of course.'

Not everything has to fade, Stella says.

'But I don't show them.'

She can see that, she says. She follows the art, she listens to the chatter, she knows that no such pieces have ever been mentioned. Just the harsh, difficult ones. Why not show these others?

He says, 'Privacy, really. The colour pieces feel like my own best work. But it doesn't feel right to show them. I don't want to, not any more. I'd rather stick to the difficult stuff.'

'That sells,' she says.

'That sells,' he agrees. Then he tells her that he forges a little. Now and again: and it turns out he's exceptionally good at it. He watches her face go still, as she polices her shock. She says nothing for a moment, and then asks why he would do such a thing.

'Lucrative,' he says. She knows the business: she must know just how lucrative it is. And not exactly uncommon. And the means of doing it getting easier, better every year. 'Though,' he adds, 'I'm small fry. You want to hear the stories about the European forgers.'

Stella doesn't want to hear the stories. 'But you don't need the money,' she says, 'do you?' And he shakes his head.

'Not really.'

And then he tells her about the theft here and theft there, and watches her expression change again. It was Etienne's idea, originally. Etienne had observed the colour drain – from his very person as from his public work – and observed the cynicism take hold: and realised that he had, once again, found his man. The expertise, and the attitude, embodied as one. And, John adds, it too is lucrative, it's enormously lucrative.

And she can see it, can she not? The seediness: he looks unwell, he looks pallid, he can pass unremarked in any environment – and this very colourlessness acts as a protection, a magical cloak, he walks unseen.

She asks, appalled now, all expressions now visible, 'Why?' But she must know why.

'Because they owe me.'

They being the world, the system, the authorities, governments and institutions: a generalised *they*. He hadn't yet been adequately recompensed for the loss of a home on Regina Road, for what they did to his parents, for the chain of events, all beyond his control, that have shackled his life. They had put a car park where his home had stood. How to explain the sense of dispossession? – and besides, she must know already. 'And besides, they deserve it.' He laughs a little. 'Provenance,' he says, 'when they didn't care about mine.'

'That's nonsense,' Stella says, ignoring the taunt, the opportunity provided to quiz him about this now-generalised 'they'. 'Nonsense,' she says again, 'what, they violated your life, so you take to a career in violation? That hardly makes sense, darling.'

He shakes his head. 'I didn't expect you to understand,' he says, and now it is her turn to shake her head.

'I understand all too well,' she says. 'The indulgence of it. I'm ashamed of you.'

He thinks of the small portrait, on copper, hanging at this moment on a Berlin wall, that would soon be his. 'I didn't expect you to understand,' he says, and they part in anger.

What in fact happened was that he mentioned Etienne, as Thatcher's brassy London marched along the pavement. 'Etienne,' he said, 'well, he always championed me. And he still does.'

'Etienne,' Stella repeated. She studied his face. 'Well, of course he always championed you; and he's quite the mover and shaker still. So I hear.' She stirred her coffee, and a silence fell. 'It's easy to hear things,' she added, 'even all the way over there.'

'I daresay.'

They sat, quietly. A mass of words, of conversation that

might yet be had, that would not be had; yet the silence was companionable rather than awkward; the coffee was strong and good.

'As long as you're happy enough, content enough,' she said at last, and he nodded. Enough could mean anything, which was perhaps the point. And they parted gently, with something like tenderness. Who could tell what Stella knew?

But this was for the future.

On this day, her hair was on end as she stood on the doorstep of her house at World's End and watched him walk slowly up the lane towards the main road. He retraced his steps to Camberwell, tube to bus, and walked from the bus stop into the college, and into his studio. He had intended to knife all the canvases, charcoal and oils, that he had worked on while Stella had been on the scene. The very many pieces, in their blacks and whites and greys. The knife was ready and waiting: it was sharp and not serrated – for nothing blunt would do when it came to slicing canvas to size – and he imagined that there would be satisfaction in the clean, economical movement of the knife, and its sound, a gasping of death, as it sliced through the fabric.

He would tuck his distemper piece away. He wouldn't even look at it.

But in the morning light, he laid the knife gently down on the table, and looked around the room. All these pieces, piled against walls: let them go out in the world, if anyone would have them. Etienne would buy the lot, most likely. Or his chums would.

So he would paint to order, his blacks and his greys: he could make some money that way. His distemper piece would remain tucked away, locked away, its colours fading year by year: nobody need see it, and Stella would tell nobody. And if it came to it, he could have it buried with him, just like Emily Sandborne.

Paint to order. Paint by numbers. Give them what they want.

After a few minutes, he took the distemper piece from the drawer in which it was rolled, and stowed, and locked away. The colours sang still, and the linen was as creamy-white as ever. He passed a thumb gently over the cloth, and after a moment he returned it to its drawer, and turned the key once more. He would hold the colours close.

Later again – it was still barely eleven o'clock – he lined up his razor knife (no serrated edges) carefully on the tabletop, vertical to horizontal, and left the studio, and walked up the hill to his gassy room, and fell on his bed, and slept.

25

*P*auldron.

It gleamed now, *The Jewel*. The pauldron, on the great silk-hung wall in front of him. The hall was lit in dimness: by the venom-green emergency signs suspended to left and to right, by the grey-yellow light that leaked from unseen high windows, though not by the blinking red of the security sensors, for these blinked no longer. Beyond these windows, the subdued hum of the nocturnal city: a police siren, a distant rumble of heavy traffic, a hiss of wheels on wet streets.

Very dim – but sufficient light to see by: to illumine the white carven figures dotted through the hall; to bring forth a poisonous phosphorous sheen from the green-white hanging silk; to cast into dark relief the doorways that opened, as if cut with shears, into the high galleries on either side. And to see the painting.

To see the pauldron, set with a green stone, flame out of a world of darkness and light captured by the artist.

And besides, John had his memory to guide him.

Only two days ago he had visited: on the very day the gallery had reopened to the public, and rapidly become thronged. He had threaded his way, his anonymity guaranteed amid such a mass of humanity, through the crowds spilling into the atrium and up the white steps to see the place. It had been closed for three years, they'd told him in the briefing, for three or four years, for ages, anyway: and they had pushed a brochure across the table at him. Voids in this venerable building now opened for the first time to public view, top-lit galleries, a thrilling development – the brochure went on and on.

John leafed and flicked in silence. He had seen it all before, and in Milan, in Basel, in galleries more illustrious than this one. He was not so easily impressed.

They pointed out the Sculpture Court, in the centre of the building: one such newly reopened void, the literature said; previously it had been a damp courtyard, useless, gloomy. Now it was glorious, silk-hung, just the one painting displayed amid a throng of marble. Just the one, the most famous of them all, maximum effect – they said. A marvel.

He took it all in. 'Floorplans?' They pushed the floorplans at him: he would study these at his leisure. He bundled the papers together; he understood, he said.

But, as he had pushed through the gallery on that reconnaissance day, he permitted himself to slough off the cynicism, the weariness. The air was charged with curiosity, with pleasure, with delightful anticipation. *Ages and ages*, one fur-coated matron said as she brushed softly past, *it's been closed for ages and ages*; she was dying to see what they'd done with it; and *it had cost a mint, a mint*. The security guards had pressed their backs against the white walls; the curators – snobby pricks, he had thought, the lot of them – had pressed their lips tightly together as these waves of the unwashed eddied through and filled the halls, had looked shocked, had wished the gallery closed again. It was all too easy to read their thoughts: it was as though speech bubbles were floating above their skulls.

Well, he thought, and *just you wait. We'll give you something to be shocked about. Your lips will be tighter still, come Thursday morning.*

He had come to get the lie of the land, to set up a nice, easy geography for himself. It was all part of the drill. There was only so much a floorplan could do, in the matter of illumination: it was necessary, always, to come and see the place for oneself. To shuffle through, a small man in anonymous clothes, drab and beige; invisible, or as good as.

The Sculpture Court, they told him, in important capitals, the Sculpture Court: just the one painting in that whole great silken hall; maximum drama; you can't miss it. The clients had run through the whole thing, as though they themselves had designed the new gallery and re-hung its collection. A real heist, they'd told him, audacious – but he said nothing in the face of their excitement. A touch of the amateur about them; it was pathetic, really. He preferred the insatiably greedy amateurs of the eighties and nineties. Time to bring in a touch of reality.

'I'll have my knife, my shoes; the computer guys will disable the security; I'll get in, I'll get out, the job'll be done.'

Puncturing words, flat tones: this was workaday stuff; this was the reality.

'You won't need the knife.'

He laughed at that. 'You always need a knife.'

It never ceased to amuse him. These were tough guys – he could see it in their faces, in the set of their bodies, he knew the sort; and they knew damn-all about art too – and yet here they were, talking as though they were setting out to do something public-spirited. *Audacious, sensational* – his brutish clients changed all the time, but the lingo didn't. As though he was after headlines.

The fact was, though – and everyone knew it – that a theft was a theft, a knife was a knife. A knife – razor-sharp, no serrated edges – would get most of the job done; add a little remote computer wizardry, and that was that. Basic tools, the equipment didn't really change, in spite of what people might think.

'It's held between two pieces of glass,' they said. 'No need for a knife.'

But he'd bring one just the same.

And there he was, in the Sculpture Court. And there it was, against green-white silk.

And yes: the painting took his breath away. Its heavy darkness, and its flaming lights; the expressions, the beautiful movements, the jewel colours. The bright welling of green at the centre. He stood and watched; the Sculpture Court began to fill up even more, as the members of a guided tour filed in and took their places. A young man slipped past him with an apology, turned to face the swelling crowd, began to talk. He ignored the bee-buzz of speech, watched the painting.

'Pauldron,' the young man, the boy said, and he took his gaze away from the painting and focused on him.

'Notice the gleam of the pauldron,' he said. He held a pointer in one hand: as he spoke, he was pushing it gently into the palm of his other hand. He had seemed composed, this boy, at first; it took him a moment to see the evidence to the contrary. He wore a polo neck, light grey; and John saw that sweat had welled from his armpits and was showing against the fine wool; he looked at the wool, at the boy, at the pointer, and the painting. At his mop of red hair, and flushed skin. What age was he? – twenty, twenty-one? No age. 'And the malachite stone set into the metal: see how it shines. It's almost the centrepiece of the whole painting,' the boy went on, 'the green against the black, the black against the colours.'

The crowd grew further, filling the broad spaces between the white marble statues, the boy talked on. Gathered a little confidence, though the woolly sweat patches remained. 'Not the figures, not their expressions. Just his pauldron; it's the gleam of the pauldron that catches my eye every time. She's looking behind their humanity, the artist is, do you see? – she's breaking down the machine.'

The boy stopped, then, and gestured with the pointer, and all eyes followed its tip, to look at the bright, blazing trail of white on black.

'And there she is herself,' the boy said, and he ran his fingers through his hair. 'There she is,' he said, and the pointer stabbed higher, 'holding the lantern. All the light comes from this one point.' He looked, they all looked, at the dark-haired young woman, bright-eyed, long-haired, dark against black, black against brilliant colour, holding her lantern aloft. 'Watching the scene. A self-portrait, they say: observing the scene she herself created. Emily Sandborne: and a true likeness, the historians say. A beautiful combination of darkness and light,' he said, and John watched as he dropped his arm and the pointer and laughed. 'Darkness and light,' the boy said, and now he laughed aloud. 'It gets me every time. The whole thing, the whole painting, the colours, the story, everything.'

Not all of them, then. This boy hadn't been a prick. He had brought the painting alive – for them all, surely. You'd almost forget the job in hand, he thought, standing there as the crowd moved against him like a breaking wave, as they packed in to see this painting, this star turn. You almost would.

'Nobody knows,' the boy said. 'Distemper pieces fade and fade to nothing, in time. But this one hasn't, and nobody knows why. Nobody knows how she did it. She took the secret to her grave.'

Not so snobby.

That was then: now, John stood in the dim light. This was the moment: the security sensors were cut; they had tapped in remotely, they had done whatever it was they did, the place was his for these few minutes. He stepped forward, he passed the fine silver cord, set at shin level, that marked the end of the public space, the space allotted to the likes of him, the great unwashed. He reached up on the wall, and touched the glass, and pushed upward.

Outside, the distant police siren had long ceased. No noise now, or not much: only the hiss of the distant traffic, and a light patter of rain. The gallery was silent as he braced his legs, and brought the painting down – to head level, to eye level – and set it on the floor.

It was smaller than it had looked, up there on the wall.

It was easy. It was always easy.

The malachite shone, the pauldron gleamed, and the linen welled with inner light. The artist held the lantern aloft, and she watched and watched as he slipped the two bracing panes of glass away. The linen – miraculous, un-aged – puckered, suddenly, and began to slide to the floor.

And now, the echo of an echo of another sound: distant footsteps on distant tiles. Plans are plans, he thought – very calmly, for he was seasoned – and plans sometimes go awry.

And he had his knife.

And that was the handy thing about knives: they were useful in a variety of ways.

Damned if he was stopping now.

He stood quietly in the dim hall; he braced himself.

The clipping footsteps came closer. It would be bad luck for him, for them, to come into this very room, of all the manifold rooms in the gallery – and yet he knew they would, and he tightened his grip around the handle of his knife. There was always a first time.

The footsteps were close now: echoes ran along the walls and into the roof. Two pairs of hurrying footsteps. One voice: female. A male voice, reassuring. Closer and closer.

He was coiled, now, for action.

A woman clipped into the room. A man – young, in the darkness, thin, tall. One younger, one older, shadowy in the darkness. And now they saw him, and for a second froze. And now one voice rose in – in anger, in furious anger. The woman, staring at him, at the glass, at the linen. Fearless, blazing.

'What have you done? What have you *done*?'

And not a moment to lose. He lunged towards her, he drew his knife, he took hold of a bony upper arm, and a scream ripped through the air – and now the shadowy young man, stronger, faster, stepped in, seized his wrist. A moment of balanced struggle: the knife caught the light and gleamed green-white: and now the woman wrenched free and made to run, and now his own wrist was free, and the young man struggled to grab him again, and there was no choice now, and the knife sliced.

A clean slice, clean, clear, across his throat.

The woman was gone, her heels echoing and vanishing; and for a second John stopped, and breathed, and looked at the silk-clad walls now sprinkled with dark drops, at the glass, at the man, ripped, on the ground.

And looked again, and saw curling red hair, and closed his eyes.

And crossed the room, and gently rolled Emily Sandborne's linen. She herself looked at him, expressionless, before he rolled her away. And without looking back, threaded his way among the statues, and vanished.

Distemper

26

The art was the thing.

Roisin said the line in her head often enough. She'd rehearsed it until she had every intonation and inflection, just right. It was convincing now, as though it were the actual, unvarnished truth.

The chatter went on, tweetling voices filling the staff room. It was three o'clock, and the dingy little room was more full, surely, than it ought to be in the middle of the working day: with mismatched furniture and people, and idle chatter, and gossip exchanged unkindly.

No, the room was not a pleasant space, and nobody could argue otherwise. It was not part of the revamp, and so it could not boast new windows or modern, stylish light sources or radiant colour schemes; the aged, antique, bulbous radiators hissed as they had always done, and they were white-hot as usual, so that the room was overheated, rank with stale air and old, old farts. The room had been dour, dark and unpleasant before the gallery upgrade had commenced, and so it had remained as the gallery had been transformed around it, and it was dour, dark and unpleasant today. Filled to overflowing with years of gossip, and bitching, and the exchange of unkind information and news of private business.

Roisin had no private business, and no life worth probing. Which was fine, because the art was the thing.

This was what she told anyone who asked. Who wondered about her life, pattern, career. She knew she had a concise reply readied – in such a way, of course, as to put them off asking any further questions. There were straightforward ways of achieving this full-stop effect. By being brisk, or brusque, or verging on the rude; by raising her voice a little and cutting in on any questions on the edge of being put: any number of ways.

And she'd had plenty of practice. She had been obliged to try out her various modes. To test them as though, she liked to think, they were a new intercontinental weapons system. An early warning array was the line of defence: it combed the skies, searching for incoming missiles. Weaponry could be deployed, then, as necessary – and would certainly see off any invaders. She'd invested heavily, over the years, in her defence capabilities, in the process using up most of her gross domestic product. I've spent everything, she sometimes thought: I've hardly a thing left.

Never mind. This was money well invested; today, her defences were impregnable. What an armoury, ready to pulverise. Sidestep a polite query from a new colleague – 'Are you married, Roisin?' – by sarcasm, by a lot of art-related blather, by one word where ten might have given the game away, or by ten words where one was more natural. How straightforward it had been, on her arrival in this place, to see them off, to stop the questions in their tracks, without even having to break a sweat.

'The art was always the thing, for me.'

Of course, few enough people were happy to listen: Roisin had noticed this about the world in general, that its inhabitants had become a good deal more inclined to talk, principally about themselves, than to listen to a word anyone else said.

She also, however, noticed how sometimes there seemed to be a – a moving away when she appeared. The movement reminded her of the way the tide ebbed on the beach. It just flowed; there was nothing much that anyone could do about it.

Why should her feathers feel ruffled so? Wasn't this what she'd always wanted? – to keep people at arm's length? Surely it pleased her.

Sometimes, she was aware of an edge of hunger, a faint growling in her stomach. But this she could generally ignore. In general, she was pleased.

She was a rare one, as her mother liked to tell her. 'Pushing and pulling, Roisin,' her mother said once, 'and all at the same time. What people must think of you, I just do not know.' That was in the course of a rare visit home – and the moral was to make these visits, even now that she was back in Ireland, even more rare.

Roisin had felt again, that day with her mother, that pain, that edge of hunger. She'd glanced across at the kitchen window of her mother's tidy new house, which looked out, these days, not at damp fields and distant hills, but at other new, tidy houses across the road. She said nothing.

It was not as though she cared very much, because what she said was the truth: the art was the thing. It trumped the business of life. It was infinitely preferable. It couldn't be put in such terms, or in any vocal terms: she had a sense of how unpleasant it would sound, how controlled and controlling; somewhere, she retained a ghost of a wish to be agreeable to those around her. She hadn't yet become absolutist about it.

She was becoming rusty, too. In the staff room, she was finding it increasingly difficult to interact pleasantly. She too was forgetting to listen (was it contagious?), to ask questions, to demonstrate interest and enquire after children, ageing parents, declining cats. A dog, the other day, who needed an intestinal operation. Were these poorly, were they celebrating this or that occasion, had they been neutered, had they been spayed, were they incontinent, these cats and dogs and parents? Had holidays been booked, had they been enjoyed? A river cruise, a Baltic cruise? Who, Roisin thought, glancing around the room, looking out the window, who cared?

Victoria, in the Education Department, had just been on a cruise around Iceland, to see the Northern Lights and all the rest of it, and had come back raving about her experience: the thermal baths, the ship, the world's northernmost botanical gardens (though these had been a

let-down, according to Victoria); the stop in Shetland where
they had been taken to see a Shetland pony – but just the
one, alone in a field; another let-down. A drunken night on
the tiles in Reykjavik, where Victoria had been swept off
her feet by what sounded like a Viking. Unlike the botanic
gardens, not a let-down at all.

Roisin had been aware then too of a noise, a little like
the high, excited twittering of swallows in the country in
summer: pleasant enough to listen to for a while, but more
pleasant to leave.

Just part of the background noise of her life. Victoria
began describing more soundscapes – the deafening sound
of rain on the corrugated-iron roof of the Viking's house, in
the very middle of the night.

Young people these days: their words, their private
activities, the details of their lives poured out of them like
diarrhoea. Roisin drained her coffee, and swilled out her
cup, and left the staff room.

The gallery these days was neither one thing nor the other.
It was neither open nor closed, neither broken nor fixed. Its
revamp – its 'reimagining', in the words of the promotional
literature – had gone on for so long now that it was difficult
to imagine it ever being completed. So the staff said to one
another: bitching and whispering on the edges of things.
Was the management up to the job? Had they bargained for
all of this – this hassle, this endlessly extended banging and
sawing, drilling and roofing, unroofing, reroofing, month
after month and year after year? So they wondered, in
what Roisin thought of as Vatican-style conclaves. All that
was needed was a guttering candle casting wild, quavering

shadows on the walls, a frescoed ceiling overhead, a phial of poison waiting in the staff fridge, and the scene would be complete.

What a pity the reimagining of the gallery hadn't included a frescoed ceiling, or a fridge kept at a perfect temperature for phials of poison.

But for Roisin, this closure could go on and on for ever. She felt that the gallery was better off closed, with its paintings sequestered from the roving gazes of those punters who, more likely than not, didn't appreciate or understand what they were looking at.

The gallery had always been closed in the years she had been here. Closure seemed now to be its natural state: strange and all as this had been at first, she had realised quickly that it was just the set-up for her. An art gallery closed to the public, a completely controlled space, a gallery bespoke, for her. There could be no better place in the world.

She moved quietly along the corridor.

She knew to keep her mouth shut. And she was good at silence. She'd grown up with it.

'Like a Virgin,' said the caption on the yellowing newspaper that lay across the kitchen table: the song had been Number One that year in every country in western Europe; Roisin remembered the girls singing it in Our Lady of Victories, all those years ago. And a photograph of Madonna, in all her youthful pomp.

But it was the other photograph that caught Roisin's

attention, that held it. A photograph of a little brooch, a little silver lapel brooch. Two tiny feet.

Philomena brought in more stacks of newspaper. What had Cormac been doing, filling the roofspace with newspaper? – but he had never been good at throwing anything out.

He was dead now two weeks, and the clear-out had begun. Patched corduroys, and voluminous underpants with the elastic shot, and books about the war and the Nazis and Pearl Harbor, darned socks, and old shirts washed into translucence that he could never stand to throw out. And bales of newspapers that he must have brought from the old house, and stuffed into the roofspace of the new one.

'Talk about a fire hazard,' Philomena marvelled. 'I never knew he crammed them all in up there. The place might have gone up like a torch.'

The kitchen in the new house faced east, and the sun poured in this morning through its wide window; and Philomena seemed to have a pep in her step. A merry widow, already.

Roisin turned back to the newspaper.

Thirty years ago and more, of course, but she could remember such brooches vividly. They had glinted and winked in the light, pinned on the lapels of half the population, back then. There was no avoiding them. And no avoiding this yellowing photograph today either: it filled half of a broadsheet page, it commanded attention.

It made her think of Maeve, and this was unwelcome. Maeve was gone, and she wasn't coming back.

Now, she caught her mother's eye, and set the newspaper down on the kitchen table.

'I'm glad you weren't browbeaten into wearing one, at any rate.'

She spoke in her now-usual flat tones, and watched as Philomena's eyes scanned the kitchen – although, who did she think was going to swish through the back door?

'Oh,' said Philomena. 'No.'

They got along, or well enough: but just the same, she would bustle away, given half a chance. This was boggy territory, where grief and memory lay just below the surface, all dark water and oozing black peat. Philomena feared being bogged down, trapped and drowned. So much was clear.

Cormac had worn his brooch with pride. Those poor English babies, he'd said, butchered, he said, by the thousand and the million. Turned into dog food, so the stories went. Well, it would never happen here in Ireland. He would wear his brooch, his two little silver feet, with pride, he'd said. And he would vote the right way on referendum day. He still had some notion, back then, that Roisin remained a religious sort of girl, apt to see statues of the Madonna moving and walking on every street up and down the land, and Roisin wasn't going to disabuse him of the notion.

But she remembered the late sunshine on the grotto walls. The wire, and the blood on the ground.

'I got myself a cryin', talkin', sleepin', walkin', livin' doll,' Maeve had sung one evening, falsetto, and Roisin could have beaten her to a pulp.

She put the memory away.

Now, she watched as her mother got to her feet, abruptly, and went to the window and looked out.

This had been the way of it throughout her whole childhood. When Maeve was alive, and when Maeve was dead; the tenor of the household remained unchanged. They sidestepped the silences, they ignored what could be ignored, and they did what they could to stop the house from falling down. From time to time, they attacked the furry mould with a bottle of supermarket bleach: it vanished and then it came back, and all that really happened was that the rooms, with their sad, shiny yellow walls, stank of bleach for a week or so. *Eau de Domestos*, Maeve had liked to call it, in another life, fretting that the smell would attach itself to her school uniform, her basketball kit, her hair.

'Be quiet,' Roisin had said at such times, an eye on the bedroom door. 'Daddy'll hear.'

He had in fact tended not to hear: though just the same, most conversations in that damp bungalow had been conducted wisely, on the quiet, even when Cormac was out about his business. The women of the family had all known that although Cormac was not, maybe, a man given to fists and whacks, sometimes he was; and the girls had seen him give their mother the occasional thump across the back of her head, where a bruise wouldn't show.

He'd punched and thumped only sometimes. Only very occasionally, because of course he was not a very aggressive man. 'I'm feeling riled,' he would say, and he would hit one of them. He never spoke with much heat: 'I'm feeling riled,' as though commenting on a result at the hurling, or a par round that morning at the golf: and then he would hit one of them a thump. It all depended on who was closer, he had no favourites – and it was usually across the back of the head. Once, a thump across the side of Roisin's head. This was what Roisin's Enid Blyton books meant when they described such-and-such a character having their ears 'boxed': it had never sounded too bad, but after this episode, Roisin knew that it was, because her ear rang as she stepped away, and continued to ring afterwards.

But that would be that, over and done with for a while.

As for the mould – they all understood that this was Cormac's fault. Their bungalow had been built badly, in some unspecified way; and built in the wrong place, in a dip, and too close to the bog. Eventually it was condemned. 'Best not to look back, a mistake is a mistake,' their mother had said – but they all knew that Cormac must have skipped over the details, and engaged a cheap builder who had used the wrong materials.

They worked it out, their mother dropped a line here and there. There was mica in the aggregate. The house, given time, would fall to pieces. The mica was there to be seen: it gleamed in the light, it twinkled pleasantly, it reminded Roisin now of a long-forgotten past; you'd hardly know that it was the mischief in all of this. But twinkling and all as it was, they were paying the price now, and would for ever more. Roisin knew this, her mother knew it, Maeve had known it. They all knew to keep quiet.

Roisin felt differently, now, about the glint she saw in the local rock.

And as Philomena used to say: never mind. It wasn't all bad. The house would crumble, but not yet. The mould only reached so far up the walls, and no further; there seemed to be a line it was unwilling to cross; and besides, there was always the bleach, the defence of last resort. The world would never run out of bleach.

And then Maeve was gone, and there were other things to think about in the crumbling house.

And now, the house was gone.

And now, Roisin looked at her mother's back, and spoke again.

'Well, fair play to you. It must have taken guts, in those days, not to wear a badge. In spite of everything.'

You had to build a bridge sometimes, and get over things – especially when you had escaped, and were well away and out of it. The old house was gone, and her father was dead, and her mother seemed set fair as a merry widow. And Roisin herself well away, and doing her own thing.

'I'm very happy for you, you know,' her mother said, turning a little in the sunny window. Her profile was black and sharp against the light. 'Your big job, and a smart girl, and you're well out of this place, and I'm glad of it. I won't lie: I never was so confused in my life as when you decided to go off and study paintings.'

'Well, art history,' Roisin said.

'But lookit, you're very good at it,' her mother went on, ignoring her, 'that's clear, and you have a career, and I'm very proud of you.' Philomena paused. 'But you don't seem very happy, and I wish you were.'

But how could I be happy? A pause, and Roisin smoothed her hand across the yellowing newspaper.

'I'm fine,' she said. 'You don't need to worry about me.'

*

And besides, the gallery would be reopening soon. This blessed period was coming to an end: the place was reopening, a date had been set, the rewiring and rehanging and reordering, the reroofing and replanting and reimagining: it was all almost complete.

And the fact was that Roisin herself had had a stake, too, in the whole endeavour. She had chosen the blues – the cerulean blue, the lapis lazuli blue, the beautiful, otherworldly gentian blues – in the third-floor galleries. She had chosen the pinks – the porphyry pink, the orchid pink, the dusty, layered pinks – in the fourth-floor galleries. It had lifted her spirits, had made them soar briefly, when she clipped up the new stone staircase to the upper floors, and saw the gallery walls decked in their beautiful peacock colours.

The rehang had destroyed this beauty – though, no, not destroyed completely, for these spectacular surfaces were still there, and the imagination could remove the paintings, could do what was needful, could bring the walls back into their glory.

The art was the thing.

This was what she said, but of course this was untrue. The walls were the thing: ordered and controlled, made beautiful, inviolate. They were not made to be violated, by the hanging of paintings or anything else. There was nothing to be done about any of this: but at least she knew her own mind. At least she knew how perfection might be achieved. At least she understood her own vision, and at least she knew how it might be achieved.

Her beautiful, inviolate walls.

As she walked, her memory pulled her back, as it always did, again and again and again, to an unviolated past, when the grain of her life was illuminated gloriously, welling with warmth, scattered with diamonds, with tiny, untouchable, unreachable points of light.

27

Roisin's house was in Portobello, only a fifteen-minute walk through pleasant Dublin streets from the gallery. She had picked up the house for a song during the crash, and she counted herself lucky. She had come over from London for a long weekend, a reconnoitre visit, with this precise area in mind, and the house was the first she set eyes on: a red-brick, deceptive in terms of space, with stairs up and stairs down, and a little garden at the back.

What a miracle.

'Adjacent to the waters of the picturesque Grand Canal': later, Roisin reflected that, while the brochure was in other ways thoroughly misleading, this particular claim was fair enough, the canal was five minutes away on foot, max. But ought water to be considered a selling point nowadays, in these times of floods and torrential downpours? *Where by a lock niagarously roars the falls...* Canal water and rainwater, getting on her nerves, under the front door. And the rats, too. Rats and canals went together like love and marriage. No, thank you.

No: better for such issues not to concern her: not floods or rats, and certainly not love and marriage. She made an offer on the house, and she knew that the offer would be accepted, and that was that. She had snuffed the air, and realised that desperation was the name of the game, here: some poor desperate soul somewhere needed a quick sale, and she had been there, on the ground. With a vacuum cleaner and her tough heel hovering over the 'on' button, ready to suck up the property. Someone had been unlucky, and she had been lucky, and someone else's despair was in any case nothing to do with her, and the house was good enough to live in, best of all. She would rent it until she was ready to make the return from London.

She hadn't told her mother about her Dublin weekend. Not until it was over, and the deed done. Philomena then took the news in her stride, or so Roisin told herself: even if her mother did not exactly like being kept at arm's length, she was surely accustomed to it by now.

'Well, I'm relieved, is the main thing I would say.' Her voice came lightly over the wires. 'It's good to have a bit of property to your name.' Was there a note of reproof in her tone? – that she hadn't so much as been consulted? If so, she might as well have kept it to herself, because Roisin wasn't about to pick up on it. 'Though,' and her mother's voice did indeed sound politely perplexed, 'I'm surprised, is what I would say, at the thought of you wanting back to Ireland.'

Roisin didn't pursue this line.

One wall of her small red-brick in Portobello was hung

thickly with paintings. The rest were bare. This single wall, running from the front door and along the narrow hall and up the stairs, was designed to overwhelm, and at the same time to stop any questions about her other walls. To provide a talking point, to prove her professional credentials. A giddying collection of nineteenth-century art in oils and pencil and watercolour, none of them valueless, and one or two of them costing a pretty penny. Picked up over the years, in sales here and sales there, for she had an eye, and the art of the period was still not as appreciated as it might have been.

There were more in boxes, wrapped and stacked neatly, in her little attic.

And the rest of the walls were bare.

She had painted them all, and expensively: a distemper paint that cost a fortune, that promised – and delivered – a slightly dusty finish, a finish that could not be sponged down to remove marks and stains, a luxurious but impractical finish. And there would be no marks and stains: there would be nobody in the house to generate a mark or a stain. No children, no annoying house guests. There would be Roisin only, and Roisin, she was prepared to say to anyone who might enquire, neither marked nor stained.

She had caused them to be painted, was closer to the mark: a Ukrainian man – Viktor – had been engaged to paint them, and he had done a nice job. He had complimented her on her choice of paint: at first, Roisin thought he was laughing at her; then, and belatedly – halfway through the job, in fact – she had realised that he was on the same wavelength. Viktor valued a distemper finish; he understood what she was after. It made it all more bearable.

For walls were her speciality, now. As Keeper of Displays at the gallery, a job which might have been designed with her in mind. It was a sort of ante-room in her profession, a sort of scullery, it was deeply unfashionable – but Roisin had come to live for her walls. For the clean sheets of matter, on which (if it came to it) a new universe of meaning and beauty might be hung, a universe that would mean nothing without the right background, the right context, the right finish. The right wall.

She had said as much in her interview. She had permitted herself a little passion, though not too much of it, and she had seen the panel look at her, with – with what: with surprise? With a glimmer of understanding? With – something, at any rate; with a something that had given her the position in Dublin, and the move back to Ireland.

In a crevasse in her memory, a stretch of granite. The mica is blank, black, in the deep darkness of this place. For Roisin, the surface was everything: but not to be touched, now. The granite, long ago, is warm, welling with Donegal summer sunshine. The donkey pulls at the green grass, wraps its squeaking stems with a long, muscular tongue, pulls it out by the roots. 'Look at his tongue!' squeaks Maeve, and they laugh together, uproariously on the grass. 'Imagine being able to do that.' The donkey crunches his apple, the granite is radiant with heat, the mica wells with glittering light.

The mica caused the house to fall.

The mica winked in the granite, in the grotto, long ago.

Roisin preferred different surfaces, now.

'We'll be in touch with you,' Dr Read had said quite coolly, and she held out a cool hand, and wished her a good day. Giving nothing away – but Roisin had seen the momentary change of expression on Dr Read's face, and had understood that the job was hers.

The house in Portobello, of course, represented a dry run. With its dusty walls, its one thickly hung wall, it was a practice run, undertaken in a controlled environment where she need please nobody except herself. She had probed Viktor: was he, perhaps, as interested in hanging paintings on walls as he was in painting the walls himself? Might he stay on for a day or two to hang her paintings? – as directed, minutely, by her? Would that be a possibility? – for a few extra quid, of course. Viktor stayed, and did the job, and now the walls of Roisin's house were as she had always wanted them.

'And this?' asked Viktor. She had baked an orange cake, and he had eaten it, two slices, and now they were assessing each piece of art.

Or rather, he was assessing them. She had set out, pencil on a piece of paper, exactly where she wanted each piece, each painting, on the distempered wall. A cheery beach scene, all bathing machines and donkeys with a blue sky shining overhead; a classical nude reclining amid a rain of delicately pink rose blossoms; ragged children with bare feet turning head over heels on London railings, the Thames a shining fish-silver in the background; more children, two of them, pointing at a stained-glass window, through which light poured in flows of green and red and blue; a busy railway terminal, alive with crowds picked out in a million hues, and overlaid with a roof of white smoke; soldiers and a cavalry on a tawny foreign field of war, the horses golden-brown and chestnut, the soldiers a feast of light.

People, and colour, and light.

'I see what you like,' Viktor said, and broke off a piece of his orange cake. 'Action,' he said, 'you like action, you like colour. Also,' and he paused for a moment to eat his morsel of cake, 'these will all look good against this paint.'

Roisin knew this already, but she nodded. 'Yes.'

'This was good paint,' Viktor had said, and nodded approval. 'Very nice to work with.' Now, he brushed a few crumbs from his fingertips, and once more ran an appreciative hand close to the dust of the walls, not touching, just hovering close to the chalky surface. 'Very, very nice. And the paintings too. Very nice.'

Roisin's thing, her big thing, she might have told him, was nineteenth-century art. British narrative art: deeply unfashionable, for the most part, though she thought she detected nowadays a renewed glimmer of interest from certain quarters. She had seen pieces in the papers, pointing out that these paintings hung – for free – in galleries up and down the land, that they ought to be looked at and appreciated anew; that the public had an obligation, indeed, to go and look at them, because more footfall meant salvation for the galleries themselves. Roisin, seated on her dark velour sofa in her house in Dublin, had read one such piece, had read with silent pleasure as her favourite paintings were brought out – as it were – from cold storage, and mentioned warmly, and petted, and permitted to pirouette on a vast stage: oil after Victorian oil, portraying the glamour, the drama of life; death and life, poverty and wealth, story after story brought wonderfully alive now in her mind's eye. Frith and Landseer and Millais, Thompson and Stanhope.

She might have wept, even, as she read. She had been alone, and her curtains pulled. Nobody could see.

If she had a fault to find with the piece, it was that it had mentioned nothing about the walls. As if such paintings could be hung just anywhere, against any backdrop, on any background! When a moment's thought would show the truth of the matter! Surfaces – and Roisin knew this, even if nobody else seemed to, even if everyone else thought that the opposite was the case – surfaces matter.

Maeve knew this, long ago. Perhaps all Irish people know how much meaning and deception and distraction can be condensed into the surfaces of things. As for Roisin's own surface: it too had stories to tell. It was one aspect of a life curated with care.

'I thought we could go for a cup of coffee some time. Maybe even today, if you have time.'

He had run into her, or she into him, between the book stacks. The first month of university, a mild autumn sun glancing through the library windows. She knew the ropes, was already in her groove, all was well. She chipped into seminar discussions, and wrote an essay, another essay; she went for dark, tar-like coffee with little groups of other first-year students, all of them finding their feet.

He – Ronan – came from County Cavan. The height of him, a mop of curly hair: he stood out. She'd caught a Galway girl laughing at his accent (as if her accent was anything to write home about), but Roisin enjoyed listening to the lightness of it, and the lightness of his voice.

'Or a drink, even.'

And they'd caught each other's eye. A couple of times, now.

She closed the heavy art book she'd been browsing, and slid it back into its slot on the shelf.

'Now, even, maybe?'

'A drink might be better; that coffee'll kill me, some day soon.' She had an essay to write. 'Now, why not.'

They crossed the road, weaving through the traffic, to Bowe's, and sat over pints of Guinness. Nothing remarkable – she thought later, tracing the drink, and the later drinks: just comparing notes about teachers and their fellow students, the bad ones, the mad ones, the obviously crazy ones. A drink; and then another drink, and a bit of a laugh. His hair was glossy black, with a bit of a curl, and he knew how to laugh; and he seemed to like her – or, as well as she could tell.

One afternoon – another mild afternoon, autumn wearing on now, after three weeks, four weeks of this, and she was easy in his company now, and enjoying the laughs – she bobbed up at his desk in the library. 'What about a drink – say, at five o'clock? Just the one.'

But now Ronan kept his head bowed to the textured plastic surface of his desk. 'I'd better not,' he said. 'I should stay here.'

At first – for the first thirty seconds, or perhaps a minute – she thought nothing of it. Though it was unlike him, to put work first. She said something else, about how all work and no play would make Ronan – but paused then, taking in the bent head, the flush in the skin on his neck.

'What's the matter?'

'Nothing. I should just get on with this.'

Roisin looked up, and across the expanse of library to where the girl from Galway was sitting, facing her, facing them, taking it all in. The avidity. Roisin looked at her, then looked back at Ronan as he looked up, and seemed to steel himself.

'I heard that – that that girl, that she was your sister. I didn't know that you were that O'Hara. My mother wouldn't like it.'

A pause.

'What would your mother not like?'

He shook his head. 'She wouldn't like the whole thing.'

But his mother was in Cavan. Which wasn't the point, exactly: but it was all Roisin could think to say.

'I'm sorry,' Ronan said. He bowed his head to his book once again. She turned and left, passing the Galway girl, whose excitement had the texture of a force field.

Never put yourself into such a situation again, was the moral of the story. Better to stay on the surface. She took the lesson to heart.

She explained none of this to any of her colleagues. Nothing about distempered finishes, and the microscopic changes that a dusty surface can reveal; nothing about shade and tone; nothing about context and background. They would hardly understand. She had said her piece in her job interview, she had won over Dr Read; she would never have to speak in that way again, except when she was called upon, professionally, to do so.

She would never be in danger, again, of giving herself away. And besides, the art was the thing. She had made certain of that.

'And this?'

Viktor's fingertip hovered, that day, over a small piece, in oils. A small patchwork of fields, in spring; a hedge, hawthorn, blooming white. A tiny piece, heavily framed; the colours breathing.

'Also very beautiful,' he said. 'The colours, they are from heaven.'

Roisin smiled a little. 'That's an Emily Sandborne,' she said. '*My* Emily Sandborne. She had a way with colours,' she said. 'This is a favourite of mine. So simple. We have another of hers at the gallery. A famous one, nowadays, on cloth. The colours,' she added, and she moved to clear away the orange cake, the china cups, 'they sing in that one, too.'

28

It was not a pre-Raphaelite number, nothing so hackneyed. No tall virgin, red and crimped of hair, with a gleaming lip. No tall virgin dead of eye – or worse, wicked of eye, dedicated to the ideal of entrapment of some man, of achieving his death by drowning, of casting him into a slumber that would last a thousand years. The Tate had enough of those, God knows, stacked in storage and pinned on walls, and Roisin had seen them all. She was, as her mother used to say (though not about pre-Raphaelite paintings), she was *scunnered* by the sight of them – for all that the last pre-Raphaelite show had the punters queuing down the steps and around the corner. Each to their own – but she, for one, found such paintings disturbing, distasteful, verging on the grotesque.

'It isn't a question of *taste*. It isn't *taste* I'm talking about,' she had told Michael Clancy, as she sat in his pleasant kitchen one hot evening. A baking London summer day drawing to a close, an August day, and the grime lying on the surface of her skin, as though she were herself a dusty old painting that was sadly in need of restoration: and Michael Clancy listening to her, and expecting her to speak.

He had called in to see her at the Tate: out of the blue; she hadn't seen him for years, for decades. He was all Londoner now, after years in the Schmoke, as he called it; he was long transformed from the gawky string bean of long ago, when he and Maeve would hang around together after school, and he'd have her in stitches. For years, Roisin hadn't heard from him at all: and now up he popped, suggesting a coffee.

She'd drawn herself up, she remembered: she had work to do, she couldn't just walk off the job. This was the *Tate*, it wasn't some factory floor.

'Wise the fuck up, Roisin,' he told her, with the same startling familiarity. 'And don't be getting high and mighty with me. It's the *Tate*. I'm not talking about going on strike, I'm not talking about starting a revolution, I'm just talking about a coffee. They tell me you're doing well here, so presumably you can have a cup of coffee without asking permission. We don't even have to leave the fucking building if you don't want to.'

So casual, as though they had been friends for years.

'Who's telling you?' she asked. 'And keep your voice down, and stop swearing.'

'Fuck fuck fuck,' he said. And, 'Everybody's telling me. Roisin O'Hara and her fancy job. Come on now, girl, move.'

His language might have been bad, but he was dressed well, even Roisin could see this – good jeans, dark, straight, nicely cut, nice jacket, nicely cut – and his hair looked good too. They went downstairs to the cafe: she felt nervous, as though he were a teacher from long ago; and she felt she ought to try to impress him – though she had no idea how to go about doing such a thing. She felt her own – wilful frumpiness, she supposed it must be, in the face of his snappy metropolitan clothes and his obvious sense of ease and happiness; frumpiness and an absence of happiness. His happiness was tangible; and surely her own absence of happiness was just as evident.

He told her about himself: he lived in Bow, he had a partner, Tim, English, they'd been together for a thousand years, they even had a little place on the north Devon coast, imagine! – and she felt herself blushing painfully as she tried and failed to encapsulate her own life in the same few easeful sentences.

Michael had always been sharp, she remembered: sharp of voice, quick to see things, to read people, to extract information and read between the lines. It had been one of the things Maeve had loved about him.

'He could buy you and sell you,' Maeve had said, long ago. 'Takes no prisoners.' He had to be that way, she went on to explain, long ago: it was that or die. A 'fruit', she called him: and a fruit needed protection in those days, in that place. A cage, a grille; you'd be pecked to death, otherwise. A fruit needed to protect himself or be protected by other people. It was the first, for Michael – and it worked, too.

Nobody talked about fruits any longer, nobody she knew, anyway – but evidently, all these years later, he remained sharp. She reflected that of course he hadn't known her so very well: not when they were children, and not later either, after Maeve, and then he had left home, never or hardly ever to return – 'I scrubbed the dust of that place from my sandals, darling, there wasn't a speck left by the time I'd finished' – but now, in London, he seemed well able to read her, to take her in, to lean in slightly across the silver, curvaceous Tate table and watch her as she haltingly spoke. As if they had known each other, had been friends, for years and years.

Also, his sharpness seemed coated now in something softer, a fleecy lining that must come along, did it? with happiness and security. She didn't relax that day, exactly, as she drank her coffee and listened to him and spoke a little when asked to do so: but she didn't keep her guard completely up either, not after the first ten minutes. She allowed him to peep over the battlements, and see the empty spaces behind the walls, and she didn't much mind that he could see them. It was a relief, really.

'Why did you come looking for me?'

They met again – for a glass of wine this time, at his suggestion – the following week. In a Shoreditch wine bar (impossibly on trend; all her rustiness and insecurity returned in a rush; one would think that she was accustomed to the company of artists, and they were here in abundance, like a flock of gulls; but not a bit of it; here she was, tense all over again), where they sat in a corner, two wide glasses between them.

'Why did you come looking for me?' she said. 'So much time has passed, and it isn't as though we were particular friends to begin with.'

Michael swirled the Riesling in his glass. 'True.'

'You were Maeve's friend more than mine, and even then: we were hardly more than children, both of you. Any of us.'

It was difficult to speak Maeve's name.

'I was back in Ireland a few weeks ago,' Michael said, 'and I ran into your mum in town. She was being a proud mummy,' he said, 'all Roisin this and Roisin that. Roisin in London, doing well, Roisin is at the Tate, of all places. Mind you, it is impressive, a position at the Tate. I'm impressed myself.'

'I had a good CV,' Roisin said, 'a few articles and a few exhibitions that went down nicely, in Leeds, in Manchester, and I did a good interview. They seemed to like me,' she said, barely able to sand the puzzled note out of her voice.

After a moment, Michael went on. 'I thought she looked, I hope you don't mind me saying this, sad as well as old, your mum, so I stopped and said hello, and after she stopped boasting about you, she told me you didn't come back all that much, so I found myself wondering how you were.' He paused for breath, took a delicate sip of wine. 'I came away feeling sad too, about Maeve, and I wondered if you felt the same way, if you've been carrying sadness with you all these years. We didn't know each other all that well, maybe, but we both knew Maeve. So I felt I owed it to Maeve.' He took another sip. 'Belatedly, of course: it took me long enough; you'd almost think I didn't owe her all that much. This is nice,' he added, meaning the wine.

Roisin didn't like to think about Maeve. She had trained herself out of it. It was of a piece with not going to Ireland all that much, of not talking all that much about herself, of holding the world at arm's length. Of not saying Maeve's name if she could help it. So now she looked at her own glass of wine – red, 'fruity', the wine list had promised her, with 'notes of redcurrant' – and said nothing, and he didn't press the matter.

After this, Michael would from time to time suggest a meeting: a coffee, a drink; in due course, she had dinner in Bow, in the house he shared with Tim. She continued to wonder, at first, what it was that Michael wanted: what could he want, from her? It took a while for her to recognise that he wanted nothing – nothing, that is, except her friendship. That she represented a connection to a past that he valued, to a person that he had loved, to a whole suite of memories and associations that they shared. And eventually, that he liked her for herself: liked her enough to want to spend a little time with her, to introduce her to his life, his partner, his home.

These were strange sensations: again, Roisin felt rusty in the face of them. It took some time to relax into his friendship, though she managed it – fitfully – in the end.

Enough to assert herself in the matter of art and paintings. This was her thing: something she knew more about than did Michael. She had opinions, and she might as well voice them.

The pre-Raphaelites. Dinner in the house in Bow: a warm evening at the end of a hot day; a green salad, tabbouleh and hummus, and cold chicken.

'It isn't a question of *taste*,' she said. 'It isn't *taste* I'm talking about.'

★

One face looks out from all his canvases,
One self-same figure sits or walks or leans:
We found her hidden just behind those screens,
That mirror gave back all her loveliness.
A queen in opal or in ruby dress,
A nameless girl in freshest summer greens,
A saint, an angel – every canvas means
The same one meaning, neither more or less...

Roisin spoke the lines with a fresh sense of indignation. Michael and Tim's garden seemed to overflow into their neat kitchen: pots of bay and thyme and rosemary basking in the warmth of this summer evening. It would be dusk soon here in Bow, but for the moment the sunshine hung on; a bar of brightness shone on the high wall of brown London brick that terminated the view from the kitchen windows. The brown wall glowed red, as if lit from within. Beyond, the unending city sound, a hum, a drone. Tim bent to lift a platter from a low cupboard, arranged chicken on the platter, drizzled a yogurt-and-garlic dressing across the chicken. He was a man of precision, of few words, and he listened: Roisin had noticed him listen to her, at any rate, to absorb her words, ask a question now and again. Chicken and yogurt, and tabbouleh and hummus; salad with a dressing, both sweet and acid, honey and lemon juice; crusty white bread; a sweating bottle of pink wine.

'Dig in,' Tim said.

Michael was a listener too, though this was not immediately apparent: he joked, he drummed his fingers on the hard glass-like surface of the modern kitchen table until

Tim gently rested his own hand on top, he was filled with a sort of energy that might set the nerves jangling were he not amusing with it, spirited, fun. But he too knew how to listen. They made a good couple, these two men; Roisin could see this at a glance. She did glance: indeed, it was difficult not to stare, to drink in what they had.

Difficult not to envy what they had.

However. She would not be rude: she could hardly just sit there, staring, or chomping her way through the meal set so generously before her, without giving something back. She must speak, she must opine, and suggest, and float. She must sing, a little, for her supper. Michael had mentioned art, the new exhibition coming up at the Tate, and she heard herself speaking, through forkfuls of parslied tabbouleh, of taste. It isn't, she heard herself saying, a question of taste. And she remembered that there was a virtue in what she had just said. The virtue was that this was what she actually thought.

'They didn't care about the actual women,' she said, watching as Tim spooned more tabbouleh, a perfect pyramid of green-flecked tabbouleh, onto his plate. She had a sense that Tim didn't know exactly what to make of her, at moments such as these: from silent to opinionated in one leap, but she could hardly help this; Michael himself had introduced the subject, and she must speak.

'I see the Tate has a big pre-Raphaelite exhibition coming up,' he'd said to her. 'Have you had a hand in that, darling? We'll go along' – a glance at Tim – 'what do you think?'

'Oh, I should imagine so,' Tim said.

'I haven't had much to do with it,' she said: and both Tim

and Michael picked up – it wasn't difficult – the reserve in her voice.

'Not a fan?' enquired Michael, with *faux* delicacy.

'Not really, no.'

How could she be? You only had to look at those paintings, one after another after another, to see what those men thought of the women they were painting – and by extension, all women. The women were as flat as the canvases themselves, was the truth of the matter. She recited Christina Rossetti's poem – and now she filled in the detail.

'She was writing about her own brother, and essentially about all the men he had around him. She wasn't blind, and she wasn't deaf; she knew what was going on.' These women were dead, or as good as: and suddenly she felt a lift, a wave of emotion, and she stopped speaking. She could tell that neither Michael – who was gazing at her – nor Tim – who was eating his chicken silently, listening all the while – had particularly thought of the pre-Raphaelites in such terms; she could tell that she had given them something to consider. And she could tell that they had detected, as she herself detected, the sudden thickening of the atmosphere in the warm, darkening kitchen.

Tim got up, struck a match, lit the candles in the pair of round glass tealight holders on the table. The glass was thick, and yellow: the candlelight shone gold, on the glassy tabletop.

She ate a little tabbouleh herself, the scent of mint, the taste of sweet onion, and parsley.

The air thick, with – with something, could she allow herself to sniff and taste this too, and decipher? With grief, and unspoken words. Not difficult to decipher, not at all. Tim said, 'Roisin, what sort of paintings do you like?'

Alive. Paintings that were alive. That teemed with life. She gave a short, dry bark of a laugh. 'Unfashionable paintings, really. The really, really unfashionable ones.'

It was all too easy to lecture, she felt – to lecture, in this case, two men with manners, two kind men, two men able and willing to listen. But this was not a gallery, nor a lecture theatre: and gentle Tim, gentleman Tim had asked earnestly, as though he truly wanted to know, as though he wanted to understand something, to put his finger on a point that was troubling him.

And she realised that she wanted to tell them too.

She looked at him: she saw what she already of course understood, that he knew about Maeve, that he and Michael were piecing her life together around this fact, this silence, and were coming to reasonable conclusions, and to the truth.

'Light,' she said, 'and colour, and life. Is what I like: any or all of these three.'

Tim nodded, didn't speak, didn't jump in, waited for her to continue.

'It doesn't have to be a period, or a style, or a name: a piece just has to capture something, something that appeals to my heart. And I only know it when I've seen it. I like the Victorians, the unfashionable stuff,' she acknowledged, 'not the pre-Raphaelites, obviously,' she said, and now both Tim and Michael laughed. 'Some of the other painting from the period: the painting that's alive, not the dead stuff.' She told them about the few pieces she had acquired over the years, filled with crowds: carriages stuffed with people, and beaches with donkeys and bathing machines and children, and railway stations filled with masses of people. People.

Michael made as if to speak, but she charged on.

'Do you know Emily Sandborne?' she asked them.

They shook their heads in unison: and then – 'Wait, yes, I do, I mean,' said Michael, 'I've heard of her. The National Gallery in Dublin has one of her pieces, right?'

'That's right.'

'I don't,' said Tim. 'I don't know a thing about her. Tell me about Emily Sandborne.'

Roisin took a breath, and told them.

Emily Sandborne was for years considered a classic downtrodden Victorian lady artist. *Mrs Sandborne.* Her work was ignored, or at best belittled; her talent was mocked and scorned; her paintings were given few airings; and in the years after her death, she was almost completely forgotten.

'For years and years.' Even though her paintings were, she said, 'magically good. And then, the colour: she had some ways with colour that nobody has ever been able to reproduce.'

And on top of that, she told them, she died, in 1839, of syphilis, passed on to her by her prostitute-frequenting husband.

'Oh yes,' Tim said, 'like Mrs Beeton.'

Just like Mrs Beeton. 'So, she died, of syphilis, and that was an end to that.'

But eventually her remains were disinterred.

'The story went around that a painting had been buried

with her, and her descendants petitioned for her grave to be opened. I suppose they sniffed money. This was back around the time of the First World War. So she was dug up, eventually, and this painting was discovered with her. On cloth, on linen, mid-century. It had been buried with her.'

Michael nodded. 'Oh yes, I remember now. Like a shroud.'

'Well, that's the idea that went around. But – no: not a shroud. It was a piece she created, that she wanted buried with her. But not a shroud: she wanted to take it with her when she went: but not to wrap herself up in. It wasn't morbid, that way. The point is,' she said, 'it was a distemper piece. Completely unblemished, as though it was some relic, some miraculous thing. Distemper pieces fade and fade with time; they don't last, they almost never survive the passage of time. But she did something to this piece, so that her colours shine – like stained glass, really. It's the most beautiful piece I've ever seen,' she said and paused.

Tim said, 'What did she do to the colours, to make them last?'

'Nobody knows.'

It was snapped up, she said, spotted by a curator at the National Gallery in Dublin. It became a small curiosity, to be shown once a year, for a month, as a sort of sweet ritual. Something to be petted, said Roisin, and wrinkled her nose. 'She still wasn't getting her due.'

And then, twenty or so years ago, the fashions swung and changed again: one or two of Sandborne's pieces were reconsidered, one or two more were put up for sale by private collectors, and fetched swollen sums; suddenly, a couple of municipal English galleries had to reassess and reinsure the Sandbornes in their dusty collections. Trendy Sandborne, suddenly.

A few historians took an interest. One such turned up a letter in the British Library: a note, a single sheet of paper, written by Sandborne and detailing her plans for her last piece. Written just before she died. Suddenly the piece hanging quietly in Dublin had a name – *The Jewel* – and a story. The gallery seemed to realise all over again what it had in its possession: its gorgeousness, its utter uniqueness. And today, *The Jewel* was to all intents and purposes – priceless.

Tim and Michael nodded together. Tim said, 'Why do you think she took *The Jewel* to the grave with her? I mean, why did she go to so much trouble?'

Roisin paused. The garden was dark now, and the candles burned all the more clearly in their yellow glass holders.

'She was taking back what she owned, before she died.' Roisin paused again and said, 'Asserting herself. She was telling the world, *I love this, you can't have it, it's too late, it's mine, and I'm taking it with me.* Of course, they did take it back in the end: so lots of people think she has been betrayed, her grave robbed, her wishes ignored. And others think that she had her way, that she took back some power while she still could. Plus she was only thirty-something when she died, and her horrible husband as good as killed her, and her work is so fabulous, and she took her mysteries to the grave with her – and, well,' said Roisin, 'you can see why she's having a bit of a moment.'

Tim and Michael nodded, and Tim leaned forward a little and asked, 'And what do you think?'

'I think it was a question of love,' Roisin said, and her voice vibrated a little as she spoke. 'She was dying, after years of seeing her work ignored; and I think that she wanted her best work close to her heart. She had lost faith in her world,' she said, 'and quite right too. How could she feel anything else? Her work and her talents were all she had. And *The Jewel* encapsulated this. And so, taking it with her was the only thing she could do.'

They nodded. That made sense. Michael said, 'So, she was renewing her love for her work, and her faith in – herself, I suppose, in the future.'

Herself, the future. 'Yes,' Roisin said, 'exactly.'

Roisin felt a faint fluttering of happiness, as she farewelled the men, in their gold candlelight, and took the tube home later that evening. Faint, tentative, but it was there; and it had only a little to do with the good food, the greens, the parsley and mint, and the lemon cake Tim had presented unexpectedly as a final flourish. The train was half empty and the carriage, hot and airless though it was, was tolerable; and she felt a glimmering of happiness. 'I hope you'll come again soon,' Tim said and kissed her on one cheek, on the other cheek, warmth leavened by English formality. 'It was lovely to meet you.' Michael walked her through the muggy night to the soot-smelling station, where he enveloped her in a hug: she preferred the two kisses herself, it was the least difficult way to be touched, but she knew he meant well. A little while later, as she changed at Embankment station for the train to Clapham, a drunk vomited almost on her shoes, right there on the Northern Line platform. But even this could not strip away these tentative feelings of happiness, which she carried with her as she rattled south.

As for Michael, as he walked the short distance from the station back to the house, he remembered the tone of Roisin's voice, the note of passion, of engagement, that seemed to hold her as she spoke.

'OK?' Tim called from the kitchen. 'She got away?'

Michael went into the kitchen, pulled out a chair, sat, poured another half-glass of wine. 'She's only half alive, isn't she? These paintings, this half-life, she's boxed in.'

Tim paused, clicked a button on the dishwasher, pushed the door closed, turned back. 'Seems so.'

'Like a shadow world.' Michael looked at his glass of warming pink wine, looked at the darkening garden, looked at the yellow candles.

Tim shook his head, shrugged. 'I don't know,' he said. 'Top me up a little bit too, will you?' He watched as Michael poured out the last of the wine. 'A shadow world: that's exactly it.'

'It's not up to me to race around feeling sorry for people,' Michael said and frowned. 'But I do feel sorry for her.'

'She came alive when she talked about her paintings,' Tim mused, 'I suppose. But I know what you mean. It doesn't seem enough.' He ran a finger around the rim of his glass, hesitated for a moment. Then he said, 'You said they found a wire, didn't you?'

Michael nodded. 'So the gossip was, around the town. That Maeve tried to deal with it herself: that's what girls had to do, back then; there was damn-all help available. And it went wrong, and she died of blood loss, there in the grotto. And Roisin was the one to find her.'

'And she never got over it.'

Another nod. 'And she never got over it.'

They sat in silence, in the yellow candlelight.

29

The Sculpture Court was practically complete now. Roisin clipped along through the galleries, the porphyry and gentian and cerulean and lapis: she swung open the heavy green-copper doors which formed its dramatic entrance, but which seemed too heavy, almost, to move – they would have to do something about that – and took a step or two into the great hall. It rang with noise: a drill was screeching against the polished floor; and a gaggle of workmen, in high-visibility jackets and wearing masks and goggles and outsize pads over their ears – they looked like aliens – were standing around another man, similarly clad and accessorised, crouching on the ground.

How many men does it take to create a Sculpture Court? – lots and lots of men. Plus electric cables, and dust, and a racket.

And yet, the hall was almost complete. She could see its final shape ghostly amid the din: white light welling from hidden ceiling windows, scale and height, grandeur and beautiful space. Statues would presently be dotted through this expanse. And *The Jewel* would be raised into its final position, just – there, the star of the show; and her eye was lifted, and caught and held by the sight of the space high on the wall. Read had pointed it out to them all, a few weeks ago, at a democratic staff meeting, at the 'big reveal', as the email had wincingly put it. They had gathered in the unfinished hall, even more dusty and displeasing on that day, and the reveal had been revealed, and they had looked, and listened to Read's voice echoing through the dusty air, and had – seeming, Roisin observed, for the most part underwhelmed – returned to their desks.

Roisin had hung on that day, for a few minutes: after the others had dispersed, and even Dr Read had slipped away – seeming dispirited; that vertical frown mark between her eyes looked, Roisin thought, even more like the line of an axe blow – she had stayed behind to take in the scene in the soon-to-be Sculpture Court. The walls were still bare: soon, she knew, they would be silk-hung in the colour she herself had selected: green, a dim phosphorus green, a shade and depth she wondered about, though it was too late now. The painting would be raised, and hung, and the courtyard and the entire building would be left open to the punters, and that would be that.

Someone else had stayed behind: a young man, hardly more than a boy, though tall for his age, and too thin. A bounce of curly red hair. He was, Roisin recalled dimly, a new person in the something department; and lumped with the task of leading guided tours around the place. Roisin had nodded at him that day, and looked at the hair and away, and left the young man to it.

Dark skin under his eyes: too dark for such a young thing. Roisin remembered this too.

His thinness and his red hair had reminded her of Maeve: and she had walked away, a little faster.

Now, today, the boy was here again. He was standing behind one of the heavy doors, against the dusty wall, as though he hadn't moved in the intervening two weeks. The air in the hall, though still full of noise, was now less full of dust; the light from the hidden windows was clearer, whiter, more radiant. Roisin's eye, accustomed as it was to surfaces, scanned his surface too: the dust in the air seemed to have settled on this boy's skin, for it looked clouded.

Again, Roisin was reminded of Maeve.

A bright voice, like a gleam of coloured light, glancing across her memory: 'I wish you'd let me help you.'

She turned to the boy, quickly, before she changed her mind, raising her voice above the screeching drill.

'So, what do you think of this room?'

The drill, the terrible screeching, it actually helped. Difficult to be – tense, inhibited, chilly, all the things she otherwise inevitably would be, now that she had to raise her voice, to almost bawl at this dusty-faced boy.

'I think,' the boy replied loudly, 'I think it'll be great when it's finished. When the place is cleaned up and completed.' He coughed, and then added, 'And when they unplug the drill.'

The slenderest of exchanges, but the boy's reply enabled Roisin to smile a little, and then the boy smiled too.

The young man. He was a young man.

'Actually, I can't wait for them to finish,' he said. 'I don't care so much about the sculptures, but I can't wait to see the Sandborne hung there on the wall. I've only started here in the gallery, and I haven't ever seen this painting, I mean, in the flesh.'

Roisin hadn't either, and said so.

'Really?' the young man said – loudly, and then stopped and blushed at the sound of his echoing voice, for the workmen had chosen this moment to pause their drilling. 'Sorry,' he added, and smiled, and Roisin smiled too.

'Oh yes,' she said. 'I've only been here a few years myself: and the paintings have been in storage all that time. Including this painting – or especially this painting. So, no opportunity. And besides,' Roisin said, 'it'll be worth waiting for.'

Like Maeve, just a little. More that there was just a touch of something that seemed to encourage a warmth, a note of colour. That was all.

She added, 'Though I can't wait either, to be honest,' and laughed again.

So trite – *I can't wait* – and yet a connection made, there and then. They talked about the painting for a few moments. A chink in the armour.

Then they walked back through the cerulean, the porphyry rooms together. The young man's name was Gerard, he revealed, a touch belatedly, as they clacked along together. He extended a hand: 'How do you do.' Gerard: a thoroughly plain name. Roisin shook Gerard's hand, and smiled kindly into his dark-shadowed eyes, and introduced herself. 'Roisin.' And Gerard said that, oh yes, he knew who Roisin was; she was the Keeper of Displays; it was nice of her to take the time to say hello; he blushed again. Then Roisin descended the new staircase, long and white and gleaming, into the lobby; and Gerard went upstairs, and that was that.

Later – after a silent walk home through Dublin streets that hissed with rain and traffic, after eggs scrambled and bread toasted and *The Archers* – Roisin sat in her painted house, and thought about Maeve. A chink: that was it. There was nothing much about Gerard, hardly a single thing if you discounted his hair, his frame, to connect him with Maeve.

It was the painting.

The colours, Gerard had said hesitantly – and then continued, seeming to gather a head of steam, build a little speed. The colours in the windows: the supernatural gleam of green and blue and red and yellow, the radiance, the lustre, the unfaded beauty. The gleam of the pauldron in the darkness, he said, and the welling green of the stone set into the pauldron: the black armour worn by the guard, and shining black amid the shadows; the glossy, shadowed horse; and the dark heel that hung down amid the fitful light of the lamps carried by the other guards; the eyes caught in this same light and glinting too, and this glint catching not their exultation at the scene, but their grief, and their shame, and their fear. Such tired faces, the black shadows pooling in the hollows of their ageing, paunching skin. Emily Sandborne herself, with her long, dark hair, alert, grieving, an observer in the shadows. All these human faces – said Gerard, and now Roisin caught a wink of a tear in his eyes as he spoke. 'Sorry,' said Gerard. 'I fill up every time I see this painting, in a book or a catalogue. It's his heel.' The leathered, rough, tough old heel, the dusty and travel-worn heel that hangs from the saddle, that says everything, that cries out for the pity and compassion that this man will never receive. 'Look at me. What will I be like when I see the actual piece?' Gerard stopped, and Roisin nodded.

'I know.'

The scrambled eggs cooled on the plate, as Roisin thought about the painting, the colours and the shadows, Sandborne watching. Maeve. Herself. The walls of the room were lit dimly: their textured surfaces were alive with a thousand gradations of light and darkness, a landscape of tiny, infinitesimal shadows and lights. She knew. She had trained herself out of looking back, of glancing over her shoulder – but no training would ever in the end suffice. The painting was alive. She exhaled.

Gerard has seen this too, thought Roisin: and God knows, there is nothing wrong with that.

Maeve would have understood this boy too. Better than most.

A fortnight passed. At the end of this fortnight, the gallery reopened – the great reopening, they said acidly in the fetid staff room, as they observed the axe-blow frown between Dr Read's eyes, the ultimate in reopenings – and Roisin saw

Gerard again. It was, yes, his role in proceedings to conduct some of the public tours of the gallery spaces: of the halls and great vaulted rooms and courtyards now resplendent in the colours and papers selected by Roisin herself, and now to be seen by the people for the first time.

Rather him than me, Roisin thought.

Already she had had her fill of this reopening business. Receptions and warming white wine, mini-spring rolls and mini-chicken skewers, complete with a peanut dipping sauce, and mini-blondies and -brownies, and an endless din of congratulatory conversation – they all made her want to dash her brains out against one of her own lapis walls. Having to conduct up to eight tours a day would have been the last straw.

Gerard, though, appeared not to mind the process too much. To be sure, the halls rapidly became airless, overstuffed and overheated – an exalted version of the staff room – and these crowds ensured that nobody would receive the experience of their dreams: but Gerard seemed to keep his cool, to maintain a semblance of grace in the midst of this atmosphere of fart and egg sandwich, body odour and damp wool.

Roisin saw him on the second tour of the opening day: the crowds already peaking, the crush dreadful. There was a pack on the long, white stairs, sharp elbows and snippets of conversation as she tried to elbow past. 'Oh, *ages* and *ages*,' one fur-coated woman said to her companion as they swept past, 'it's been closed for ages and *ages*; I'm *dying* to see what they've done with it. Apparently, it cost a mint, a *mint*.' Roisin abandoned her attempt to gain the top of the stairs independently, allowed herself to be carried along with the crowd, her feet hardly touching the floor, noticed two of the security guards pinned against the walls – and then saw Gerard apparently in charge of this throng of humanity.

A Pied Piper, leading them up and in.

'Just follow me, please,' he said lightly – but his voice carried surprisingly well, and his flock seemed disposed to obey. Let's have a look at this, Roisin thought, and was carried on and in, coming to rest at last in the Sculpture Court. How beautiful it looked! – even on this packed day, and her heart swelled with something like pride. And how fine the painting looked, suspended there against her green silk walls, below the welling white light. The pools of shadow, the gleaming eyes, the bars of black light. Let's see this.

Gerard turned to face the swelling crowd, began to talk. The buzz of conversation died away.

'Pauldron,' he said, and Roisin watched as he began to speak.

'Notice the gleam of the pauldron,' Gerard said. He held a pointer in one hand: was it nerves? – for he was pushing its tip into the palm of his other hand. He was wearing a polo neck, fine merino, light grey; and perspiration at his armpits was darkening the wool. 'The pauldron: it's almost the centrepiece of the whole painting,' Gerard went on. 'Perhaps I shouldn't single out one feature like this, but' – and here he paused for a moment, 'it's really how I feel.'

Roisin had been preparing to feel pity for the boy – a mere boy, really; too young for such a task; what was Read thinking about? and that sweater ruined, surely – but now she saw that pity was not in this case required. Gerard had their attention. He didn't give a damn about his wet armpits.

Maeve, again.

The crowd grew further, filling the broad spaces between the white marble statues, the boy talked on. 'Not the figures, not their expressions. Just his pauldron; it's the gleam of the pauldron that catches my eye every time. That catches in Sandborne's colours. She's looking behind their humanity, the artist is, do you see? – she's breaking down the machine.'

He stopped, then, and turned, and gestured with the pointer, and all eyes followed its tip, to look at the purity of green and blue and red and yellow, the bright, blazing trail of white on black.

'And now look at the foot hanging down, look at the sole, the heel, do you see it?' – and he ran his fingers through his red hair. 'There,' he said, and the pointer stabbed higher, 'just the sheer humanity of it. The hard skin, the leathery sole, the dust.' He looked, Roisin looked, they all looked, at this hanging emblem of humanity, at the shining light and the darkness, at the slash of the pauldron, and the glimmering lamps, brightness and darkness against jet. 'A beautiful combination of darkness and light,' he said, and Roisin watched, they all watched as Gerard dropped his arm and the pointer and laughed. 'Darkness and light,' he said, and now he laughed aloud. 'It gets me every time.' He paused. 'Every time: you'd think I was an expert – but I only saw *The Jewel* for the first time this week!'

The audience tittered.

'And there she is, we think,' and again the pointer rose, and wavered, and pointed. 'Emily Sandborne, and nobody knows how she captured this distemper painting, and managed to keep it alive, and unfading.' A pause. 'She took this particular secret to the grave.'

He had them: the crowd moved, exhaled audibly – and now there was, spontaneously, a round of applause; and Gerard flushed, and lowered the pointer, and nodded. He knew his mind: that was it. Like Maeve, he had his opinions. Roisin looked over the heads of the crowd at the sparks of light in the painting, and then she slipped away from her green silk walls, and out into the corridor, and away.

30

Another week passed – and now in the gallery, the lights were burning into the night. Only in one office, and that office faced away from the city and into a void. Not indeed – Roisin had all too frequently grumbled to herself – a void, a courtyard made over glossily by architect and builder and curator, full with silk and paved with Italian terrazzo: it was nothing like that. This void was damp, and gloomy; a line of bins in varying shallow hues, green and brown and black, stood ranged against a wall, along a stretch of which moss crawled from the damp ground. The public would never see this particular void, not if the gallery had anything to do with it.

Dr Read had offered a touch of apology on that first day, as she showed Roisin around her new domain. 'We're not planning work on this wing,' she remarked as she opened a fire door and revealed a dingy corridor, murky light, low ceilings – and beyond, a warren of small, partitioned office spaces. 'It's a pity, but—' and she sighed a pitying sigh. Roisin would later discover that Dr Read occupied a corner office high in the building, with sheets of windows offering a clear, cool north light. Later: that first day was all poor ventilation and grimed windows, with the stuffy staff room as the pièce de resistance.

Tonight, in her office looking into a void, Roisin was working late.

It was all the gallery's fault. She had no call to be working late, she had no call to be working after five o'clock at all; she ought to be in bed. But instead, she was here. Instead, the gallery's reopening had put, as she had reflected loudly to anyone who would listen, the cat among the pigeons. Rejigging and rehanging and remodelling: it had been almost too much.

Roisin expected no sympathy from her colleagues – and this was as well, for there was none to be had. They had become (in spite of themselves, in spite of their sarky comments, day after day and month after month) excited by the swirl of these last weeks: by the finishing touches applied, the clearing of wires and scaffolding and dust, the lighting of lights, the rising delight engendered by this upcoming reopening, the full and thrilling rehang of the collection, the rising energy in the building. They were delighted, and they avoided eye contact with Roisin, and avoided listening, and having to reply, and moved away.

Roisin did not appear to notice; or at any rate, gave no indication of having noticed.

She noticed that Gerard alone listened, paid attention, sympathised. She noticed silently, and was grateful.

Now, tonight, she sat in her low-ceilinged office. Beside her sat Gerard. He looked tired, was saying little; Roisin, on the other hand, was saying a great deal.

She was at her worst – and she knew it, and hardly cared.

'And now the other file – no, the other one, the red one, give it to me. No, never mind, I'll find it,' and her hand riffled through a hillock of multi-coloured plastic files on her desk. She pulled out the red file, and opened it, and a collection of photocopied articles and images spilled out and onto the ground. Roisin preferred at all times a paper trail – but now she clicked her tongue with exasperation. 'No, never mind,' she said again, 'I'll do it' – and then she sat back, and closed her eyes for a second. Opened them, and tilted back in her chair, and watched Gerard on hands and knees on the tough, institutional carpet, filling his hands with papers.

No, not a power thing. Roisin's eyes had filled with tears.

Although: perhaps a power thing, perhaps a little.

It was late. It was very late; this had been going on all day, and Roisin was very tired.

But still.

'Gerard. Please: I'm sorry,' she suddenly said. 'This isn't your job: it's never your job to be on the floor picking up after me, or after anyone. Please. This is my job.' Then she was on the floor, and Gerard – and the shadows under his eyes were darker than ever, now – was back in his chair, and the sudden, shocking imbalance was cleared away.

They had become friends, in the course of two weeks. After a manner: *friendly colleagues* was perhaps a better description – but even this meant the occasional coffee together, and the occasional conversation that veered away from art and art history into other areas. It was all rather surprising.

All the more reason, then, why Gerard should not be found on hands and knees, picking up bits of paper that he hadn't even dropped, that were nothing to do with him.

'I'm sorry,' Roisin said. This was all to do with a temper, a sourness. None of it was Gerard's fault. Gerard nodded, mildly enough.

Now Roisin went from her knees to her feet, and back to sitting, and pulled a set of floorplans across her cluttered desk, and compared them to another set of papers, bundled on her desk: text panels, which she had been working on for days – for days and days – and which were late being displayed. Late! – and she the Keeper of Displays! Roisin wanted to weep: the rehang of the collection was complete, and the panels were incomplete, and it was all her fault. Her walls were being violated. The shame and disgrace were immeasurable.

'Look,' she said, and she gestured first at a text panel, before pushing an index finger into the floorplan. 'The Sculpture Court: I put down that *The Jewel* is hanging on the south wall, when it isn't.' Her voice rose an anguished notch. 'It isn't. It's the west, the west wall. I haven't corrected it!'

It was a dispute from a day, two days previously – worst of all, picked up by Read herself.

'Are you sure it's the west wall?' Gerard couldn't read maps.

'Making a fool of myself,' Roisin said. Her precious dignity, her precarious self-respect, all of this was slipping.

'A bloody eejit, as my mother would call me, and she'd be right, too. I had to sign off on' – and she pointed at the bundle of files, at the papers, at the disordered desk – 'all of this; and now I'll have the Board saying I don't know my south from my west.' She fetched breath. 'Oh God,' she said, 'I'll have to go and stand there, and see if I can't work it out. And sort this out once and for all.' She stepped over the papers, she moved to the door.

'I'll come too,' Gerard said, 'and then we'll call it a night.'

The young man, the boy, rose to his feet slowly, and followed her out into the corridor, and through the swing doors. Her fingers moved quickly across the key pad of the alarm – so rapidly, indeed, that she failed to realise that the alarm was in fact unset. She stepped into the main gallery. A suite of rooms, the colours shining even under the dim lights, stretched ahead.

'Come on then,' and they set off along the corridor.

It was pleasant to have a friend. Remember that. Not someone who chatted and who needed a chat – for Gerard, as they paced these beautiful, dim rooms, was quiet, happy to take in the spaces, the shadowy paintings, the airiness, the mystery and wonder of a beautiful, wondrous place. Not someone who needed endless attention, and not someone who probed. Just a young man who reminded her a little – a very little – of Maeve: who in spite of a fragility, had a sense of himself. Who had, when it came to it, a set of shoulders, and a pair of lungs, and a degree of passion.

'I don't mean *taste*,' Gerard had said. They had been in the Sculpture Court, looking up once more at the painting now installed there. No pointer, no perspiration marks. 'It isn't *taste* I'm talking about.' He hadn't had to explain:

Roisin knew. There was truth there: there, in that hanging, leathery heel.

This was what she had told Michael Clancy, sitting in his darkening kitchen in Bow. Strip away the blather, the technique and the brushstrokes, the materials and the application, and look for the truth. He had listened and Tim had listened, and the candles had glowed in their yellow glass holders. How pleasant to have a friend, how pleasant to be on a wavelength. Her life had stripped away all of that: all of it, and her whole life, ever since she had lost Maeve. She had pushed Michael away too. Perhaps she might claw back some of these feelings, and acquire herself a second chance.

Their feet clacked on the hard, glossy floor, and echoes ran clacking along the walls. There were the heavy copper doors of the Sculpture Court – and besides, who cared, really, whether the painting was hanging on the west wall or the south wall? She would try to work it out now: then, she would pack Gerard into a taxi and send him home; and she would go home herself; and west wall or south wall, Roisin thought, I'll fix it in the morning.

I need to wise up.

Her hands met the cold copper of the doors. She pushed, straining a little, and then the doors swung silently on their massive hinges, and opened, and they entered the vast, silk-hung room.

Cane

31

Ward was old enough to remember the days when there was only one way of getting into this gallery: a sort of minor-key imposing entrance on the square around the corner. But nowadays, most visitors used this spiffy new entrance, all white Portland stone and modern lines, which opened into the gallery's tall and dramatically top-lit new wing.

He'd been glad to leave Dublin behind.

Rob bustled, now: he began wheeling his little suitcase – natty – towards the gallery doors. 'Where'd you get it?' Ward had asked the moment he had laid eyes on it: covetous eyes, he wanted this exact model for himself; but Rob had refused to divulge.

Now he glanced over his shoulder. 'I'm coming,' Ward said; and Rob rolled his eyes, and vanished through the doors.

The gallery, of course, was closed to the public. Barely opened, and now closed again: a slashed throat had a way of messing up plans. A couple of policemen stood stationed just inside the doors. Rob now spoke to one of them – Ward was still busy with the doors – and the policeman spoke into his radio. They waited, standing by their cases: the two policemen didn't seem especially keen to chat, and Ward felt this as a mild surprise, accustomed as he was to Irish informality.

Well, whatever. They would have to wait, standing there by the wheelie cases. We probably look like cabin crew, Ward thought – although he knew they looked like no such thing. Too old, for one thing; though at least he was in decent shape, while Rob enjoyed the sort of strapping superhuman physique that God seemed to reserve for New Zealanders and Australians.

The gallery was in good shape too: as a minute, two minutes, ticked by, and still nobody seemed to be in any hurry to meet and greet them, Ward passed the time by looking away from Rob's physique (Rob himself was glancing over some gallery literature detailing upcoming exhibitions, for all the world as though he had just arrived on a weekend away) and taking in the surroundings. The gleaming whiteness, the daylight, even on this glum afternoon, welling in from above, the dramatic staircase which led away into the main part of the building – it was all beautiful, and confidently modern.

Ward had been accustomed to spending a fair amount of time here, back in the day. No complaints here: he retained fond memories of the gallery, though not of Dublin. He thought of the little flat he'd had for a couple of years, just

by the canal, a fifteen-minute trot into his lectures every day
– the easiest of commutes. He'd been in the habit of pausing
in the gallery for a few minutes, most days, and taking in a
painting or two. You can do that, he liked to say – to French
or German colleagues, or to European pals of Martin, in
London to attend some clinical seminar or other – you can
do that when a gallery or a museum is free: you can just
drop in for a few minutes, *en route* to somewhere else; you
can perk up your day, he would say.

The French would shrug, and turn the conversation;
the Germans would think that they were being invited
to participate in an exchange of views and opinions, and
would press on, until Martin enlightened them. 'One of his
old hobby horses, darling,' he'd remark as he passed, as he
refreshed a Caipirinha or a designer gin, 'I wouldn't pay any
attention. Let him go on. Olive?'

So, go easy, Ward thought now, go easy on Ireland. At
least the museums and galleries are free.

And now, time to snap to attention. Finally, someone to
greet them. Someones: a man, a woman. The man, younger,
the woman, older; the man, police – Ward could see that at
a glance, though he wasn't in uniform – the woman: well,
he couldn't place the woman, though he guessed she was
attached in some way to the gallery. She was fiftyish, tall
and slim – willowy would be the word – and well groomed.
Tweed. Pearls at neck and ears, hair expensively though
subtly tended. Interesting bone structure.

He'd mentioned bone structure to Martin once, and
Martin had never let him forget it. Had begun to make
cracks about the shape of people's heads, and to ascribe
such an interest to Ward himself, as though Ward were an

olden-days white South African racial supremacist making a note as he prepared a lecture in his Pretoria office; or one of those eighteenth-century observers of the physiognomic scene, piecing together theories about the races based on the shape of a skull, the cast of a brow.

'Yes, Dr Mengele, ma'am,' was one of Martin's expressions, nowadays. Designed to stop a conversation, to bring it juddering to a halt. Created especially for those occasions when Ward was tilting back on a chair in the kitchen at Despard Road, having a drink at the end of a long day, needing to talk. Martin would listen for a little while, attentively, with the courtesy he had learned at his school. And then, 'Yes, Dr Mengele, ma'am, it's all in the forehead, ma'am,' he would say, and proffer another Pringle. 'Stop,' Ward would say, and Martin would select a Pringle himself, judiciously, and crunch, and then say, 'I think you'll do the right thing by the lower orders, we all know we can trust you,' or something of that sort.

Ward would manage the situation: a laugh, and move on.

And cry, later, when he was alone. This was more frequent, nowadays.

'Mr Ward, Mr Atkinson?'

Ward nodded, and there was Rob nodding too, the two in unison, once more like schoolboys caught in the act. Charlotte, all over again. She set the tone, this new person, in a mere syllable.

No.

Look at me, Ward thought, as he shook her hand: here I am taking against her. Just like Charlotte.

Maybe I do have a thing against women. You want to be careful.

'I'm Emma Read, director of the gallery.' The woman dropped his hand, she took Rob's hand. 'And this,' and she nodded vestigially to the policeman, 'is Patrick Walsh, who is leading the investigation.'

Patrick Walsh was black of hair and blue of eye. He looked tired.

'Good to meet you both,' Rob said.

'Yes indeed, thanks for meeting with us,' Ward added.

Emma Read, who seemed to be the sort of person who would take charge of any situation, now spoke again. 'We thought,' she said, 'that you should come immediately and see the Sculpture Court, see where all of – of this,' she paused, 'took place last night.' Emma Read clearly believed in direct action; no blather here about whether anyone had had a good flight. She turned and led the way through the white, dramatic atrium, and up the stairs.

Rob and Emma Read were talking quietly now as they walked, and Ward said, 'Can you tell me, I mean generally, what you think of this whole situation?'

Patrick Walsh slid a glance. 'Well,' he said, 'it's bloody mad, isn't it?'

An accent from somewhere down the country, as they liked to say in Dublin, somewhere culchie, as they liked to say; slightly modified, maybe by a couple of years in the city, though not too much.

Ward only said, 'Mad: that's about it,' and they kept walking.

The white staircase gave way to an upper hall, then to a broad sequence of rooms, overwhelming, with oxblood-painted walls and oxblood-tiled floors, and hung with seventeenth-century oils – a few landscapes but mainly portraits, the sad, sleepy eyes of their subjects tracking the quartet. Too much colour, Ward thought: this is what it must feel like inside a stomach.

'We think,' Patrick Walsh added suddenly, 'and I may say that we hope, that this crime, this near-murder, is a case of simply being in the wrong place at the wrong time. We hope that's what it turns out to be.'

The two men looked at each other for a moment.

'OK,' Ward said. 'Can I ask how he is? – the victim?'

Not nearly as bad as was first thought, thankfully.

Up ahead, Emma Read was holding open a vast copper door. Rob had already passed through into the room beyond, and now Patrick Walsh followed him.

They were in the Sculpture Court.

The walls of the Sculpture Court were hung with silk: white, at first glance, Ward thought, though when you looked at them again, they seemed to hum with a sheen of green, an unpleasantness that reminded him of scum on a pond. The silk was clearly devastatingly expensive. What a mistake.

The hall was thronged with figures in white marble, which were not Ward's thing any more than seventeenth-century portraiture or oxblood paint were his things. And it was filled with actual living people: police in uniform dusting for fingerprints, down on hands and knees on the floor, on the glossy white paint of the far doors. 'This is one of the new spaces in the gallery,' Emma Read went on coolly, as if she were leading a guided tour, 'in fact, it was opened to the public just a few days ago. The scene,' she added, again unnecessarily, 'is over there.'

It was obvious enough now – to Ward, and he assumed

to everyone else listening – that Emma Read had an issue with taste, or with tastelessness: that she regarded this whole affair as a lapse in taste. That there was a colleague involved was a little way down her list of priorities; this was obvious too. That the colleague chose to have his throat slit here in the brand-new Sculpture Court was more than regrettable – it was a disgrace.

And now, look: the silk-hung walls were ruined.

Not that Emma Read said a word of all this: but, Ward thought, she might as well have been parading a sandwich board with her grievances listed in bold, black print.

Over there: Ward glanced at Rob, and the two men threaded their way through the marble figures towards the living figures, towards the area on the floor.

No silhouette outlined in white, for this was no television murder scene: but the detectives had marked the edges, the corners of the area. He had been tall, the victim, if the marked area was anything to go by. Nothing much here: and yet Ward felt his eyes glisten a little. Twenty-two: he was barely more than a child. Ward had all too frequently felt moved at the sight of an empty space on a wall where a precious, well-loved painting had once hung. He was used to the blaze of anger he felt at the sight of an empty frame, its contents ripped away contemptuously. But the sight of an empty space on the floor, where someone had lain in pain and fear a few hours before – this area of emptiness brought with it a wave of grief. This was a surprise.

Now Emma Read glided up behind him, spoke at his shoulder, caused him to start.

'The alarm was activated at 2.15 a.m.'

Not that he was about to lose it. It wasn't his style

– especially not in front of strangers, and this stranger in particular. Rob had already moved from the space on the floor to examine the green-white silken walls, which carried now a wide arc of black blood droplets.

'And the painting was here,' Emma Read went on, and Ward glanced at her as she pointed to the wall. 'The only painting in the room: it was, if you like, one of the gallery's glories, and was hung here for maximum impact.' Perhaps she saw something in Ward's eyes, in his expression, because for a moment her hauteur seemed to sag, and she said, 'Mr Ward, I'm not without feelings. But you are here to survey the scene, and I'm trying to give you the bare facts, all the facts I can.'

A bluff Kiwi accent can come in handy at such tight moments: now Rob stepped across the tiles and said, 'And we appreciate it, Dr Read,' and Ward began to exhale.

'And the glass that held the piece – is here.'

This was more their thing. Ward and Rob had seen plenty of such discarded frames and the like. They were usually lying – all too obviously flung – on the ground: but this one, these two pieces of clear glass, had been set carefully against the silk-hung walls. As though in atonement, Ward thought at that moment, looking at it: but carefully set or not, the glass signified – no, it bawled, it roared and shrieked – desecration.

When people asked Ward why he did what he did – and they occasionally did ask; for example, men used to ask him in bars, if they were especially keen to get him into bed, it was worth the trouble of a supplementary question – he had a stock answer ready. 'Because at heart I'm a zealot,' he would say, and this tended to sort the wheat from the chaff, the sheep from the goats. The chaff, the goats, they didn't like words like 'zealot'; the others didn't mind it.

He was with Martin by this time though – so into bed, never.

Hardly ever.

A zealot.

Yes: the chaff, the goat, the man at the time would usually back right away. Sometimes, the fundamentalism positively attracted them: but Ward, more often than not, found at such times that his own ardour diminished; and he would make his excuses and his stumbling way out onto Old Compton Street or Shoreditch High Street, and go home to Martin, with relief.

And this was the thing: Martin was the only one who'd engaged with the question correctly, in Ward's view. *What do you do?* He did this by leaning forward on the heavy, black, cast-iron, Victorian chairs on which they were seated – on that first night, their friends now far away in the Spanish restaurant in Farringdon – seats so heavy they could hardly be moved. Possibly to stop them being thrown about late at night, by drunken punters? Terrible chairs: very rapidly, Ward's bum felt cold and sore; and Martin's bum obviously was too, judging from the way he began, after a few minutes, to wriggle on his chair, and shift from buttock to buttock. But then he paid Ward the ultimate compliment, the gargantuan compliment of seeming to forget about the discomfort, of seeming to actually listen.

And then, of course, he went home with Ward, or rather, he permitted Ward to go home with him, and of all compliments this was the best.

'Oh yes,' Martin said, sitting forward in the iron chair,

'I've read about this.' About the trade in stolen art, he meant – it really was a huge trade, wasn't it? A huge international trade, an extraordinary and extraordinarily profitable trade. 'I read a piece about it in the *Guardian*: didn't they steal something from, where was it, was it Boston? – just lately?'

Not too lately – but yes, that was one of the most recent biggies.

'The Isabella Stewart Gardner Museum, that's right. In Boston.'

'What was it they stole again?'

'You name it,' Ward said, and rubbed his nose in embarrassment, as though the responsibility for the theft was his. The gallery staff had actually let the thieves into the building in the middle of the night, he said. They had knocked on the door, posing as policemen, or looking to borrow a little milk, who knows, and been let in, just like that, and then they tied the staff up and stole more than a dozen paintings.

Worth half a billion dollars.

'Half a *billion*,' Martin said.

'They sliced them out of their frames. Vermeer, Rembrandts, the lot. The gallery left the empty frames hanging on the walls. I saw them,' he added.

Martin was watching him. 'You saw them?'

'When I was nineteen,' Ward said. 'A student summer, a work visa, I went to Cape Cod, me and half of Ireland.'

Ward remembered the warm sand between his toes, on the beach at Provincetown. But it didn't stay between his toes, it got everywhere: sand in his bed and in his hair, on his bread, between his buttocks. 'I couldn't stand the place,' he said. 'I went into Boston whenever I could. And one day I went to the Gardner.'

How to explain the shock, the moment of revelation? He saw again the planted quadrangle with its tiled floors and Italianate facades. The sage-green, richly embossed wallpaper in the Dutch Room, the polished furniture. The hush and the opulence.

The frames, hanging naked on the wall.

Martin leaned forward a little on his heavy iron chair. 'And what?'

His head swimming.

Martin said, still leaning, still intent, 'What is it? What are you remembering?'

An image of the Rembrandt, that Rembrandt, in a glossy art book, he'd studied it, marvelled at the speed and pitch of the boat, the foaming of the waves, the panic and the human frailty. He said, slowly, 'One of the stolen Rembrandts. *Christ in the Storm on the Sea of Galilee.* They say Rembrandt painted himself into the picture, looking out at us. Very calm. It felt as though he was looking right at me.'

He paused. Their first date. Martin might laugh.

But no. Martin was still sitting forward on his heavy chair, still intent. 'Go on.'

Ward said, still slowly, 'I just mean – then to see the empty frames. The desecration of it, the empty *frames*. I couldn't take it in.' He sat back now, in his own uncomfortable chair; the chill of the iron pressed through the fabric of his clothes.

'So, that was that, was it? That was the moment?'

Ward nodded. It was. His own course set, in that shocking

moment. 'I suppose it was,' he said and he tried to smile a little; Martin ought to stop gazing; better to shake up the conversation, he didn't want Martin thinking he was a freak. Mention the Nazis. 'And then, the Nazis too.' They would be on happier, less personal ground with the Nazis. They were great ones for stealing artworks too, the Nazis, and bunging them into the Austrian salt mines for safekeeping.

Everyone enjoyed a conversation about the Nazis.

Martin smiled too, and studied his drink. He said something quietly.

Ward said, 'Hm?'

Martin looked up, and smiled more broadly. '"The empty frames," I said. The empty frames.'

Shortly after that night, thieves executed a heist in Paris, another hair-raisingly expensive painting, and it was all over the papers; and now Martin seemed positively impressed that his new boyfriend was working in that line.

He hadn't heard of the agency, of course, before that night. Nobody had ever heard of it. Which was fine by Ward, though he knew that it annoyed certain of his colleagues.

'Art Investigations, no, definitely not, I mean, until now,' Martin said politely.

'The Art Investigations Agency, is the full title,' Ward said. 'Or, if you prefer, L'Agence d'enquête sur l'art.'

'I think I prefer the English version, if that's OK,' Martin said, very politely.

'So do I, really.'

'And so—' Martin prompted.

'Well, the French bit is important, because we receive funding from the Council of Europe. We're pan-national;

but lots of countries fund their own similar agencies, we're not unique by any means.' Martin was looking at him so very earnestly that Ward felt a dark flush – not attractive – creep up from his neck.

'Golly,' Martin said. 'You'd think I'd know something about it. And it's based here, is it, in London?' He did seem surprised, and fair enough too: any agency with European funding, whether based in London or not, tended – as Ward knew well – to get pilloried on a weekly basis, these days, by the tabloids. But his agency prided itself on keeping its collective head down and its profile low, partly for this very reason: Ward was fairly sure that the papers hadn't yet sniffed them out, and relieved too.

'London is a sort of centre of the art theft trade: so when it came to establishing the agency, it made sense to base it here. And they did.'

'I see,' Martin said.

The next morning – one of those first Sunday mornings, in Tufnell Park, they were still in bed – Martin asked some more questions about the agency: and Ward was pleased to see that he really was intrigued, that his questions hadn't been – as they so often were – mere steeplechase hurdles to be surmounted with a leap and a splash, on the track to sex. Martin didn't possess an encyclopaedic knowledge of art: but he did go to galleries sometimes, he did like to 'sniff around', as he put it, and he could understand where Ward's interest came from. More than that: he respected it.

He was a member of a strange, careful tribe: he was an English Catholic. Quite an old family, in fact: from Northumberland; they'd held on to their lands when all about them were losing theirs; and had kept a fair bit of money intact too. Educated poshly, a Catholic boarding school.

'So, all those cassocked priests queuing up to pounce on you, right there on the altar: what an exciting schoolboyhood for you,' Ward said, quite early in the relationship, before catching on to the fact that Martin didn't much care for this sort of humour.

'There was some of that, yes,' Martin said, 'but I managed to sidestep them.'

Ward wasn't even surprised to hear this, Catholic priests being Catholic priests, and all too good at pouncing, but Martin went on:

'I think my school was a bit more careful though, probably; the priests were more likely to pounce on each other. Anyway, nobody pounced on me – not priests, anyway.' He went on to say that he did a bit of pouncing himself – 'in my final year, only with other age of consents, of course, we were all at it, I think the school offers it as an A Level.' But he didn't seem too keen to continue this topic. Later, Ward realised that this was down to those deeply ingrained English Catholic instincts of self-preservation. Don't talk too much, and don't give anything away.

Martin did open up, like a blossom in warm sunshine, once he found himself in a solid, secure relationship – or so Ward used to tell himself. He reassured himself that Martin was comfortable in his skin, the evidence being that he was happy to slip into falsetto in front of his friends, to make jokes about Dr Mengele, to essay from time to time a mocking lisp, to have fun.

Yes, Martin's was a bright, sunny face, one that he was

happy to present to the world. As for the shadows: these he showed only to Ward, who was glad to see them. These shadows, these pools of darkness behind the closed door of the house on Despard Road: their existence, Ward told himself, indicated trust, meant that Martin trusted him.

He trusted Ward, and Ward trusted him.

So Ward once thought.

32

'Gerard Boyle was the name. Right?'

'Right,' Patrick Walsh said. They were now convened – Rob and Patrick Walsh and Ward – in a grimy little office in what Emma Read had introduced as the administration wing. She'd brought them all the way there herself: away from the Sculpture Court, and through one top-lit gallery and then another, the walls changing from oxblood to crimson to what was, all things considered, a very nice green, and then up a flight of modern stairs. The art changed too as they walked, in a way that discombobulated Ward: he held, he'd realised, in some filing cabinet in his brain, grainy memories of certain paintings hung in certain rooms, long ago, but all of this was now swept away. The place had a new smell, too. Brand new. He sniffed the air as he passed through the galleries in Emma Read's perfumed wake. Surely art galleries ought not to smell so new.

Perhaps Emma Read could read minds – or perhaps she had noticed Ward's head turn and turn and turn again as they walked. Whichever it was, she soon spoke up. 'The entire collection has been rehung,' she said, as she glided along. 'In chronological order, now: it's best international practice; they did it at Tate Britain a few years ago, and it seemed to work quite well, so we thought we would give it a go here too. Perhaps you've seen the results at the Tate?'

He had, of course. She ushered them through a door, a stitch in the building – was the best way, Ward thought, of putting it, thinking suddenly of his mother long ago, stitching silently and silently pressing. The building suddenly slid from new and restored glory into an environment less salubrious – a low-ceilinged corridor lit by yellow fluorescent tubed lighting. Emma Read smiled briefly. 'This wasn't part of the restoration: this is where, where the staff, has its offices. The public don't come here. It isn't very nice, I'm afraid.' She stopped, opened a door. 'I've set this office aside for you. It seemed the most appropriate space.' She paused for a moment. 'I hope I haven't been indelicate; it was difficult to know what to do for the best.' Ward must have looked puzzled, or Rob must have, because she added, with gentle apology, 'I mean, this is where Gerard works, and Dr O'Hara.' With that, she was gone.

Patrick Walsh didn't seem puzzled: he was rather more on top of the context than either of his companions, and now he pulled a chair across, and sat and rustled some papers. Importantly – but this was to be expected, because nobody had exactly been taking time so far to listen to what he had to say. Ward and Rob sat too, took in the grubby, down-at-heel little room, with its strip lighting and dispiriting view of a gloomy, damp courtyard.

'So,' Rob said.

'So,' said Patrick Walsh, and Ward caught Rob's eye. There was a patter in which they had been trained: at a morning workshop run by – inevitably – Charlotte, plus a communications person brought in from outside. ('From outside, Ward,' Charlotte had said, glaring at him, 'so you'd better turn up.') Now Ward watched as Rob switched himself on and ran through the drill in his New Zealand tones.

'Just before you begin, Patrick, could we just make a few clarifying points?'

'Go for it.'

'You know that our focus – our prime objective – is to assist in the recovery of the Sandborne,' he said. Patrick nodded, and Rob went on. 'This is why we're here. We pool our resources with you, needless to say, and help in whatever way we can; our systems, our databases, will be using whatever information we can pick up here. I feel I ought to underscore this, because needless to say this crime, this near-death, is your turf and not ours; but our experience is that our parallel presence can sometimes feel unusual to the home police force.' Rob paused to fetch breath, and added – rather limply, Ward thought – 'Does that sound OK to you?'

'No worries,' Patrick said, that Australian usage rising unthinkingly to his lips. 'We know all this: we know the systems, we know how it works. We've never worked with you guys before, obviously, but I'm sure we'll make out fine.'

Make out.

'So,' Patrick said again. 'I thought it would help to run

through the facts we have so far. I know you have some of the details – they were sent across early this morning – but we've brought together some additional material in the period since.' Again he ran a finger through the papers on the desk in front of him – Dr O'Hara's desk, perhaps, though there were three other desks crammed into this ugly, tiny office – and, perhaps with a touch of relief, set to work.

The crime had been committed between 2.05 a.m. and 2.14 a.m. Unusually precise timing, but an unusual crime. It had been witnessed at close quarters, for one thing, and the witness had lived to tell the tale. It had been witnessed electronically: the alarms had been remotely deactivated – which was, as Rob knew and Ward knew and everyone in the unit knew, a piece of cake nowadays; a spotty teenager in his high-smelling bedroom could deactivate any alarm, anywhere. 'It was a state-of-the-art system,' Patrick added, and his tones indicated that he, too, understood how little this meant. But the video cameras were working just fine: and so they recorded all the necessary comings and goings – and now, to demonstrate their proficiency, Patrick pulled his laptop towards him, fiddled, and brought up a greyish video recording onto the screen.

There was the young man, there was the older woman, making their way down the very corridor outside the door; there they were yanking open the fire doors and disappearing from view. There they were reappearing now into the sight of another camera, and disappearing again, and reappearing again: CCTV hardly ever works, as everyone knows and nobody ever says, Ward thought, the guilty little secret of our modern times – but the gallery's cameras were in extra-good working order, with nothing left to chance. You had to hand it to them – though, granted, it was a pity about the crappy alarm system. Ward scratched his head.

Patrick must have read his thought, because now he said, 'The gallery concedes that it cut corners with the alarms.'

Ward said, 'No, really?' – and Patrick grimaced a little.

'I know,' he said.

Now he pulled up the images of the Sculpture Court. There was the man – as bold as brass, as Ward's mother would have said – manhandling the Sandborne. Now there was the knife, and now there were the empty panes of glass that had once held *The Jewel*. The man – small, slight. Ward hadn't expected to see a balaclava or the like – they didn't exactly wear balaclavas nowadays, there being other perfectly good and simple ways to occlude one's identity, one's features: and this small man had the glasses, the little hat, the scarf. 'You can ignore the Bourne films,' Ward had told Martin on that first night, long ago, their stomachs full of good Spanish food and their warm blood full of good Spanish wine, 'if you can't get an iris, if you can't get a fingerprint, if you can't get a good, square, full-on shot of someone's complete face, then you're back at zero.' Even Agent Bourne would be back at zero looking through these greyish images: and Ward knew it, Rob knew it, Patrick Walsh knew it.

But no: because now he watched Rob sit a little forward, his attention focusing further.

'Now here they come.'

The ugly bit, the seldom-seen bit: and now, Ward felt himself moving back – he actually moved the chair back from the desk until a look from Rob ('perhaps he used to shear sheep back in New Zealand, do you think?' Martin asked him once) brought him inching forward again.

They entered the frame – burst into the frame, really – and while there was a great deal to look at, God knows, all Ward was able to see was the spray of blood from Gerard Boyle's throat, bursting through the air in an arc, filling the air, staining the silk walls. The video was silent, of course, but he could imagine the noise, the screams, the bubbling of blood in an open wound. Gerard Boyle fell to his knees, and then to the floor: how amazing that he had lived, after that.

'Then the companion runs away, then the – the wannabe murderer, the thief, whatever you want to call him, leaves too: and it's all over in another minute.'

Patrick Walsh spoke evenly, in the tones of a man who has seen it all before: but Ward thought that there was none of that macho carry-on that you sometimes got from guys in his position. There was an awareness, a respect, whatever you wanted to call it. Someone might have died, that someone had a name, his name was Gerard Boyle, and Patrick Walsh gave the impression that he was aware of the gravity of these facts.

Rob was still looking at the screen: but now he sat back slowly and said, 'What else?'

'Dr O'Hara, Roisin O'Hara: appointed four years ago,' Patrick Walsh said, lifting a sheet of paper on the desk, setting it down again. 'Highly thought of in the art world, but—' He paused, and Ward added the subordinate clause.

'Not great in the real world?'

'The staff don't like her. And she doesn't like them either, and she doesn't disguise it. I gather she thinks it beneath her to have to interact with them, so she sends memos instead. Dr Read reports that she is excellent at the technical aspects of her job, but yes – terrible on the human side.' Patrick Walsh paused again, and then added, 'Which is neither here nor there, but when people take the opportunity to bitch and bitch like – really, like *crazy*: well, as I say, it doesn't make it any easier. For example,' and Patrick shook his head, 'they're saying that it's all Dr O'Hara's fault for making the victim work late in the first place. Terrible stuff. Anyway, my hope is that we can wrap this up as quickly as possible, and that you can too, on your side, and that all these politics become, frankly, irrelevant. So, fingers crossed for that.' Patrick smiled, a very little, but there was no disguising the sense of disgust that he felt.

Ward said, 'So the atmosphere is tense, really, and we'll have to deal with that.'

'Exactly,' Patrick said.

'And what about Gerard Boyle? What do we know about him?'

Nothing much, seemed to be the answer. Gerard Boyle was twenty-two, he too was from 'down the country', which Patrick seemed to think was a satisfactory reply. ('Where down the country?' Ward asked, and Patrick lifted a paper again, but in surprise this time, and finally said, 'Roscommon, apparently.') Nothing much: or rather, there was nothing much to tell. A degree – and then straight into a minor job here in the gallery.

'Twenty-two,' Patrick said. 'In the wrong place at the wrong time. He was working late: the fact is, I think, that there was still a degree of behind-the-scenes chaos here, in spite of the fact that the building was open, the rebuilding job over, all that sort of thing.' They were all still running around like headless chickens, Patrick said, and Gerard Boyle had been one of the headless chickens. It was an unfortunate analogy, given the context, and Patrick seemed to realise this himself after a moment, because a reddish blush bloomed on his cheeks for a few seconds before he returned to himself.

'We'll be asking more questions about him, of course,' Patrick went on, as though to disavow any notion of incuriosity, 'and we haven't had a chance to speak to his colleague, to Dr O'Hara. She's in hospital, they tell me; just for observation. So that will have to wait – perhaps tonight, or failing that, tomorrow.' He paused and said, 'She seems to think it's all her fault.'

Rob nodded. His eyes, as they returned to the screen, glinted a little.

33

Ward looked at Rob, then, and he took the cue – besides, Patrick seemed to be running out of things he could tell them – and indicated that he, at any rate, needed something to eat. 'Of course,' Patrick said, and he tidied up his files and stood up politely. 'I'll be here,' he added, and they made their way down the corridor and out into the main gallery once more.

'What is it?'

'Just a little hunch. A little click. Let's get outside.'

They continued to clack from one expensive room to another.

'It's so much better looking than I remember, this place,' Ward said. 'They really must have spent a fortune.' They found the white stairs again, strode through the white atrium again, tugged open the heavy doors, passed the police and the cordon and the onlookers, and headed off up Clare Street.

Patrick Walsh hadn't mentioned the Sandborne. Which was to be expected, perhaps: an attempted murder trumped a stolen painting, every time: but Ward noticed it just the same.

He had seen the look in the eyes of some listeners: a suggestion he was a princess, wailing over his lost art. But it wasn't like that at all: Ward understood the notion of moral gradations; human blood would always sit above stolen paintings in the moral order. Of course he understood that – he was no sociopath – but he also understood that art wasn't something to be so quickly discounted, either. 'It's part of our lives,' he'd told Martin, home in Despard Road after a night out, after he'd caught this judging look in the eyes of an acquaintance. 'It's all part of our history and—'

'I know,' Martin said. He was perched on the end of the bed, taking off his shirt. 'Our common humanity, our patrimony: it's a vio*lation*, a form of rape. You don't need to convince me. But you don't always have to convince the already convinced, you know,' he added, 'not every time,' and stretched out his long arms and yawned.

Certainly Ward was aware of how the air was able to sour rapidly: how close he could come to having his head kicked in, by men and women alike. Rape? 'Hardly,' was a common response, the G&T turning to pure alcohol, the slice of cucumber to a gherkin. 'It's hardly the same.' The most common, the mildest reply. Though sometimes not mild at all. 'That's offensive to me, as a person,' or a variant thereof. 'That's a typical man thing to say.' Or the much less varnished, 'You don't know what you're talking about.'

Not in the agency, obviously. Rob and all the others – even Charlotte – got exactly what he meant, no questions asked, no swear words blazing in the air. These paintings were part of us – that was it, essentially. Yes, our patrimony, to turn a sexist phrase. And when they were stolen to order, as nowadays they almost invariably were, they left a gap, a violation in their wake, that could never be filled until the painting was returned. If it ever was, and too often it never was. The painter's sweat and tears and sleepless nights; the painter's vision; and then the years and years heaped on top of that, of other people, other nameless people, gazing and staring at the painting, and allowing it to connect with their lives, memories, hopes, tragedies through which they'd lived, bruises they'd sustained, the happiness they'd witnessed and experienced. And the way in which a painting, like any piece of art, was able to connect with that, and provide clarity, and understanding, and buoyancy, maybe, where there was no buoyancy before, so: no, Ward thought, and sometimes said, 'don't tell me that the theft of a painting isn't rape. When it's stolen, and laid in a safe in America, or Russia, or India, never to be seen or displayed again; or burned when the ransom money isn't handed over. Don't fucking tell me,' as he had all too often said, quite coolly, across a table in a pub, or a table in someone else's house, across the lemon roulade, the cheese, the wine glasses: 'don't tell me, don't fucking lecture me about what a painting can do, and what the loss of a painting can do.'

Martin, he had once thought, enjoyed these very occasional tirades. Very occasional: they weren't Ward's style, frankly: but sometimes he saw red, such as when he was made out to be a shit, a sexist and chauvinist pig, a bastard (and he'd been baptised with all these names), when people clambered up onto the moral high ground and swung around and spat down on him. Martin saw that sometimes Ward saw red, and that fire would then spill forth.

Did Martin understand, really? He liked to sit by the fire and watch it burn. He did, truly, enjoy the occasional conflagration – but no, perhaps not in the way that Ward had once imagined. He remembered the empathy of those early days, the cocked head and furrowed brow and the nods, the listening manner, the air of understanding. Not so very many years ago – but what a gap, a crater in time, as it now seemed! Martin seemed like a different person: though Ward was understanding now that his partner was, in fact, the same now as then, the same as he had ever been.

'Ward fights *crime*, is in fact what he does.'

The mocking upward inflection, the shrillness of the *crime*.

'Our common *humanity*, our *patrimony*. The empty *frames*: it's a vio*lation*, a form of *rape*.'

The stress on the words had come later. I wasn't completely stupid, Ward thought.

There actually had been a lemon roulade once: only half eaten, its meringue as chewy on the inside as all good meringues ought to be, and with almonds scattered, and the curd properly tangy: and he had his eye on a second slice, but got side-tracked. Martin helped himself to a second slice though, and enjoyed it – he told Ward, later – all the more for the accompanying sourness in the air as the argument blazed on. 'Lemon on the inside, lemon on the outside,' he'd said, 'it was the full experience, really it was.' Recollecting the evening now, Ward didn't think their hosts saw it quite that way though: certainly they were never invited back, which was a pity because it really had been a terrific lemon roulade.

How Martin had egged him on. And their hosts: that was two more friendships down the toilet.

He paused, there on the street.

'Where'll we go? Where do you recommend?' Rob asked. 'And hurry up, I'm bloody starving.'

'Hadn't you better tell me about your hunch?'

'Over coffee.'

Ward sighed theatrically. 'There used to be a cafe just a bit further along, the Pied Piper, let's see if it's still there.'

Rob frowned; his parental sensibilities were offended. 'What sort of name is that?'

'A good sort of name,' Ward told him; Rob knew his views on modern children. 'The Pied Piper had the right idea. They should teach his story to policymakers.' *A Vision for Today*: Ward could just see it on the PowerPoint, accompanied by a slide of a rat, and another of a pigtailed girl. And the Pied Piper was still there: they went in.

The place seemed unchanged. It was kitted out in carved wood and stencilled fairy-tale scenes; baskets of scones, of muffins, a top-of-the-range coffee machine added which, Ward thought, certainly hadn't been there in *his* day. The stencilled scenes were for the benefit of the adults: there were no children among the clientele, which of course was the point. Just tired-looking tourists, a few suits, Ward, Rob. The owner hadn't liked children, in Ward's day: he had explained this to Ward one slack afternoon; explained how he disliked children and didn't want them in his cafe, but that of course it was against the law to ban them entirely. So instead, he kept them out by means of subliminal messages directed at their parents.

It worked.

Ward had loved the place. It had been a refuge of sorts.

Martin, of course, knew about his past, his childhood, in the same way as he knew about Martin's past, his childhood, his schooldays. They had talked and talked, talked a good deal until they got their heads around each other. This was a big deal in itself: Ward had been accustomed to going through life clutching a cattle-prod, using it as appropriate. There was no point letting people get too close: that was Ward's silent motto, his credo, because they were just looking for an opportunity to hurt you if they could, and a cattle-prod meant that they couldn't do this, or not so easily.

Don't have friends, only have acquaintances. His family's motto. Again unspoken, because the Wards, silent in their semi-detached, pebbledashed suburban Dublin house, were not the sort of people to sit around discussing mottos. They just got on with things, using a minimum of words in their dealings with each other and the world. This was the way of things. *That's just the way of things* might have been another motto, because his mother used it a fair bit. It encapsulated her view of the world: *that's just the way of things, they can't be changed, they certainly can't be bettered, there's no point talking about them.* By *them* she meant prices and politicians, the weather and the news from the great outside world that occasionally leaked through the aluminium windows of their semi-detached. It meant just about everything, and it meant that his mother was no fun to be around. Long ago – he gleaned – she had nursed dreams of becoming a primary-school teacher: but she came from the wrong side of the tracks, and her chance of gaining a scholarship to big school was quashed by the snobby nuns, and that was an end to that. No education, no prospects: the biscuit factory for a few years, and then early marriage, and children. And that was it.

That was just the way of things.

Martin asked, 'What about your father?'

This was over pizza and a bottle of Montepulciano in Tufnell Park. They were on (though who was counting? – Ward was) their fourth date; their previous three had all ended in bed, but now Ward felt himself begin to freeze.

But Martin wasn't having any of it. 'Tell me,' he said.

'There's not that much to tell,' Ward said. He took another slice of his pizza, folded it, took a bite. A little bite and put the slice down again. 'Well, there is,' he said, 'but I don't suppose you're going to like it very much.'

Martin said nothing, just looked at him, his own pizza cooling on his plate.

Ward's father was no fun to be around either.

'Not – that,' Ward said to his pizza. 'I don't mean that.' An effortful snort of laughter. 'I'm not a complete cliché, you know.'

Martin took up his pizza again.

'It was just physical, mental stuff,' Ward said. 'Really, nothing else.'

Just. In his peripheral vision, as he trained his gaze on his pizza, he saw Martin nod.

'Sometimes I think I was lucky, really,' Ward said.

Martin shook his head. He said, 'Tell me.'

'He worked in the biscuit factory too,' Ward said. 'Daddy did.'

That was where his mother had 'met her fate', as she put it. This was on the occasions she discussed such topics – seldom, and then never. The background to her marriage, their marriage, had to be gleaned. A wedding photo, all slicked, oily hair for the men, and simple lines for the women. A honeymoon weekend in a Wexford caravan, and then a new life. Daddy packed the biscuits into lorries and drove them around, and acted as caretaker, and general helpmeet. He laid the poison to kill the stray dogs that scavenged around the grounds of the factory; he killed the otherwise useful feral cats when they became too numerous; and he sacked and drowned any kittens born inside the factory perimeter.

A helpmeet: in Ward's memory, Daddy's proud declaration that the biscuit factory 'couldn't manage without him'.

'They couldn't manage without Daddy,' Ward said. The playground corner, out of the wind, out of a mizzle that flew with the wind through the air, and two minutes, three minutes, before the teacher rang the great wooden-handled school bell, and they could run back inside and warm their hands and their damp feet against the radiators.

'He says. He said that they can't manage without him.'

'You hold your corner,' his mother said to him, that morning. 'You keep your backbone straight. You answer right back, and don't take any rubbish from anybody.' And there, his backbone is as straight as straight can be. He wouldn't go near the handball alley. He never was picked to play; he'd stay away. And today, an audience: the wind and the rain have kept them all in the corners, in the angle of two walls; an audience today, if he speaks up, if he can keep his backbone straight. 'Ramrod-straight, is the way to do it.'

'Why, what does your daddy do?'

'What does your daddy do?'

He lifted his chin, he remembered his backbone. He'd seen the lorry. The size of it! – and the shininess!

'Can I drive it, Daddy?'

'You can not.'

A sinking heart – but what a chance now to boast about the size of Daddy's lorry.

'He drives a lorry.'

Snuffles of laughter, and he turned and stared.

The biscuit factory smelled of sweetness. Malt and sugar and sugary milk. He'd been there, and they'd given him the broken biscuits in a paper bag to bring home. Sugar, and broken biscuits and milk.

'They couldn't manage without Daddy.'

'A lorry?'

And now the ground was slipping away. He'd said something wrong but he didn't know what it was. The sound of the wooden-handled bell rang in his ears. It clanged and clanged. It cut out the sound of the snuffling laughter. But he saw the nudges, the elbows nudging, the smiling mouths – and not nice smiles, either.

The biscuit factory was an old-fashioned sort of place. He was able to see this, later: to measure and understand that the blood of its original Quaker owners still coursed in the corporate veins: the management didn't much like sacking people, and avoided doing so wherever possible. Otherwise, Daddy would have been first to get the boot: the very first. A 'gulpin', to use Ward's mother's language, meaning a feckless, idle fool.

'And a bit of a drinker,' Ward said, and Martin nodded, listening and listening.

'So I surmised,' Martin said. 'Go on.'

His brother and sister, Dermot and Anne-Marie, seemed to know how to stay out of the way: leave it to the middle child, the bookworm child, the vulnerable child, to be at home, to see it all, to hear it all. Why hadn't he been more clever?

'There's always one,' Martin said, kindly. 'Usually, anyway. You wouldn't believe the patterns. You'd better eat,' he said, 'before it gets cold.' He topped up Ward's glass. 'Go on.'

Ward took another wedge of pizza. 'They were just smarter,' he said. 'Smart enough to keep their heads down, smart enough to leave me and my mother to it. I was a bit of an eejit, really,' he said. 'Too pious for my own good, an altar boy as soon as I had the chance, good at school, a total swot: you get it.'

It wasn't a question; Martin nodded.

'So I was the one, is the long and the short of it.' He looked up now, at Martin looking at him. 'The eejit who didn't know how to get out of the way. And here I am now, putting such a premium on cleverness, and I never was clever, not when it counted.'

Martin held his gaze. Each held the other's gaze. Ward

found himself examining Martin, scrutinising him for signs of shrinkage, a shrivelling from unpleasant facts. But no: nothing like that. No false, cheery bonhomie either. Martin just sat and waited; he showed a bit of respect. This would be OK.

'We moved to the wrong part of town,' Ward said slowly. 'By which I mean the right part of town. And there he was, driving a lorry around, and drinking all weekend, and drowning kittens in his spare time, and the middle-class neighbours watching and watching, and,' he took a pull on his glass of wine, 'and I think he lost it.'

'You're making excuses, surely,' Martin said.

Maybe he was.

'Go on,' said Martin, and Ward watched as he leaned forward a little, across the red-and-white checked tablecloth. 'Go on.'

The long weals rubbed and rubbed against his shirt. Daddy had broken one of the cane kitchen chairs. He had broken it against the wall, so that splinters flew, and then he had taken one of the broken cane legs and beaten Ward with it.

The cane leg was yellow, and shiny with varnish. It shone yellow in the yellow of the kitchen light. His mother – no, she didn't scream. You couldn't scream, otherwise the neighbours might hear. So she spoke instead, low.

'Don't belt him.'

Usually she was the one belted.

'Don't, don't belt him.'

'If he won't eat his potatoes, then he has to be belted,'

Daddy said. And the chair didn't make too much noise when it broke. It was only voices that made noise. 'Take off your shirt,' Daddy said.

'He'll eat everything after this.'

'Take off your shirt.'

And then the air was filled with yellow.

After that first evening, Daddy seemed to get into the swing of it. He kept the cane leg: it was special, and just long enough, though not too long. The cane left red marks, but it didn't leave blood, and that was alright. And he only did so much beating. He stopped after only a few whips. He knew how to do it so that nobody would see or hear anything.

Later, his mother rubbed cold, pink lotion into Ward's back. Dermot was asleep in the upper bunk, or pretending to be asleep. It was pretending, Ward knew: but his mother spoke in a whisper anyway.

'We'll just ignore it, and it won't happen again,' she said. 'Your father has a temper on him, that's all. Just a temper. You'll eat your potatoes after this, love, won't you?'

He ate his potatoes, after that, but the cane was kept handy, and used now and again. Always on his back, on his buttocks, where the red marks could never be seen. 'I'll beat the queerness out of him, if it's the last thing I do.'

And it was the same when he pulled his mother by her hair about the place: he would grab a handful of hair at the very top of her head. Nobody could spot anything if you did it this way; and when he punched her, he did it above the hairline. There was never any need for the bruises to show.

'Stop it, Daddy.'

'"Thtop it, Daddy,"' and Daddy would go for him, instead.

Or, as well as.

Daddy, you bastard.

Daddy wasn't always drunk when he set to them with his fists and his cane, and with his grasping hand. Only sometimes. It was worse when he was drunk, but it was also better: you could count the minutes before he fell asleep on the sofa. Ten minutes, twelve minutes, fifteen minutes: he never reached fifteen minutes. Anne-Marie and Dermot would stay quiet upstairs, but Ward couldn't: he couldn't leave his mother alone; he had to sit on the stairs, and watch through the bannisters as Daddy arranged his broad, golden signet ring on his finger, and began to push, to thump it into his mother's head, until she fell over.

'My head's ringing,' she would say, would whisper. 'Stop now.'

Once Ward said to her, 'Can we not go away?'

She looked scandalised. 'We can't do that. And go where? Where would we go?'

Although, they did go away. Once. They went to the chip shop. Only once, when Daddy had been very bad, and taken the barometer from the wall in the hall, and smashed it against the bannisters until it broke into very many pieces. Its shining face, and its silver and iron inside bits, spread out across the hall floor.

The barometer had been a wedding present.

He fell asleep soon afterwards: and she came up the stairs, very quiet and very calm, and bundled them all into trousers and jumpers and coats, with their pyjamas still on, and warm underneath their clothes, and they left the house together, and caught the bus down the hill towards town, and got off the bus at Cafolla's, and went in and sat down, and she ordered chips for them all, and milk, and went and brought down the squeezy plastic round tomato-bottle of ketchup from the silver counter, and they had their chips and drank their milk, all silently, and she sat there, saying nothing and watching them, and crying only a very little bit, and when they finished, she lifted her chin the way she did when her mind was made up, and she gathered them up again, and paid, and left, and caught the bus again, up the hill to the corner of the road, and they went back into the house, and stepped over the dead barometer in the hall, and past his snoring, and back to bed again.

His bed was still a little tiny bit warm.

In the morning, the barometer was gone.

So, that was the only time she'd left: and that was only to take them to the chip shop. After that, she hardly ever lifted her chin again.

'Yes,' Martin said, 'I see.'

Ward couldn't, he said, remember everything, every detail. He couldn't remember, in fact, long stretches of his childhood: there were holes like honeycomb. 'Nothing,' he said, looking at Martin, then shifting his gaze left and down onto the red-and-white tablecloth, the ruby depths of the wine, the cooling mushrooms on his pizza. 'I mean, I know what happened – but I can't actually remember. It's a very strange sensation.'

Martin said that this was what happened in response to trauma: the brain closed down, shut sections of itself off, it was all about protection. It was fascinating, Martin said, what was happening nowadays: the research into how the brain and one's memory worked under conditions of stress. The neurological researchers had discovered all sorts of interesting things about how neural pathways fired, how they opened and closed at such times. Martin talked about disassociation. About exactly what the brain did to keep itself safe. The brain was pretty great: it knew what to do and it did it; and later, when life was safe (or as safe as it was ever likely to be), it provided the means to open up the neural pathways into memory, into experience. It understood that a permanent blank was not much use, though a temporary blank was, and acted accordingly.

'Which is pretty cool, I think,' Martin said, and Ward agreed. It was pretty cool.

Later, Ward set about remembering – recovering – his lost memories. He wasn't surprised by their content, when they eventually emerged: events took place in a loop. A beating, and another beating. The queerness being beaten out of him. *Thtop it, Daddy*. A cane, usually. Sometimes Dermot's hurley stick, though this was for special occasions, because the bruises left by ash wood proved slower to clear from the skin; and they were all the colours of the rainbow, and had to be explained away.

'What else?' asked Martin.

A steadily increasing sense of brutality, as though his father had a dial in his head and was turning it up, slowly, to see how high it could go: which accounted for the closing of the neural pathways. But he realised that one form of brutality was just the same as another, regardless of that ghostly dial. Brutality was brutality, however you looked at it – and having looked at it, and examined it, and understood it completely, with professional assistance, Ward was happy to set it aside. There was no need for these memories to define who he was.

'Go on,' said Martin.

The violence stopped – not when he reached a certain age, or when he stretched sufficiently to be able to look his father in the eye. It carried on well into Ward's teens, past the age when he ought on paper to have been able to defend himself. Better that he put up with the strikes and the punches and the welts and the dark bruising, than his mother have to take all of it instead.

'Yes, exactly,' said Martin. 'That's the way it works.'

The beatings stopped, in fact, only when his mother died, and when his father began to drink so very excessively that he could no longer adequately handle a cane, or a chair leg, or any weapon. When he stopped representing a credible threat.

'Gosh, this is all so interesting,' said Martin.

Ward carried his father's coffin, when the time came. There was no need for any dramatics about it all.

Later, much later, when Martin's paper was published in the *Lancet* – the paper which helped to establish his reputation, the paper peer-reviewed and found wanting on no counts, the paper about forgotten-and-remembered trauma, about brain science, about healing and empathy and peace and clinical repair-work, as though the brain were under the bonnet of an old car, for the likes of Martin to tinker about inside of, the paper which sealed Martin's position professionally and at the clinic, the paper the existence of which I (Ward thought, again and again and again) myself knew nothing about until its appearance

– later, much later, Ward tried not to mind. As Martin said, this was Ward's tangible contribution to their future, to their financial security, to the good life they'd have together.

'I mean, talk about silver linings,' said Martin, and smiled. 'I'll take you on holidays.' Now they could get a real top-of-the-range Danish kitchen. 'Right?'

'You might have asked.' How sullen I sound, thought Ward, like a spoiled child.

'What, and have you say, *No thanks, darling, I'd rather not?*'

'You might have asked.'

Martin rose, folded his *Times*. 'You'll feel differently in a few days,' he said. 'I think that this is part of the healing process; and you will too, in time.'

Well, and this explains my attitude to Dublin, Ward thought. He looked around, at the wooden curlicues of the Pied Piper's interior. Rob knew about this story: Ward had told him, in dribs and drabs, over the months: and this, needless to say, gave Rob another reason to dislike Martin. Ward sensed too, though, that Rob assumed everyone in Ireland had a similar story to tell: that Irishness was a sort of useful shorthand for unhappiness in and frustration with early life, with workhouses, and bones lying in shallow graves in the fields. Probably Rob imagined a sexually perverted priest buggering his way through the annual cohort of altar boys, including Ward; perhaps he thought that Daddy's fists and Daddy's cane marks were better than the other available option.

Well, and he would just have to think whatever he wanted to think.

And who cared, really. He took in Rob, sitting there on a high stool in the Pied Piper, and clearly feeling better. An Americano and a good chicken sandwich followed by a caramel square had worked their magic, and that murderous, faint-with-hunger look had gone, at least for the moment.

'Tell me,' Ward said, 'about your hunch.'

34

The Jewel was discovered in, Rob said later, a place that was not very jewel-like. Not very *englamoured*, as Rob said: and Ward looked at him with a degree of surprise: *englamoured* was not a word that Rob would ordinarily use.

A long evening of checking databases, following Rob's hunch that led from one forged painting to another to a small theft in Spain, in France, in England; looking again at the gallery camera records, gleaning information, and clicking its sections together like individual pieces of Lego. A profile emerging, as Rob searched precise avenues, sniffing after a scent: that older man, slicing and stealing on the gallery recordings, had been in the building several days previously, casing the joint, taking it all in. He had even joined a tour that Gerard Boyle had headed. He had, Rob noted, really looked engaged.

The Jewel was destined for a private collection. A safe, there to moulder for, perhaps, decades.

It deserved better.

And this older man: Rob had been seeking him now for some months. Following his shadow through the darkness. An occasional player, Rob said, not habitual, but skilled; called upon for the occasional special job – not a high-profile theft, but niche. *The Jewel* was the exception to the rule. He studied the data, he added a little of his own: a pattern was forming, he would be tracked down, some day soon, now; even these shadowy guys couldn't expect to get away with it for ever.

This was not, Ward thought, what Emily Sandborne had wanted.

She'd wanted none of this. Surely to God. Not the unearthing, the sordid digging around in her grave for her treasure to be taken away from her. Not the rehanging on a gallery wall, not the biography, not the slashed throat, and not – this being a woman who seemed to know her fabrics – the spoiled green-white silk on the walls of the Sculpture Court.

All this had happened in spite of her.

He kept these irrelevant thoughts to himself.

'We can go back – tomorrow, even,' Rob said. 'The painting is gone – but only for now. We can leave your friend Patrick to deal with his crime; and we can go home and put out the call. I have a million connections in my head, look,' he said, and he swung the laptop around. 'Look at the pattern: Leeds, Rouen, Salamanca: regional galleries, lucrative but low-key thefts. I bet he's behind them all. He should never have gone near *The Jewel*. He must have been mad.' Rob pursed his lips. 'And he's no habitual murderer either, in spite of what this looks like. We can complete a profile in ten minutes and send it out, and bingo.'

'Not ten minutes.'

'No, not ten minutes. A day and a half, and Charlotte will be happy too. We should see Roisin O'Hara,' Rob said and paused. 'Just because.'

Ward nodded. 'Yes, I'd like to, if we can.'

'They tell me I can go home tomorrow,' she said. 'I told them I'm fine to go home tonight, right now, but.' Roisin smoothed her hands over the thin hospital coverlet. 'A night in hospital will set their minds at rest, they tell me.'

'Well, you've had a shock,' Rob said, 'so I'm not surprised they want to keep you in. Always do what the medics say, is my motto.'

He was perched on the edge of the bed; around them, white hospital light, and the life of the building proceeding smoothly. Visiting time had just begun and the ward was filling up decorously. She nodded.

'Of course you're right.'

Ward was sitting in the one chair. She looked smaller, he thought, than the woman he had watched clipping along, brisk and silent, through the camera footage, and she looked younger too. Slight – too thin. Dark, with just a few silver hairs. She looked tired, which was to be expected, and she spoke more softly than he for some reason had imagined. A light, musical accent, western.

She had added a few details. She was a good witness, a noticer: the height, the size, the clothing, she had retained a good deal in spite of the trauma of the moment; and Rob had listened intently and nodded, his eyes gleaming. She had explained, quite calmly, that the responsibility for the whole episode lay on her shoulders; and she had refused to be comforted. The only good thing was, she said, that her friend had escaped with his life. But everything else was bad.

Rob took her hand at this point. Hardly the professional thing, but she grasped his hand in return and held it.

'You have to go easy on yourself,' he said gently, as Ward watched him.

She grimaced. 'That's a thing I've never been able to do. And I don't think I deserve it in this case.'

Rob said nothing. Ward looked on: a tableau, seen at a slight distance. She still had a tight hold on Rob's hand, but now there was a detectable shift, a movement in the air, as if she was speaking in dialogue with herself.

'Not for years and years now. Easy: ease is not a thing I feel I've earned in my life.' And again a shift of focus, as she looked at Rob and he gently removed his hand, and she ran her hand now through her dark hair.

'That seems very cut and dried,' Rob said gently.

She shook her head. 'I just mean,' and now another shake of the head, as though she herself hardly understood what she was saying, 'have you ever felt as though your life was bound up in something else, in something that was completely beyond your control?'

Rob nodded. 'I suppose so. Sometimes,' he said, 'in fact, yes, frequently, now.' He looked at her. 'Is that how you feel?'

She nodded.

'My sister died, you see,' she said, 'and I wasn't around for her very much just before she died, and ever since then,' and again she ran a hand through her hair, 'I feel as though I don't deserve to have a life of my own. As though I've been touched by frost. And now, Gerard. It all feels part of some destiny. So that's what I mean about ease: it's not something I connect with my own life.'

A pause.

'I think I know what you mean.' Rob cleared his throat. 'Though, remember that your friend is going to live, he isn't going to die, and that none of this is your fault.' She opened her mouth to speak, and Ward continued to watch from his slight distance as Rob went on, 'But that isn't what I wanted to say.'

She looked at him. 'What did you want to say?'

'The things that you can't help, you leave in the past, like a load of suitcases that you don't want. The things you can help – the future, the present day – you take with you. You lighten the load, you stride out, you reach out with both hands.' Rob laughed a little. 'And I'm mixing my metaphors a bit now. I'm not so arrogant that I'm going to lecture you about your sister, but I do know that you have a responsibility to yourself and your life. To, how do I put it,' and Ward watched as Rob moistened his mouth with his tongue, and paused for a moment, 'to renew your faith in yourself, in the future. If you can.'

She gazed at him. 'A friend said something similar to me, not so long ago.' She paused. 'I assume you're speaking from experience.'

Rob said, 'Well, not exactly. Though I have been thinking along those lines.'

She looked at him. 'Well, I will too, I'll do some thinking too.' And then seemed to shake herself a little. 'But you're not here to counsel me, gentlemen. I'm sorry. Is there anything else you need from me?'

Ward shook his head and smiled, and Rob rose. 'I don't think so,' he said. 'And you've heard enough advice from me.' He smiled now, too. 'We're fairly confident your police will find this man, perhaps with the help of a little information from us. And the painting – confident there too.'

'I'm glad,' she said. She looked exhausted, suddenly, and they took their leave with hands shaken and smiles. When Ward glanced back, her eyes were already closed.

'You did good,' Ward said; and Rob nodded very slightly.

Very late in the evening, Patrick Walsh rang with the news. It had been located, *The Jewel*: it had been swaddled carefully in heavy-duty brown paper, and handed into a city-centre charity shop, which had taken all day to get around to unwrapping and discovering it. 'It seems undamaged,' said Patrick Walsh. 'They seem clear that it's undamaged: we have it in front of us now, in Dr Read's office.'

'We'll come up, if we may.'

'Dr Read will meet you at the main stairs, she says.'

They walked through the peacock-coloured galleries – Roisin O'Hara's colours, Ward thought now – to where Emma Read stood at the head of the flight of white stairs. No reserve now: she was smiling, and flushed.

'If you'll follow me, gentlemen.'

She led the way through the sequence of oxblood halls, and into a lift to the top floor. One wall of her office was a sheet of glass, a single pane through which the lights of the city glittered. Patrick Walsh sat, very upright, in a chair in the corner. He too smiled.

'And there it is.'

A piece of fine linen, a tinge of porridge-grey – and a tableau of figures surmounted by brilliantly illuminated stained glass. Black-gleaming armour, shadowed faces, downcast eyes.

'We've had it checked over. Of course it'll be done again, properly, slowly, in the days to come. But it seems fine.'

Emily Sandborne, glancing at them from the furthest shadow, the furthest darkness. The beginnings of a smile, perhaps: yes, he still saw this in her visage – but now Ward saw something else, too. A steeliness, a challenge in her eye.

'Before it's displayed again.'

A challenge?

'Thank God,' added Emma Read.

A challenge. Definitely, yes.

'May I?' said Rob, and Emma Read nodded.

The green of the malachite, set into the armour there at the fabric's very centre: as Rob bent over the fabric, Ward saw that the malachite seemed to catch the light, casting a profound glow upward to chime sweetly with the green of Rob's eyes. A perfect match.

Coda

John stood on the pier at Holyhead. In the distance, the cliffs of Holy Island gleamed black.

He might have ended it that morning without even getting on the boat, without going through the trouble of the crossing – the 'voyage', as he had heard one passenger say to another, as though they were setting sail for the South Seas. There being no point prolonging this life, if you wanted to call it that.

But several things had held him back.

Ireland was foreign soil, an alien land. So, for that matter, was Wales, where he had disembarked, and wandered the streets of Holyhead before making his way out to the pier. But Wales would do. A different island, though: that would have been another matter altogether.

The harbour walls at Holyhead were impressively long. Plenty of scope there. Nobody would be watching. It had been best, yes, to make tracks for home, and to pause well before he reached where home had once been, to remember that there was no home available any longer.

So, where he was would have to do.

There would be kelp swaying and moving in these deep, cold waters. Like the tidewrack by the Thames, long ago. Waving strands of kelp, to welcome him in, and entangle him, and draw him willingly down.

He had cut himself as loose as possible: passport tightly wrapped in plastic in his zipped jacket pocket, to make it easy on them. But nothing else. Everything else left behind.

Stella would be pleased with this gesture, if she knew. *Well done, darling*, she would say, if she were here on the pier with him, the salt wind lifting her hair. *Let it all go. Bravo, say I.*

And, *Do the right thing, John*, Gran would say, remembering Northumberland. *Listen to yourself, and do the right thing.* She'd provided the perfect example.

And then, old Etienne. Fool. Letting me down at the end, old man. They told me you were too old.

Etienne would be in hot water with them now.

Cold water was better.

Behind him, the afternoon ferry to Ireland was leaving a trail as it moved slowly through the harbour waves. The sun was shining oblique on the waves: a pale grass-green where the light fell on the water; heavier tones, not green so much as black where the rays did not reach, a white wake.

The boy wasn't dead, as he had feared. The radio, the newspapers had been clear: gashed and marked for life, most likely; the blade of his knife had been keen. He ought to feel – violent, searing sensations, rending and tearing and ripping: but in fact he felt nothing like that. If anything he felt calm, or quite calm. Not distressed or agitated, anyway. He had a solution: an atonement, it occurred to him to call it. He had dropped into the charity shop, for all the world a good citizen, and set his neat parcel on the counter with a smile, and headed off for the ferry terminal, a solution in mind. Atonement was a natural word, given what had just happened, in someone else's life.

And he hadn't even known the boy's name.

But, *solution* was better.

He was weary of all this. He had existed, and soon he would no longer exist. His gran, and his parents, and even Stella in her way: each had existed, and then stopped existing. Soon it would be his turn. In his mind's eye, the strong flow of the Thames as it rose and fell, the flow of brown river water on shingle. A home taken away. A lack, an absence – covered over, successfully enough for years, by activity and money and a sort of bitter satisfaction – but resurfacing, in the end. And a solution; and a sense of relief that he need pretend no longer.

A verse surfaced too, emerging from the sudden calm of his mind.

For he maketh the storm to cease, so that the waves thereof are still. Then are they glad, because they are at rest: and so he bringeth them unto the haven where they would be.

He stepped forward.

He would be able to wash himself clean.

Roisin sat and looked at her dustily distempered walls.

Her heart had fallen, sinking into her stomach. There was nothing much wrong with her, they said, other than shock. She had her pills, and she needed to keep taking them – but really, she might as well be resting quiet at home as remaining here.

They were satisfied that she'd be fine.

Gerard would be fine too, they said, and that had made her heart easier. He would have a scar, of course – there was no way that he couldn't have a scar – but better a scar than the other thing.

He had said so himself. Quietly: the knife had missed his windpipe, but he'd been told to speak very quietly, to rest himself. She had taken the lift upstairs, and visited – during visiting hours, of course – and he had told her that, apparently, there were people out there who would quite go for scars.

'Like war wounds, in the old days, you know. My friends say they'll help me with the dating apps.'

Roisin said, 'They have?'

Gerard smiled, swallowed gingerly. 'I'm only joking.'

Roisin scratched her head. Maybe they'd invent an app for people like her, too. Though no, there wouldn't be a market for it. And the technology wouldn't exist.

In the meantime, Gerard seemed, well, surprisingly chipper. Surprisingly so, yes. 'And they found *The Jewel*,' he added.

She nodded. Just left there, she said. On purpose, they supposed. But Gerard shrugged a little at that.

'Who knows,' he said. 'We don't know. He might have. Dr Read seemed mighty pleased, anyway.'

'Yes, I bet she was.'

'My job waiting for me, she said, just as soon as I want to come back.'

'Well, I should bloody well think so.' Roisin cleared her frown and added abruptly, 'I want to apologise. If it hadn't been for me, you wouldn't have been there in the first place.'

But Gerard shook his head, and smiled a little, and said something about fate. About destiny. It was just meant to be, he said. She shouldn't give it another thought.

Roisin would think of nothing else, for a while; afterwards, she would see. She remembered the friendly New Zealander and his words. And the bottom line was that there was no need to burden Gerard with any more of this. She moved to go, hesitated, spoke. 'Maybe, when you're better, you can come over and have tea,' she said. 'I make a mean Madeira cake.'

He nodded. He'd like that, and he smiled again, saving his voice.

Now she sat in her shadowy sitting room. Dim lamps played a little on the dusty surface of the distempered walls; through the open door, she could glimpse – were she to look that way – the thickly hung wall of the hall, the framed paintings marching up the stairs. Gilt gleamed a little in the lamplight: tiny, microscopic points of light. Were she to look that way.

She had taken down the relevant catalogue – earlier, by daylight – and studied *The Jewel*. Why, she hardly knew: to take it in in its entirety, to look at its colours and its gleaming lights and dark pools of shadow, to watch the almost-smiling of Mrs Sandborne, to watch her as she watched the future.

What would she make of all this? *You survived*, she might say, *and I did not. Make the most of your survival.*

She might say.

It might get better.

Who knows what she might say.

Emma Read had been filled with joy, she'd been told. Perhaps this joy was in bad taste: what about Gerard's neck, what about the ruined silken walls of the Sculpture Court? Bad taste – and yet, perhaps not so. Gerard was alive, and the silk could be replaced, or done away with entirely, and the walls left bare. She had never, after all, been entirely comfortable with that shade of phosphorus. She might have made a mistake, there.

And they had all survived.

'Tell me something,' Maeve had said, long ago. 'Just this: what do you want to do with yourself?'

'What, just that?'

'Just that.'

'See a little bit of the world,' she'd said. 'That's all; and try to be happy. What about you?'

Maeve considered. 'Just to survive,' she'd said, 'would do me.' And roared laughing.

Roisin looked again at her walls. She could do more than survive, now that she'd been given another chance – and now her doorbell pealed. When she answered it, she saw Michael Clancy on the doorstep, smart in a car coat and dark jeans. He'd heard she was poorly, had had a shock, the grapevine had been working overtime. He thought she could do with some company – so here he was, just off the plane. Hoping to stay in her spare room. 'Amn't I great?'

She nodded.

'You'd better ask me in, then. And I've a lemon cake, too, in my bag: Tim baked it and sends it with his best love. His warmest love. Again, aren't we great?'

'You are.' Roisin nodded again. 'You'd better come in.' She held the door wide, and he stepped in, and she closed the door behind him, and they stood in the cloistered hall.

'Poppy seeds and everything,' Michael added, and looked around in undisguised appreciation. 'Well! This is nice, isn't it? My God. Very, very nice.'

She smiled a little, and considered for a moment. 'You both are. Great, I mean. You're great,' she said. 'Come on through.'

They checked in using one of the self-service machines, trying their passports one way and then another way, bending, typing in sequences of letters and numbers, all around them people doing the same thing, until the machine allowed them to carry on. Then they began walking towards the security area.

Ward said, 'Englamoured?' – and Rob didn't seem all that surprised to have this word fished out of the ether, seemed to be almost expecting it, expecting the challenge.

'I heard it used once. I can't remember where. I thought I'd use it when some special occasion came along.'

Ward nodded.

He had dialled Martin's number from outside the gallery,

while awaiting the taxi. He had tried again when they clambered out of the taxi in front of the terminal building. Now he tried again. 'I'll just make a call,' he said.

Rob had been calling too – phoning Jane, and he'd had more success at getting through, if not in actual conversation. He could take the kiddies this weekend, after all, he told her – but from the gleaned fragments of conversation he could overhear, it seemed to Ward that Jane was on her high horse, that the new plans that had been made could not now be unmade, that Rob wouldn't be seeing the damn kiddies this weekend after all.

'Never mind,' Ward said.

'Never mind, you,' Rob said. 'What, is His Lordship for the, now, what would this be, third time not picking up?'

'It doesn't seem like it.'

'Do you know where he is?'

'He said something about going to Kent.'

'Oh yes, that's right. To Nige, the ex, the Kentish oast-house dweller.'

Ward flinched. 'Nigel.'

'Because you could go to Southwold after all now, couldn't you? For your weekend?'

But somehow Ward doubted it: and his doubt must have registered in his expression.

'Englamoured,' Rob said now. 'Ward, did you know that this word has two definitions?'

Ward shook his head. What?

'It means "rendered glamorous". Glamorous, in the modern, Hollywood meaning of the word. OK?' Rob took a breath and said, 'And it means "surrounded with illusion". Englamoured.' Ward watched as Rob studied his face: watched, aware of a stepping back. 'What I'm saying is: that's you.'

Ward said nothing, but his mind took another long step back – and now Rob shrugged in sudden irritation. 'Oh, for Christ's sake.'

'For Christ's sake?' Ward repeated, and stared. 'For Christ's sake what?'

'For Christ's sake, how many times are you going to call him? Three times now: how many more times? Do you think he'll be waiting for you at home tonight, glass of whisky in hand? You know he won't. He's punishing you, Ward. He's sitting in some oast house punishing you. What are you even doing with him?'

Stared and stared. The airport terminal reverberated and flowed around them. What?

Rob repeated, 'What are you even *doing* with him?' A beat of silence, and then, 'Ward, I don't think you should be with Martin. I think you should be with me.'

With you? Standing very still. 'What?'

Rob spoke hurriedly now, the harshness gone, tripping over his words. 'I've been thinking about it for some time; I've been looking for some opportunity. This trip, this Ireland thing, made it all clear. The painting, I dunno,' and he ran a hand over his mouth. 'It's about taking the opportunity, Ward.'

Ward said again, 'What? – what, is Emily Sandborne directing you from the grave?'

But it was no time for heavy humour: now it was Rob's turn to flinch. That was a line Martin might have used. 'I'm sorry, Rob, I didn't mean – but I'm with Martin. I've been with Martin for years.'

'But you shouldn't *be* with Martin,' Rob said. No turning back now; now his agitation was plain to see. 'Ward, you should be with me.'

'You said that.'

'You should come home with me.'

Home?

'Home with you?'

'Yes, Ward, that's what I'm saying.'

'But I have a home,' Ward said.

But Rob said that, no, he had a house. A very nice house, but a home was a different matter.

'I don't know,' Ward said. 'This is too much to take in.' He said, 'Martin trusts me.'

'He put your life into an article without even *asking* you. He mocks you. He goes out at night, Ward, and doesn't come back.'

'I shouldn't've told you that.'

'Yeah, well, you did.'

They stared at each other.

'Home with you?'

Rob nodded – and now the shock seemed to recede a little, to be replaced with something else. A glimmering of colour, perhaps. A lifting of the light. His eyes were so green.

But – no.

'This is insane. I mean, what if it doesn't work out?'

'Then it doesn't. At least we'll have tried it. Life's too short, Ward. It really, really is too short.'

'And what about *Felicity*?'

'So, we'll go to your place, and pick up Felicity, and go home.' Now Rob paused, and selected the words. 'I'm offering you something else, Ward. The possibility of something else, anyway. That's all.'

Ward stood, and looked, at the crowds and the shop fronts, and the glaring lights. 'I need to ring Martin again,' he said, and he watched as Rob's face fell into folds of exhaustion and something that might have been grief, and humiliation.

But, not watched from far away: instead, he had a sense of space collapsing, falling in on itself, of the two of them standing not far apart, not gulfs and gulfs apart – but, suddenly, forehead to forehead.

And so, instead of turning away, as he would normally do, as he always did, to make a call: instead of turning away, Ward looked at Rob as he dialled Martin's number and held the phone to his ear, and he continued to look at Rob as the phone once more rang and rang and rang, before cutting, again, to voicemail.

Acknowledgements

Significant sections of this novel were written at the Tyrone Guthrie Centre at Annaghmakerrig: this, the result of the Jack Harte Bursary awarded to me in 2018. My thanks to Valerie Bistany, Maureen Kennelly, and Conor Kostick; to the Irish Writers' Centre which endows and administers the Bursary; and to the Director and staff at Annaghmakerrig for their friendship and hospitality.

Thanks to my agent Veronique Baxter at David Higham; to Helen Francis, for sensitive editing of this novel; and to Clare Gordon, Chrissy Ryan, and especially Neil Belton at Head of Zeus.

I am grateful to Catherine Toal, for reading and commenting on a draft of this novel; and to Ruth McDonnell, for discussing with me modes of painting using the medium of distemper.

Last and most, love and thanks to John Lovett.